ACCLAIM FOR THE NOVELS OF
DENNIS KOLLER

THE RHYTHM OF EVIL

"A fast-paced, can't put the book down, suspense thriller. If you liked the Harry Bosch series by Michael Connelly, you'll love this book. The Rhythm of Evil is a top-notch thriller! The suspense escalates in Koller's fast paced tale of a simple murder that turns out to be anything but simple. Tight writing and believable characters will keep the pages turning."

—*Vivian Roubal*
Columnist, Martinez News-Gazette

THE CUSTER CONSPIRACY

2017 INDEPENDENT PRESS AWARD
DISTINGUISHED FAVORITE

"Intriguing."

—*Publishers Weekly*

"A first-rate thriller! Koller ratchets up the suspense in this fast-paced tale of history gone awry. Crisp writing and intricate plotting will keep you turning the pages."

—*The Martinez Gazette*

"The Custer Conspiracy is a fast-paced crime novel, played against the backdrop of history, which races to its conclusion at a fever pitch. A must-read for fans of historical novels, with a conspiracy twist tossed in just for the fun of it."

—*Curt Nettinga*
Editor, Huron Plainsman

"If you like suspenseful, fast-moving detective stories, I would recommend this intriguing tale. The author blends mystery, murder, guns and beautiful women (into) a fun ride."

—Bismarck Gazette

"The writing and story ideas remind me of a cross between Dan Brown and Michael Crichton."

—Dave G.
California Writers Club State Past-President

THE OATH

2017 SILVER MEDAL MILITARY WRITERS SOCIETY OF AMERICA

2016 BAIPA BOOK AWARD FOR BEST FICTION

"Dennis Koller's mystery-thriller debut is a strong one. The novel has it all; intrigue, politics, murder and romance. Combined with characters and dialogue that are ultimately believable, *The Oath* is a real page-turner."

—The Irish Herald Book Review

"A dying former POW, four dead women, a world-weary homicide cop and the Vietnam War are expertly woven together by Dennis Koller in a masterful piece of storytelling that will leave you guessing right until the last few pages of 'The Oath.' An excellent book with just the right amount of social commentary woven into its pages to make it not just another murder mystery."

—Mike Billington
Author of "Corpus Delectable"

KISSED BY THE SNOW

BOOKS BY DENNIS KOLLER

THE
RHYTHM OF EVIL

BY
DENNIS KOLLER

PEN BOOKS

DALLAS

Pen Books
A Division of Pen Communication
Providence Village, TX

This book is a work of fiction. Names, characters, places and incidents either are products of the author's imagination or are used fictitiously. Any resemblance to persons living or dead is entirely coincidental.

Pen Books paperback edition August 19, 2020

Edited by: Adele Brinkley, K. Boston, K. Peticolas, D. Almeida
Cover Design: Jonas Mayes-Steger

Visit Pen Books on the World Wide Web at PenBooks.biz

Manufactured in the United States of America

ISBN-13: 9780998080819
ISBN-10: 0998080810

Thank you for purchasing this Pen Books paperback.

Please remember to leave a Review
at your favorite retailer.

To Sarah—
My wife, Muse, best friend,
and the love of my life.
With her, everything is possible.

POPPY

2007

Thank god for drunk twenty-somethings, Poppy Garcia thought as she happily emptied the contents of her zippered pouch on the kitchen table. It had been a good night. The grave-yard shift was, indeed, the cash cow of all enterprising cabbies, and from the heft of her pouch, this night promised to be better than most. She smiled at the vision of guys hurriedly throwing her cash while yanking their dates out of the back seat, hoping to get laid before either of them passed out.

Her smile turned to a scowl when she heard footsteps climb-ing the front stairs of her duplex. She glanced at the clock on the stove: eight-fifteen. Had to be a solicitor. Her friends knew never to disturb her until mid-to-late afternoon. The doorbell rang. She ignored it and opened her laptop, firing up Excel. The doorbell rang again.

"What the hell!" she grumbled, slamming her laptop shut.

She walked across the living room to the front door. Looking through the peephole, she saw a middle-aged man in a blue shirt and brown sport coat holding a leather portfolio in one hand and a wallet in the other.

"Yes? Can I help you?" she asked through the door.

"Police officer, ma'am," came the reply. Securing the portfo-lio under his left arm, he used both hands to open his wallet, re-vealing a badge on one side and an ID on the other.

"I'm sorry, can you bring it closer? You're standing so far

back I can't read it."

"Certainly." Holding it steady, the man moved closer to the peephole. "My badge and ID, ma'am." He waited a moment and said, "I'm sorry to bother you so early. My partner and I are knocking on all the doors in this neighborhood to alert residents there was another robbery here last night."

She scrutinized the man in front of her. Clean shaven. Medium height. Full head of hair, neatly combed. Late forties to early fifties. Not bad looking in that pretty George Clooney sort of way.

She still had trouble reading his ID through the peephole's curved glass, so she slipped on the chain lock and opened the door. "What can I do for you, Officer?"

"Forgive the intrusion, ma'am. I'm . . ."

"Before we get any further, you can knock off the 'ma'am' thing. It's such a cliché. My name is Poppy. Poppy Garcia."

"Forgive me, Ms. Garcia."

"And forget the 'Ms. Garcia,' too. Call me Poppy. Everybody else does."

He nodded and smiled. "Be happy to, Poppy. My name is Michael Ryan, San Francisco Police Department." He paused, holding out his badge and ID again, closer this time so she could read it. "Robbery Unit." He waited until she read and internalized the information on the ID and then said, "As I was saying, we had a burglary last night around the corner." He turned and pointed to his right. "Down 24th Avenue. Third home invasion in this area in the past two weeks. There is no doubt a gang has targeted your neighborhood. My partner and I are going door-to-door, cautioning folks to keep their doors locked and asking for assistance in apprehending the perps."

The word "perps" made Poppy shiver. She'd heard it on television, of course, but having a real-life policeman talk to her like that, like an insider, made the hair on the back of her neck stand up.

"I would love to help, Officer," she said through the narrow opening, "but I just got off work. I'm really tired and just want to go to bed. Would it be possible for you to come back this afternoon? Say around four?"

"If it were possible for me to come back, I would." Ryan said. "Unfortunately, the crime rate in this part of the city is climbing, and the whole department is stretched to the max." He stepped back, put his wallet into his coat pocket, and held up the leather portfolio. "I've got pictures in here of two of the suspects. If we can identify them, we might be able to roll up the whole gang. Keep you and the neighbors safe from these scumbags."

"The perps," she said with a grin.

"Yes, the perps," Ryan replied with a chuckle. "I can tell you watch way too much television."

"You're right," she said, flashing a toothy grin. "I'm a sucker for cop shows. I'd watch 'em twenty-four-seven if I could."

"Have any favorites?"

"*The Wire*, for sure. Oh my god! It's so good."

"Yeah, my favorite, too. But I also like *Law and Order*. You watch that?"

"Oh, I do. Unfortunately, I'm at work when it's on, so I tape it. Don't get to watch it until the next day, but I never miss it."

"Tell you what I can do," Ryan said with a big grin. "Since you're a police-procedural junky, I can make you an honorary San Francisco police officer if you'd like."

Poppy knew he was teasing, but still smiled. "That would be so cool, Officer. My girlfriends won't believe it. Can I see your badge and ID once more?"

"Absolutely." He took the wallet from his pocket and passed it through the opening. She carefully compared the man standing in front of her with the officer pictured on the ID. Satisfied, she handed back the wallet, removed the chain and opened the door.

He slipped his wallet back into his pocket and held up the portfolio again. "I have a few pictures to show you, Ms. . . . ." He caught himself. "To show you, Poppy. Would it be a bother if I came in? I promise not to take much time. Three minutes, in and out, max."

Poppy glanced at her watch, thought a moment and then moved aside to let him enter. "Of course. Can I offer you some coffee?"

"That would be wonderful," he said with a smile. "Thank you."

She led him into the kitchen. "Don't mind the mess, Officer." She pointed to the table. "I drive a cab at night. Just got home a little over an hour ago and was counting my tips when you rang the bell."

"Looks like you did well. Do you enjoy driving a cab?"

"Actually, I love it. I get to meet so many interesting characters."

"I hear you. Same with my job." He nodded his head toward the table. "Have you finished counting?"

"Not yet. I'm guessing though there's probably three hundred here. Give or take. May not seem like much to you, but for me it's a good night."

"Congratulations."

"Thank you. Have a seat, please." She nodded toward one of the chairs. "I'll get you some coffee."

As Poppy walked across the kitchen toward the coffee pot, she didn't hear Ryan place the portfolio on the table. Nor did she hear the sound of the suppressed Sig Sauer as it sent a 9mm round into the back of her head, blowing out a portion of her forehead.

Careful not to step in any of the blood spatters, the man who claimed to be Officer Michael Ryan calmly unscrewed the suppressor, picked up the shell casing from the kitchen floor, and placed them both in a plastic pouch that fit neatly into his jacket pocket. As he walked toward the front door, he glanced at his watch and smiled.

"Just as I promised you, Poppy Garcia. In and out in under three minutes."

CHAPTER 1

PRESENT DAY

Becky and I had planned on going to the Giants game that afternoon, but decided to pass when my right thigh got pretty badly chewed up playing in the Police Athletic League's soft-ball game last night. Note to self: never slide on a dirt infield while wearing cut-offs.

We had just plopped on the couch to watch the game when my cell chirped from the back bedroom. As I struggled to stand, my thigh brushed against the couch's armrest, sending a sharp pain shooting down my leg. "Shit," I barked, as my leg buckled under me.

Becky reached over and patted my shoulder. "Rest your leg, hon, I'll get it." At the kitchen door, she turned and said, "But you've got to start watching the language again, okay?"

I nodded apologetically. Becky had been trying for some time to make me more conscious of my word choices. I rebelled at first, using the go-to excuse that I'm a cop and live in a relatively male-dominant environment. To me, using the F-word, S-word, A-word, C-word or hell, pick-a-letter word was nothing more than normal, everyday male conversation, and, truth be told, increasingly female conversation as well. At least in my world.

I had to admit, though, her constant reminders had unquestionably improved my vocabulary. I wasn't perfect, but Becky, smart woman that she was, always gave me kudos for making progress.

"It's your nephew Bobby," she mouthed as she handed me the phone.

"Bobby," I said, my grimace folding into a smile. "Been too damn long, my man. How the heck you been?"

Bobby was my brother Bill's only child. A terrific kid. Had been born with cerebral palsy, but I can honestly say I'd never once heard him complain. He simply accepted his handicap and pushed on. I admired the hell out of him.

"Hi, Uncle Reg. Yeah, been a long time. Sorry I haven't kept in better touch. I know you and Dad talk a lot so figured you'd be getting an earful about me whether you wanted to or not."

I laughed. "Hey, I talked to your dad a couple of weeks ago. He told me only good things about you."

"Must have been a short conversation," he replied with a chuckle.

"That it was," I said. "But seriously, he told me you're not only graduating from college in a few weeks, which I already knew, but you've been offered a full-ride to UCLA Law School. Pretty darn impressive. Your brain musta come from your mom's side, 'cause your dad ain't that freakin' smart."

He laughed softly, then said, "It's been fun catching up, Uncle Reg, but I really called to ask you a question. You got a few minutes?"

"For you, my man, I got all the time in the world. What's up?"

"I heard something yesterday that really blew me away. I talked to my dad about it, and he suggested I call you." The timbre of his voice had changed. More serious now. *Sounding almost attorney-like,* I thought with a smile. "Do you remember when I was like three or four years old?" He went silent, allowing my mind to wander back in time. "You had just returned from the military and were living with us while you went to college. I was attending a special school for handicapped kids run by the

2

Shriners."

"Of course, I remember. You got picked up every day by your own personal cabbie. A young woman, if I remember correctly."

"Yeah. Her name was Poppy Garcia, and she's actually the reason I'm calling." He took a deep breath and then said, "Poppy picked me up and took me to school every day for almost five years. I'm guessing she was probably about twenty or twenty-one at the time. Around there, anyway. I'm surprised you remembered her."

"Funny. I can't remember what she looked like, but I do remember her lifting you into that damned cab every day."

"Yeah. For over four years. Rain or shine. Believe me, she got me through some very difficult times." I detected a slight catch in his voice. "I owe her a lot, and got to thinking how cool it would be to reconnect. To tell her how appreciative I was for everything she did for me."

"That's really nice, Bobby. And, hey, if you need help locating her, just ask."

I heard him take another deep breath. "Thanks, but I've already located her."

"Congrats, on . . ."

"No! Hold on, let me finish." He went silent for a minute, then said, "I looked her up on Google. It said she died in June of 2007."

"Died? Oh, Bobby, I'm really sorry."

"She didn't just die, Uncle Reg. She was murdered. In a home invasion robbery."

That caught my attention. "Son-of-a-bitch." I looked over at Becky with pursed lips and a *not now* scowl. "Did the article say who the perp was?"

"No. The killer was never caught."

"Dammit. When I get to The Hall tomorrow, Bobby, I

3

promise I'll check it out."

"There's more." He went silent, like he was trying to find the right words. "Do you know what Twitter is?"

"Twitter? Come on, Bobby, of course I know what Twitter is. What's that got to do with Poppy Garcia's murder?"

"I'm a heavy-duty Twitter fiend. I'm on it a lot. It's my window to the world, so to speak. I woke up yesterday morning to a tweet from a guy who lives somewhere in the Bay Area near you. I've never met the dude. We're only connected through Twitter."

"And?"

"And, he's accusing your department of being overtly racist, sexist and homophobic because Poppy Garcia's killer has never been brought to justice."

"That's utter nonsense, Bobby." Becky heard the anger in my voice and looked over. I waved her off. Taking a deep breath to calm myself, I said, "How the hell could this jerk-off make an accusation like that?"

"I have no idea. That's why I called you. Hoping it's not true."

"And the department is being condemned as racist-slash-sexist-slash-homophobic because we never solved her murder? Where'd that . . ." I wanted to say "crap come from," but knew I'd get *the look* from Becky, so instead said, . . . "bull come from?"

"Well, for one, Poppy was an Hispanic female. That's where the race and gender accusations came from." He paused. "And she happened to be gay. I found that out by accident a short time ago. I don't want to get into it, just know she was."

"Personally, Bobby, I could care less about any of that. Wanna know what I *do* care about, though?" Not waiting for a response, I said, "I *do* care about *you*. And because this woman cared about you, I now care about her. I'm sorry about the

Department didn't find her killer. I'll look into it, I promise you."

"Thanks, Uncle Reg. I'd really appreciate it if you could."

"Don't get your hopes up, though. Thirteen years was a long time ago. Light years in our business. Can't promise you anything. In fact, I can't promise they'd let me poke around in it for even a day or two."

"I was afraid of that."

"But there may be light at the end of the tunnel," I said. "That Twitter jerk-off, unbeknownst to him, may have just helped us get this case reopened. His contention the police department didn't solve a murder because we didn't like the victim's gender or nationality or sexual preference is a trifecta that the Brass isn't going to be able to ignore." I paused for a moment, then said, "Bobby, you never met the dude, right?"

"Yeah. Never. I called to let you know the accusation was out there, and the guy's tweet, at last count, had over 100,000 retweets. Most of them critical of your department."

"Son-of-a- . . . ," I said, before catching myself and saying ". . . gun."

Becky leaned over and pecked my cheek. "Keep up the good work, champ," she whispered with a smile. I almost caught myself blushing.

I nodded, patted her on the knee, then continued. "Fill me in on the whole 'retweet' schtick. Is 100,000 a lot?"

"Well, it's not the most I've ever seen, but it's getting there." He paused, then in a quieter voice said, "Uncle Reggie, I need to have your word that your department will still pursue finding Poppy's killer."

"I can't give you an ironclad promise, Bobby, but I will promise you this—if I'm allowed to reopen the case, Poppy's killer will be brought to justice."

CHAPTER 2

I climbed out of bed at 4:35 a.m., grumpy and acutely pissed off. Grumpy because my leg was still oozing pus, forcing me to spend an additional thirty minutes in the bathroom cleaning and rebandaging the damn wound. And pissed off because this Twitter jerk-off wouldn't let go of a thirteen-year-old murder that I was certain no one in the department would even remember. But I promised Bobby I'd get on the Garcia case at first light, and, dammit, I was going to keep that promise, gimpy leg or not. Becky stirred, turned over, and asked what time it was. I told her to go back to sleep, that she had another hour before she had to get up. A hint of a smile creased her face. "Gladly," she murmured, and snuggled back under the covers.

By 5:17, I was on the freeway headed toward the Hall of Justice. On the fifteen-minute drive, I replayed in my head the end of the conversation I had with Bobby.

After repeating the Twitter dude's accusation about the department being homophobic and racist, I patiently explained how the department worked. First off, we don't play favorites; we treat all homicides the same. I told him the television shows had it right—if a murder wasn't solved in the first twenty-four to forty-eight hours, there was a good chance it would never be solved. I explained to him that because the department didn't identify a perp in the Garcia shooting, it didn't mean they didn't try or didn't care.

When he told me the Garcia woman was murdered in June of 2007, it gave me the opening to switch gears. Even though I wasn't in the Homicide Unit back then, I did know the statistics. Hell, every cop did. In both 2007 and 2008, homicides in San Francisco doubled, caused mostly by gangbangers shooting and killing each other in record numbers. I told Bobby his lady friend unfortunately picked a terrible year to be gunned down. In 2007, the year she got herself offed, the City and County of San Francisco recorded ninety-seven homicides. It was the city's second highest murder rate in fifteen years, with only 2008 being worse, and, thank god, by only one. Needless to say, the Department was overwhelmed. As a result, it solved a dismal thirty-nine percent of that year's cases. Poppy Garcia's case obviously wasn't one of the thirty-nine percent.

My passionate explanation quieted him down some, but he still begged me to look into her murder. That all he wanted was to bring closure to those who, like himself, had been affected by Poppy Garcia's generous life. I told him I couldn't guarantee I'd find anything, but I'd give it my best shot. Getting up at four-thirty in the morning proved, at least to me, I was giving it my best shot. And the guy who was going to be the recipient of my best shot was that damn Twitter idiot. No matter what, I wasn't going to let that son-of-a-bitch off the hook.

~~~~~~

I pulled into the Hall of Justice of the City and County of San Francisco parking lot a few minutes after six, hobbled up the steps and took the elevator to the fifth floor. Turning right past Robbery, I entered room 504 – Homicide. Even though it was barely 6 a.m. on a Monday morning, half of my colleagues were already at their desks. This was not unusual. I'd been in the SFPD for over

8

fifteen years, in Homicide for the past six. Only in Homicide did members routinely show up two hours before their scheduled shift.

When I joined the force in the early part of this century, major disruptions were occurring in many of the SFPD units. The Homicide Unit, thankfully, had remained relatively stable. When I heard in 2014 the Unit had an opening, I quickly applied and, to my surprise, got the job. As a rookie, I got partnered with Tom McGuire, who, at the time, was the longest serving homicide inspector in the history of the department. I served two years with him, and like a sponge, absorbed everything he taught me.

When he retired, I was partnered with a contemporary of his, an officer named Manny Morales. Manny and I have been together for the past four years. He's known in the department as *Gloves* because back in the day he wore gloves that were filled with seven ounces of lead shot. All he had to do was slap a suspected perp, and that perp went down. On the street he was known as Superman. The gloves were strictly illegal, of course, but in those years, most supervisors looked the other way. Manny's had a good career. As of last week, he was officially two years shy of retirement.

I saw him as I hobbled into the office. As I got closer, he looked down at my leg. "You okay? You're walking funny."

"As well as can be expected," I replied, trying to play the sympathy card. "Played in the Department's baseball game last night. First inning I got a hit and thought I could stretch it into a double. Ended up sliding into second on a gravelly dirt infield wearing cut-offs."

"That was a stupid-ass thing to do," he said. *There goes the sympathy card*, I thought.

"Were you safe?"

"Actually, I was. Felt good taking one for the team so we

9

could score," I smiled, trying to reclaim the sympathy angle. Morales was having none of it so I changed tactics. "See you brought donuts." I nodded to the open box on Morales' desk. "Was wondering why you were in here so early, Gloves. Your turn, huh?"

He nodded. "Yep. First Monday of the month. My turn. You want one?"

"Nah." I laughed. "You know me, ordinarily I'd be all over that fritter, there. But last night? Last night taught me a lesson."

"So, you tear up your leg in a softball game, and now you're on a diet?"

"In the old days . . . old days being like six months ago . . . that hit would have been a stand up double. No slide. No torn-up leg." I shook my head. "I just gotta get back to eating better. These damn donuts everybody brings have been slowing me down."

"That and the beers after you get home."

"Well, that, too," I said with a chuckle. Pausing, I took another look at the box of donuts. "Okay, you got me. I'll take that fritter there."

"Hmmm. Now that's the Decker I've come to know and love," he said, passing me the donut.

"Yeah. I'm a wuss," I said, taking a bite of the fritter. "So, what's on the docket for today?"

"Only the Morrison murder, as far as I know," Manny responded.

"You're the lead, right? Anything in particular I can help you with?"

"Don't think so. Why, you got something else going?"

"Could be." I took another bite of the donut. "Got to talk to the Deputy Chief about this one, though. You follow Twitter?"

"I have an account, if that's what you mean. But I don't pay much attention to it. Why?"

"My nephew Bobby, my older brother's kid, called me

yesterday. He was born in the City, but now lives in L.A. Told me he'd been trying to find a friend of his from the time when he and his family lived here. A female named Poppy Garcia." I shrugged my shoulders. "It's a long story so bear with me. My nephew has cerebral palsy. This Garcia woman was a taxi driver that picked him up, both literately and figuratively, every day for three or four years. Drove him to a special school out in the Avenues. He wanted to reconnect and thank her for all the things she did for him."

"How long we talking about here?" Morales asked. "How much time between then and now?"

"The relationship goes back to when he was like three or four years old, so maybe eighteen or nineteen years. Bobby's in his early twenties now. Just about to graduate from UCLA."

Morales put up his hands to stop me. "So, remind me again why are we even talking about this?"

"Because when Bobby searched the Internet trying to find out where this woman lived, they reported she'd died. Murdered in two-thousand-seven."

Morales looked at me with a weird expression. "She was murdered in San Francisco? In '07?"

"Yeah. And not murdered while driving the damn cab like you'd expect. But in her own duplex out in the Avenues. That's the reason why I asked you about Twitter. A tweet came out yesterday morning accusing SFPD of being homophobic, sexist and racist because we never solved the case. And as of early yesterday afternoon, it had been re-tweeted over a hundred thousand times."

"Son-of-a-bitch, Deck. I actually remember that case. My partner at the time, Barry Egan, caught it. Yeah, out in the Avenues. The Twitter dude is correct. We never did solve that damn case."

"I know. I looked it up. But just because the case wasn't

11

solved, doesn't mean that Egan or you or anybody in our Department punted on the Garcia murder just because she was gay, or a Hispanic female. You and I know that's not true, and I'm gonna find the idiot who's tweeting this garbage and kick his ass good. Screw 'em. No one's gonna slur me or you or anybody in this room with that crap." When I heard the anger in my voice, I thought of Becky and knew it was time to get a grip. So did Morales.

"Hey, calm down, partner. I hear you. I know you weren't with our illustrious group back in the day, but you're obviously aware 2007 wasn't one of our better years for closures. And if I'm remembering correctly, the stats were even more gruesome in '08."

I paused and took a deep breath. "Yeah, I know. I looked that up, too. There's no doubt those weren't the best times to get whacked in this city." I stood, touched my pant leg to see if any bodily fluids were seeping out of my wounds and then delicately brushed the last remnants of the donut off my pant leg. I sat back down and said, "Geez, Barry Egan! There's a name outta the past."

"Yeah." Morales laughed. "Like I said, I partnered with him. We were paired together for four years. Just like us. I gotta tell you, he was a tough son-of-a-bitch to work with. But even with that said, I still liked him."

"I never met the dude, but knew him by reputation. Heard the same thing about him that you just referenced. That he was a tough son-of-a-bitch to work with." I paused, then asked, "When did he leave us? Two-ten? Eleven?"

"Eleven."

"I knew what he looked like. Heard about his reputation, and forgot he'd been your partner. He's been gone now for nine years." I gave a soft whistle. "Damn, a long time ago."

"God, time sure flies when you're havin' fun, doesn't it?" He laughed. "And who woulda thunk a case of his would come up thirteen years later? I'm guessing it's gotta be classified not only 'cold' by now, but 'frozen'." He laughed again.

"This Twitter nonsense has to stop," I said, feeling myself getting angry again. "Makes us look bad. I'm going to ask Bristow for permission to rummage through the case file. If for no other reason than to find a choice morsel or two that'll stop that SOB from tweeting out slanderous lies."

Morales nodded. "I remember the number of cases we had in '07. Man, seemed like hundreds. And the way things were back then, if Egan hadn't been assigned that particular case, I never would've heard the name Poppy Garcia." He took another donut and tore it in half, offering me one of the halves. I shook my head. He took a bite and then said, "Given the tweet, the Deputy Chief may actually agree to reclassify the case as open-slash-pending. But you know he's not going to let you anywhere near it given your nephew's connection."

I nodded and smiled. "In the old days, you'd be right. But in the age of Twitter and going viral, I'm hoping it's not going to be a problem." I pointed to our breakroom in the back. "You want coffee?"

"Nah!" he said. "But I can get some for you if you want. Save your leg a little wear and tear."

"Appreciate it, Manny, but I'm mobile enough to get my own freaking coffee."

The room was empty when I got there. I took the pot to the sink, scrubbed off the burnt-on sludge as best I could and refilled the reservoir with water. No sooner had I put coffee inside the filter than Deputy Chief Matt Bristow walked in.

CHAPTER 3

"Hi, DC." I said. "If you're after coffee, afraid you'll have to wait a few for it to brew."

"Not a problem, Deck," he responded. In the Department I was known as *Deck,* for Decker, my last name. "Glad we got guys around like you who'll make the damn stuff." He shook his head. "Some of the newer guys we got now think they're privileged."

"You be a hankerin' for the good old days, huh?" I replied with a smile.

"Nah. I was around in the *good old days.* I can tell you, for the most part, them days weren't all that good. With that being said, however, there are some of the good old days I wouldn't mind resurrecting. Like the ones where I could pick my own people and get the job done. Like I did for you." Bristow and I have had our run-ins, but his deciding vote got me into Homicide. For that reason alone, I'd go to the wall for him. "So how you been doing?"

"Busy, Matt. In and out too many times a day. You know the drill."

"Only too well." He paused and then said, "Did I notice a limp when you walked?"

"Yeah. My leg got all chewed up playing in that damn softball game last night." I was telling him about the game when the coffee pot beeped. Bristow wanted coffee more than he wanted to listen to my tale of woe, so he walked over and poured himself a cup.

"Sorry," he said, offering to pour mine. "I interrupted your story."

"Wasn't all that interesting," I said. I do have something I need to run past you, though, if you got a minute."

"Shoot," he said, taking a sip from his cup.

"Do you remember a female murder victim by the name of Poppy Garcia? She was capped in late '07. Before my time, but I thought maybe you might remember her. Lived out in the Sunset."

"I don't. But if this is going to take awhile, could we meet in my office in five minutes? I've got to take a leak." He held up his cup and shook his head. "This is what it means to get old. Take a just one sip of this stuff and you gotta pee." He put the cup down. "Give me a minute, Deck, then come to my office. We'll chat about your murder case."

~~~~~

"Come in," Bristow called out as I softly rapped my knuckles on his half-closed door. He noticed the look of surprise on my face as I looked around his office. "Pretty cool, huh?" he said, sweeping his hand over the room. "The place got redecorated over the weekend. You like?"

I didn't know what to say. Every damn piece of furniture in the office was the color of midnight.

He took me by the elbow and escorted me to a black round table by the back wall. "So, I ask again. What do you think?"

"At this moment . . ." I stood next to the table and did a complete pirouette. "I'm thinkin' I'm glad I don't have to dust this damn room."

He laughed and gave me a slap on the back. "Yeah. Good thing the city supplies janitorial help." Then, pointing to one of the chairs, he said, "Sit." I did as he commanded. "I know the motif is slightly on the dark side, but that shouldn't surprise you. You and I have been together for what now, six years?" I nodded. He smiled and said, "So, you know what a dark kinda guy I am." When I didn't respond, he changed subjects. "Okay, so tell me again why you're asking about an old murder case. I thought you and Morales had already been assigned?"

"We have, Matt. But I'm talking about a case that happened back in two thousand and seven, before my time. A cab driver named Poppy Garcia got herself popped. The case never got solved." I spent the next ten minutes telling him about the call I received from my nephew alerting me to the tweet accusing the Department of being homophobic, sexist, racists pigs.

"So, what's the big deal?" Bristow asked dismissively. "Not the first time some idiot accused us of all that. In fact, I'm wondering why 'baby killers' didn't make the list. They're all goof balls, Deck. Get used to it. Goes with the territory."

"This one's different, Matt. You're familiar with Twitter, right?"

"How can I not be when we have a President addicted to it."

I laughed. "But this is different. I checked before I came in this morning, and this guy's accusation has been re-tweeted somewhere north of a quarter million times. I can tell you the Twitter universe is on fire. The tweet is on the verge of going viral. We don't deserve this nonsense, Matt. Especially since it's being engineered by some jerk who probably jacks off at the thought of making the SFPD look bad. I'm pissed and want to squash this idiot."

"If your numbers are correct, I'm surprised the yahoos in PR haven't been up here yet."

"They will be, Matt. It's only a matter of time. And the brass will be all over our asses to do something."

"So, you're asking me to reopen a thirteen-year-old cold case?" Bristow sat back in his chair. "That's gonna be tough to do. First of all, there are procedures to follow. You know that. And second . . ."

"Nothing you can't override, Matt," I interrupted. "Look, all I'm asking is for a couple of days. Don't know about you, but I'm fed up with us taking the brunt of these conspiratorialist nut cases. Give me two days to show what a bunch of crap these idiots are spewing, and it'll all be over."

Bristow hesitated. "We can't reopen every damn cold case because some half-wit makes a stink, Deck."

"I know, Matt. But I'm not asking to open every damn case— only this one. The one with half a million re-tweets accusing us of not doing our job." I butted in before he could respond. "And only for a couple of days. Manny said whatever you do is okay by him since he doesn't need me right now."

Bristow steepled his hands under his chin and sat back in his chair. "Thirteen years, huh?" I nodded. "I'm really skeptical about this, Deck. Let me take it upstairs first. See what they have to say."

"We both know what they're going to say, Matt. Let's just you and me put out the Twitter fire before it goes any further."

He pursed his lips and looked at the ceiling. "Okay," he finally said. "Do what you have to do. I'll square it with the brass. You sure your partner is copacetic not having you around for a day or two?" I nodded. "Then I'll go along with it. But no more than two days. We clear on that?"

"You bet, Matt. I appreciate it."

"Okay, let's see what we got." Bristow walked to his desk and hunched over his keyboard. "The vic's name is Garcia?" I nodded. He fingered a few keys and watched as pixels showered the screen in a rainbow of colors. He scrolled downward. "Yeah, here it is. I don't remember the case. Not to be heartless, but she's nothing but another number on my screen." He leaned in closer as he scanned the case outline. "Don't see much here. Poor lady got herself killed at a bad time. Not only were the gangs shooting each other with abandon, but it was right around that damn off-year election that everybody was worried about. Lots of angst about our budgets. Cuts in the department. You remember what it was like."

"As you know Matt, I wasn't in Homicide at the time. But every damn department in the building was running scared that budgets might be cut in half. Would have threatened a lot of our jobs. The department would have been in deep doo-doo." I smiled inwardly at my choice of words. Becky would be proud.

"Yeah, particularly this one. Thank god the good guys held the high ground." He chuckled and looked back at his screen.

"So, says here Garcia got whacked in her home." He kept scrolling. "Says here she drove for the Lake Merced Cab Company and didn't show up for work. They called her cell, but she didn't answer. Ditto her landline. Finally, the office calls the emergency number. It goes to her mother who lived in the flat upstairs. The mother goes to the daughter's flat and finds her on the kitchen floor. Says here Poppy had taken one in the head." He looked up at me. "Damn, Deck. Imagine a mother finding her daughter with her head blown apart. How utterly devastating would that be?" Not waiting for my reply, he looked back at the screen and continued reading quietly for the next few minutes. He finally stood and stretched. "I could go on, Deck, but there's nothing here you can't get yourself. Says here Barry Egan handled the case. He's been long gone, but how convenient having his old partner, Manny Morales, as your partner. You have any questions about the case, you can just ask him."

"Yeah, right. He'd love that." I laughed then said, "Thanks

19

for letting me have a look-see."

"As long as Morales is okay with you leaving him for a few days, Deck, that's all I care really about. If he tells me he needs you back, you go back. No questions asked. Otherwise, I'll give you a few days to see if you can silence the noise and give the department some rest from the assholes who simply want to criticize us. And we owe it to the victim's parents, too. They deserve peace of mind knowing we did everything possible to bring their daughter's killer to justice. But after you take enough of a look to show those Twitter jockeys are full of it, get your ass back with Morales on the Morrison case. He'll need you."

I nodded and stood up, knowing I was dismissed. As I turned toward the door, Bristow stopped me. "Wait a minute, Deck. Almost forgot." He opened the top drawer of his desk and pulled out an envelope. "Earlier this morning, I found out the brass scheduled a damn meeting at City Hall this Wednesday night. On your birthday, of all things. Can you believe it?" He laughed.

I held up my hand. "Birthday's on Thursday, Matt."

"Whatever," he said with a wave of his hand. "This meeting is a command performance. Unfortunately for me, I happen to have two tickets to the Giants game that night." He waved the envelope at me. "Rockies in town. Thought maybe you could use them." Knowing my answer, he handed me the envelope.

"Thanks, DC," I said. "Never let it be said I turned down free Giants tickets." I put them in my coat pocket. Didn't want anyone in the squad room thinking I was Bristow's honey boy. "I'll take Becky."

"Great idea." He put his arm over my shoulder and walked me to the door. "Tell her I said 'hi.' And some day you'll have to tell me how a guy your age corrals a beautiful young woman like her." He emphasized the word "young."

"Matt, you'll be the first to know the whole story," I said with a smirk.

He smiled, patted me on the back and said, "I'm gonna hold you to that."

CHAPTER 4

I checked my watch as I left Bristow's office. Half past nine. Gloves was on the phone, but hurriedly hung up when he saw me coming.

"How'd it go?" he asked.

"As well as could be expected. I told him you were okay with me spending a day or two wrapping this up. Then I'll be back helping you on the Morrison case."

"Sounds good. Got one question though."

"Shoot."

"To reopen a cold case, the regulations say you've got to be in possession of new evidence. You have new evidence?"

"Nah. And Bristow's not reopening it. Just gave me two days to shut down the conspiratorialists out there. Stop the chatter once and for all. You got a minute so I can pick your brain about what you remember? Like what your impressions were back then. A drug deal gone awry? Pissed off boyfriend? Maybe stuff that didn't make it into the murder book?"

"Well, let me suggest you read the murder book first. Egan was lead on the case, and I'm pretty sure all the answers you're looking for will be in the book. If not, you know where I live."

I smiled. "Who would have thought as of this very minute I would be the lead on a thirteen-year-old cold case?"

"Lucky you."

"Lucky? Let me show you what lucky looks like." I reached

into my coat pocket. "Lookie what da man just gave me for being such a good, loyal homicide inspector." I fanned the two tickets in front of him. "For Wednesday night."

"And I know you're gonna invite your partner and now your best friend to go with you."

"Sorry," I answered. "Deputy Chief commanded me to take my wife. Besides, I know if you really wanted to go, you'd just call up one of your marks. Probably get better seats than these."

"Let me take a look at those." I passed them over. "Geez, man, these are open air seats. You're gonna freeze your ass off out there. I mean, if these were club house tickets, maybe I would have asked nicer." He laughed. "Oh, well. Have fun. Remember to bring lots of blankets."

I walked back to my desk and called the person I really wanted to take to the game.

Tom McGuire answered on the first ring.

"Tom," I said. "Reggie Decker."

There was a pause on the line and then, "Decker? Hey, man, what a surprise. How the heck you been doing? It's been a while since we last talked. Hope you're not calling for a donation to the Police Athletic League or something."

We both laughed. "Nope, something a lot better, Mac. Bristow, you remember him, don't you?" That triggered another dual laugh.

"God, Deck. Been trying to forget the SOB going on two years now. No such luck. Tell him I said hi."

"Will do, Mac, for sure. Actually, it was Matt who gave me two tickets to the Giants game Wednesday night. Playing the Rockies. I know it's short notice, but I was wondering if you'd like to go with me. Would be kick-ass to see you again."

There was silence on the other end, then, "Damn, Deck. Of all nights. I'm scheduled to give a talk in front of some old fogies over at the Athletic Club on Steiner. About how to keep busy in retirement. As if I knew. Anyway, sorry I can't make it. It was nice of you to think of me, though. Let's plan on getting together sometime soon. Maybe for lunch at Original Joe's? You up for that?"

"Would consider it an honor, my friend. Sorry about Wednesday, though."

"Take that pretty young wife of yours. You can pretend it's a first date."

I laughed. "Sounds like a perfect substitute, Mac. I'll tell her you gave up your seat so she could go."

"You do that. And give my best to the guys."

I hung up, disappointed about McGuire, but knowing I would be scoring points with Becky. It made the tradeoff worth it.

I sat back and called Bristow's secretary, Carolyn Knecht, known to everyone as "CK." She'd been a fixture in the Unit for what seemed like forever. Over the years, she was given more and more responsibilities, one of which was being the keeper of the keys that unlocked all the department's official records. The 'record' I needed was Poppy Garcia's official murder book.

Every homicide that occurred in the City and County of San Francisco had its own murder book: a day by day paper trail of the case that had been put together by the assigned Investigator. If you wanted to look through a murder book, you had to call CK. If she liked you, it would be on your desk within thirty minutes. If she thought you were a pain in the ass, it might take her three to four hours to find the particular book you were looking for.

Lucky for me, CK and I were buds. After checking with Bristow for an okay, the storage box containing Poppy Garcia's murder book was on my desk twenty minutes after I called.

"Dusty," I teased as she placed the banker's box on my desk.

"Am I supposed to apologize?" A half-grin creased her face

25

as she ran her index finger over the cover twice, making an X. The several ornate rings that adorned her fingers flashed in the glow of the overhead florescent lights. While CK wasn't a woman you'd call a *looker*, she had a certain earthy sophistication that made her a treat to be around. "Been lying in the vault for the past thirteen years," she said. "What did you expect?"

I took the top off the box and peeked inside. "Not much of a murder book," I stated, staring down at a single three-ring binder.

"Another Barry Egan masterpiece," she hissed. Seeing my look, she quickly added, "Okay, okay, so I couldn't stand the son-of-a-bitch. Sue me!" She paused and then added, "Glad we got rid of the prick."

I sat back in my chair and chuckled. "Oh, CK, you've got such a colorful way with words. But you know," I whispered conspiratorially, "he wasn't 'gotten rid of.' He quit."

"I know," she whispered back. "But that makes no difference. He was still a prick."

I smiled, wondering what would've happened if CK and Becky had become roomies. Her bawdy mouth would have driven Becky to drink. That friendship would've gone belly up within three weeks.

I shook off the image as I felt her fingernail tap my shoulder. "You can use the small conference room if you want. More privacy. No one scheduled until after lunch." She glanced at her watch. "You've still got a few hours."

"Any chance I could take this home?"

"Well . . ." she replied as she walked away. "You know you're not supposed to, but if I don't see you again today, have a good one."

I blew her a kiss, stuffed the binder and a yellow legal pad into my briefcase and limped out of the office.

CHAPTER 5

I pulled into my garage shortly after noon. Carefully trudging up the back stairway, I turned off the alarm and plopped my briefcase on the kitchen table. I opened the refrigerator looking for something to eat, but instead grabbed a beer and limped into the dining room. From where I was standing, I could see virtually all of the city's southern waterfront. As a wedding present, Becky's mom purchased a new home for us right below Twin Peaks. Never let it be said I didn't marry well.

My leg started to bother me so I took the beer into the bathroom and peeled off my khaki's. The gauze pads covering my leg were crusty with blood. I gingerly replaced them with new bandages, hoping the leakage phase was finally over.

Once finished, I swallowed two aspirin with the beer remaining in my bottle, walked to the bedroom and put on my loosest sweats. *If I have to work all afternoon and night,* I thought, *might as well be comfortable.*

Back in the kitchen, I snagged another beer, placed it on the table, and opened the murder book. The inside front cover featured a 5 x 7 photograph of a dark-haired woman in her early-to-mid-twenties, wearing rimless glasses and a hopeful smile. "Nice to meet you Poppy Garcia," I whispered. While I wouldn't have called her beautiful, I could see why my nephew wanted to reconnect. A sense of goodness radiated from her, detectable even through the sterile photograph.

Curious to see who besides me had checked out the book over these past many years, I turned to the plastic sleeve attached to the back cover. Only two names were listed; Carolyn Knecht had checked it out twice and Barry Egan once.

As required, CK placed a handwritten note into the sleeve. The time-stamped read: 12:02 p.m., August 25, 2008. It stated an email had been received in the Department's general inbox from a woman named Maria Garcia inquiring about the status of her daughter's case. CK's note mentioned she gave a copy of the email to Inspector Egan so he could respond. She also noted she put the original email in a plastic sleeve and filed it in the evidence section of the murder book. Two weeks later, on September 6, 2008, Inspector Barry Egan signed the book out at 11:36 a.m., and returned it at 2:29 p.m. the same day. CK wrote a notation indicating the book had been returned.

I wanted to read Mrs. Garcia's email, so I searched the divider tabs and found the 'Evidence' section. There were sixteen separate plastic sleeves in the section, some containing only a page or two of notations, while others were stuffed with evidentiary interviews, letters Poppy Garcia wrote or received, the early twenty-first century paper trail of human existence. I went through every piece of paper in the sixteen sleeves. Nowhere could I find an email from Poppy Garcia's mother. I grabbed my legal pad and made a note to ask CK what might have happened to that particular email.

I sat back and finished off my beer, deciding how I was going to attack the Garcia murder book. It was in a standard format, starting with the Preliminary Report and ending with C-OC, which I knew stood for Conclusion - Open Case. Someone with a marker, no doubt CK, crossed out the OC and substituted CC for cold case. Didn't change a thing for me.

I thumbed open the book to the first tab. It was, as I knew it would be, a simple summary of the case: name of the victim; location of the body; who found it; the time the police were notified, and the first officer(s) on the scene. A waste of time. I needed to know more about the case before I tackled this part, so I put it aside for later.

Next, I took a quick peek at the Coroner's Report. It was issued six days after the murder. The coroner's office established the victim died in the kitchen of her home between nine and eleven on the morning of June 26, 2007. The cause of death was a gunshot wound to the back of the head from a 9mm handgun. Interestingly, they recovered the slug from the kitchen wall halfway between the free-standing stove and ceiling, but didn't find the shell casing.

What the hell? I thought. *The shooter picked up the brass?*

On my yellow pad, I wrote, "The perp or perps picked up the shell casing. WTF?" I figured Becky wouldn't find abbreviating the words as objectionable as writing them out longhand.

The report contained photographs of the bullet hole in the wall, as well as a number of photos of the back and front of Poppy Garcia's ruined head. The blood splatter pattern suggested the victim had been standing and facing the opposite wall when the shooter fired. The shooter stood approximately five feet behind and slightly to her right. A broken cup and coffee splatter on the floor suggested the victim was drinking coffee at the time and must not have sensed the danger behind her. There were no bloody shoeprints on the kitchen floor, suggesting the killer or killers were either extraordinarily careful or left right after they shot her. Or both. The coroner's office found no evidence of sexual assault or battery. Blood samples from the victim showed no drugs or alcohol in her system at the time of death.

The next few pages chronicled the crime technician's report. I didn't feel like plowing through page after page of the items the techs collected, so I put the report aside. For now, my curiosity extended only to the conclusions their analysis suggested.

I tabbed open the Summary section.

Egan entered his summary in the book two weeks after the murder, and it included a bombshell. While no useful DNA samples were found in the house—no fingerprints, no hair, no footprints, nor any other technical or scientific evidence—they did find a quarter kilo bag of cocaine in the back-bedroom dresser. SFPD Narcotics considered a quarter kilo to be borderline dealer size.

Am I imagining this? I thought to myself as I paged back to reread the last sentence of the Coroner's Report. "Blood samples from the victim showed no use of drugs or alcohol, at least for the twenty-four hours preceding her death."

"Let's see if I got this right," I mused aloud as I sat back in my chair. "A quarter kilo of coke in her bedroom drawer, but no evidence of drug use for at least twenty-four hours prior to death."

While it made no sense to me whatsoever, I guessed it was theoretically possible. So, I flipped back to the Preliminary Report, looking for the cops who arrived on the scene first. It wouldn't have been Egan or Morales; they would have been called only after Homicide was notified. In my relatively short tenure as a homicide inspector, I'd found it useful to try to get a feel for a murder scene before it was overrun by the tech guys. Getting the impressions of the officer or officers who first arrived at the scene was more often than not helpful.

With the drug issue still rattling around in my brain, I needed to ask those first responders if they remembered seeing any evidence that a drug deal had gone down in the house prior to the shooting. Given the number of years that had passed, it would be a miracle if the first responders were still with SFPD, let alone remember the state of Poppy Garcia's house. Instead of being discouraged, I decided to wade through Egan's notes detailing how the murder was discovered.

Those notes revealed the first inkling something was amiss at the Kirkham Street address was registered by the victim's place of employment. Poppy Garcia was scheduled to work the night shift but hadn't shown up. According to her supervisor, Garcia had never been late to work. Half an hour after she should have been there, her employer placed the first call to her cell phone. Records showed someone from her place of work called her every ten minutes over the next hour. Finally, the supervisor, knowing Poppy's mother lived upstairs, placed a call to her. That call was logged by their system at 9:14 p.m.

At 9:19 p.m., a hysterical Maria Garcia called 911 dispatch, crying and screaming at the operator for help. Her daughter had been shot. The operator notified the police and stayed on the phone with Mrs. Garcia until they arrived at the house. The dispatch operator's call to Central Station logged in at 9:22 p.m. and was relayed to the Taraval Station at 9:23 p.m. At 9:24 p.m., Taraval Station ordered an ambulance to meet their officer at the Garcia household. At the same time, the Station dispatched Officer Maxwell Graser to the Kirkham Street address. Egan posted Graser's arrival at 9:38 p.m.

Maxwell Graser! My mouth broke into a wide grin. Small world. Graser had been a cop for twenty years. And a good one, too. Worked himself up from a patrolman to the Investigative Unit. He and I had worked a few cases together over the past decade. Then last fall, out of the blue, he quit the force and went to work as a property manager for the Port of San Francisco. Huge surprise to everyone.

He and I weren't what you'd call soul mates, but certainly buds. Primarily drinking buds, if truth be told. At least in our early days. When Becky entered my life full time, having a few beers with cop friends like Graser came to a screeching halt. Not because Becky objected to me drinking. It was me wanting to be home with her more than I wanted to be scarfing down a few beers with Graser, or anyone else for that matter.

I sat back in my chair and gazed at the ceiling. The coincidence of having an old compadre being the first cop on the scene of a murder that occurred thirteen years ago was off the charts. I couldn't have scripted it any better. If he remembered the case, and I figured the odds weren't in my favor, Graser could give me a feel for what it was like inside Garcia's house the night she got capped. I had doubts about Egan, but I needed an insight from someone who had no connection with the down and dirty investigation of this particular murder. Someone who could look at Poppy Garcia through unfiltered eyes. Hoping Graser could act as my eyes and ears that night, I pulled out my phone, hoping I still had his number. I did.

He answered on the third ring. "Damn! Reggie Decker! When your name popped up on my phone, I freakin' fell over. Listen, would love to talk to you, but I'm in a meeting right now. Shouldn't last more than thirty minutes. Can I call back? Will you still be available?"

I assured him I would and hung up. Knowing I had at least half an hour, I put the murder book aside and emptied the contents of the two 8 x 10 envelopes on the table. I was looking for photographs of Poppy Garcia. I remembered seeing one in the front of the murder book. It was a posed shot, not quite what I wanted. Digging a little further, I found a bunch of candid photos. I spent the next twenty minutes looking carefully at each one. I wanted to see the Poppy Garcia my nephew Bobby knew. The woman he thought so much of that he tried to reconnect with after all these years, for nothing more than to say *thanks* for what she did for him both emotionally and physically.

The first photo that caught my eye was Garcia's senior class picture from Abraham Lincoln High School. A color shot of a smiling, attractive young girl with jet black hair and soft brown eyes. The hair had an artificial look, but the eyes and smile were genuine. *A nice person lives here,* they said to me.

There was also a story about her from the *Chronicle*. The headline read, "San Francisco's First Hispanic Female Cab Driver." The article identified the cab driver as Poppy Garcia and made a point to mention that she volunteered to drive handicapped children to school each morning. I wondered if Bobby ever read this article. I looked at my watch. *Got at least ten minutes*, I thought. *Why not call and ask?*

Bobby answered on the second ring. I told him about the article. He couldn't remember ever seeing it, but had found a video on YouTube that was shot by the Merced Cab company back in 2003.

"You do know what YouTube is, don't you?"

"Come on, Bobby."

"Hey, just checking," he said with a laugh. "If you have time, I'll send it now. Hold on." He came back within twenty seconds. "It's on its way. Take a look and call me back. I'm in it. When I was four, I think. Wonder why I never received any movie offers." I could hear him chuckle. "Anyway, it's pretty cool. Someone filmed it from the top floor. I think you'll enjoy it."

I hung up and walked back to the office. Sitting at the desk, I turned on the computer and clicked the link Bobby sent. For the next six and a half minutes, I sat transfixed, watching a video of Poppy Garcia and my nephew play out before me. Bobby was right. It had been filmed from a classroom on the second or third floor. It showed a cab driving up to the front of the Sunshine School building in the pouring rain. The cab driver walked to the passenger side back door and lifted out a young boy. The camera zoomed in to a close up of both the boy and driver. The driver I recognized from her high school picture as Poppy Garcia. The young boy was my nephew, Bobby. *God, he was so small,* I thought. Garcia set him down on the sidewalk, reached into the back seat for his crutches, got him settled, opened her umbrella and started walking with him up the path to the school's front doors. What caught my eye was Poppy Garcia holding the umbrella over Bobby while leaving herself totally unprotected. The camera followed them to the front door of the school where they were met by someone, probably a teacher. It then followed Ms. Garcia back to the cab, her dark hair plastered to her head. The final shot was of her wiping her eyes with some kind of cloth, taking a final look at the school and driving away.

I took a deep breath, went back to the kitchen and called Bobby. "Thanks for sending this to me. You're right; she was a good woman, and I'm gonna find the son-of-a-bitch who killed her."

CHAPTER 6

I looked at the clock on the stove. Figuring I had at least an hour before Becky got home, I pulled another beer from the fridge. No sooner had I popped it open than Graser called back.

"Hey, Deck," he said. "Is this an okay time to talk?"

"Hell yeah, MG. I'm at the house havin' a beer. How the hell you been? Thought about you so damn often, but just never got around to calling. Feel bad about that, too."

"Don't worry about it. Life has a way of getting in the way of even our best intentions. How you been doin'? How's the wife? Uh . . . Becky, right?"

"Yep. Becky. And she's doing well. Teaching at a Catholic school out in the Mission. She'll be home in an hour or so. You still married?"

"You bet. Same lady you knew. Sixteen years now. Don't think I ever mentioned it to you, but she's the reason I left the force. Our marriage had started to implode. Too many nights out with guys like you." He laughed. "And if I'd kept it up, you'd be talking to a single guy right now."

"Then you made the right choice, man. And I'm guessing you enjoy what you're doing?"

"Amen to that, Deck. I'm working normal hours now. Man, who woulda thunk, huh? Home by six every night. No more being called out on emergencies at two in the morning. You of all people understand what I'm talking about from the inside."

"That I do, my friend."

"So, I'm guessing you didn't call me out of the blue to sell me a ticket to the policeman's ball. What's up?"

I laughed. "You guessed right, Max. I caught a case. Well, truth be told, I didn't catch it. I requested it."

"Requested it? What kinda case we talking about here?"

"A case that's been classified cold for the past eight or so years. You know the drill. Maybe they'll reclassify it; maybe they won't. Happened back in '07, when I was still in White Collar crimes." I took the last sip of my beer and went to the fridge for another. "Hold on a minute." I put the phone on the counter, opened the beer, took a quick swallow, then put the phone back to my ear. "Sorry. Had to get something."

"Oh-oh. Same old Deck. Did I detect the sound of a bottle being opened?"

I laughed. "And not my first, Max. But hey, I'm home. Becky's still at work, so there's no need to start counting yet." I took another swallow, then said, "Hope you ain't countin', either."

"God forbid," he chuckled. "So, tell me about this cold case."

"It's actually one you were involved in, to tell you the truth. And I'm not officially working it either. Just take a *look-see*, as Bristow put it."

"A murder, I'm guessing."

"Yeah. You were the first responder. From a 911 call. When you were at Taraval Station. A woman named Poppy Garcia. Ring a bell?"

"Poppy Garcia? Hell, yes, it does. Damn, Deck! That was way back in '07, wasn't it?" he asked. "Freaking ages ago, but I still remember like it happened yesterday. One of those cases that never leaves you. Somebody pumped one into that girl's head, if I remember correctly. In her own place, too. Mom found the body.

36

Called 911. Tragic."

"You remember those days, Max. I was new on the Force, but I knew guys in Homicide. Felt sorry for them. They were so overwhelmed a bunch of those damn murders didn't get solved. the attention they deserved. I'm glad I wasn't working the Unit in those years. They just didn't have the manpower to do justice the cases they had. Anyway, I'm involved in the Garcia case for two reasons. First, my nephew knew this Poppy woman. She was a very special person to him. And, since the department didn't get it solved, he asked if I would take a look."

"And the second?"

"The second is because there's some local jerk off who sent out a tweet yesterday saying the department purposely didn't solve the Garcia murder because she was a Hispanic female who happened to be gay, proving we're all racist, sexist, homophobic pigs."

"Ouch."

"Ouch is right. To be completely honest, Max, I'm revisiting the case only to prove the Twitter prick wrong. Him and his half-million followers."

"You'll get no argument from me. What can I do to help?"

"I got the murder book here in front of me. Barry Egan caught the lead. Did you know him back in the day?"

"Not well. He left the force in what, two thousand ten?"

"Close. Two-eleven."

"I knew he caught it 'cause I met him in the house when he showed up. Probably an hour or so after I got there."

"It's the hour you were in the house alone I want to talk about. I've been reading the murder book, and to tell you the truth, I'm none too impressed with how Egan handled the case. Sloppy, if you know what I mean. Sloppy enough to give some credence to the Twitter prick's accusation. Makes my teeth hurt to even say it." Graser didn't respond, so I continued. "I'm sitting here think-ing how awful it had to be for the mom to see her daughter on the kitchen floor with half of her head missing. I still shiver at what she must have felt."

"I'm with you, Deck," Graser replied. "I felt the same way."

"Can you imagine how life-crushing it would be to walk into the house and find your child that way? Shot while standing in their own damn kitchen. Even if this woman was a drug dealer, or worse, you'd still want to do what you could to save the mom from that horror."

"Absolutely," he replied.

"Max, I have a lot of faith in you. I need to know if you re-member anything about the murder scene. Anything that didn't look right. You know what I mean, right?"

"Tell me what you're thinking."

"Well, I haven't been through the whole book yet, and I'm not what you'd call a disinterested third party. My nephew, whom I love dearly, adored this woman. But it was a long time ago, and this Poppy lady could've gone to the dark side without him ever knowing. I just don't know the answer. I need your help."

After a short silence, Graser spoke. "Well, Deck, I only saw her bloody remains. As I remember, I spent most of my time deal-ing with her semi-hysterical mother. And as far as my impres-sions? Again, as I remember, everything looked normal. I kept the mother in the living room, not only so she didn't have to look at her daughter's corpse, but because I didn't want her to mess up the scene. The ambulance came within ten minutes of my arrival. One of the EMTs took Mrs. Garcia up to her flat and called a friend of hers to come over. The other dude looked at the body, said there was nothing he could do for her, and left.

"I didn't see any sign of a fight. No overturned chairs, no pa-pers strewn about. The victim was fully clothed. Except for all the blood, tell you the truth it was a peaceful scene. Not a robbery, since there was a bunch of money and other stuff laying on the kitchen table. I'm guessing a few hundred dollars in bills and another fifty or so in change. Quarters, nickels, dimes—that sort of thing.

"On the table next to the money was a laptop. Dell. One of the high-end models. I remember because it's the make I had at the time, but mine didn't have all the bells and whistles hers did. In any case, the screen was black. I noticed the power light on, which meant the laptop was in sleep mode. I became curious as to what the vic was doing when she was so rudely interrupted, so I put on a glove and tapped a key. Given the money on the table, it didn't surprise me the screen opened to an Excel spreadsheet. Turned out to be tip money. I'm not guessing here, Deck. The Excel title read 'TIPS'. The rows contained the June dates. Last entry was on the 26th. She never finished counting the day she died."

"Anything else laying around?"

"Yeah, her cell phone, and on the counter near the coffee pot was a fairly large camera bag. I didn't look in it though."

"Did it look to you, or feel to you, like a drug house? I mean where transactions went down?"

"Nah. And I can tell you with some certainty that if the money I saw came from drug transactions and not taxi tips, she was a piss poor drug dealer. Like I said, couldn't have been more than two, three hundred dollars, not counting the change. I mean, come on. You ever see a dealer worth his, or in this case her, salt deal in small coins?"

I laughed and shook my head. "What about drug paraphernalia? Pipes? Bowls? Sniffers? Anything like that laying around?"

"No, no, and no. Didn't see anything of that nature."

"Would you be surprised if I told you Egan found a quarter

kilo of cocaine in her back bedroom?"

"You and I were in the business a long time, Deck, so we both know we're generally immune from surprises. But in this case? Yeah, I'd be surprised."

"Surprises me, too. Doesn't make sense on any number of levels. But let's suspend the skepticism for a minute and agree this was a drug hit. The money on the table, forget the denominations, woulda been long gone, right? Whoever did the lady would've taken it. And then Egan wants us to believe they wouldn't have rummaged around to find other valuables? Like, for example, a quarter kilo of coke laying in the top drawer of her dresser? Come on. To say this had the characteristics of a drug hit, at least for me, doesn't make it."

"Well, I never asked myself about motive, but you're right. It doesn't smell right."

"Yeah. Just wish we had the answers, Max. But I appreciate your help and insight. I'll finish up the book, push back hard on the Twitter dude and then make a decision about whether I should pursue this case any further."

"Lots-a luck, my friend. You need anything else, you know where to find me."

"You'll be the first number on my speed dial." I heard the key in the front door. "Max, got to run. Becky's home. Tell you what, the four of us should get together one of these days. Talk to your wife, then look at your calendar. We'd love to entertain you over here. Becky's a great cook."

"Sounds great, Deck. I'll ask Debbie tonight. Be back to you soon. Say hi to your wife for me. And good hunting on the case."

CHAPTER 7

B ecky walked into the kitchen as I hung up. "Well, this is a pleasant surprise. When did you get home? And did I hear my name mentioned in the same sentence with the word 'cook'?" She put her briefcase on the chair and gave me a hug. "Already had a few, huh?"

"Hey, only three or four. See?" I pointed to the kitchen counter. "You can count the bottles." She took a peek and smiled. "I took most of the afternoon off. Brought home the Garcia murder book. That's the woman Bobby called about. Decided I could concentrate better here without all the office distractions. And yes, your name and cooking were mentioned in the same breath. You remember Max Graser? I worked a few cases with him." She shook her head. "Didn't think so. As soon as I got into Homicide, he fell off our social calendar."

She snickered. "You sure it was a cop you were talking to?"

"Yep. A cop and a drinking buddy. Too much of a drinkin' buddy, to tell you the truth. It was either demon rum or you." I reached over and pulled her to me. "And I knew demon rum wasn't going to get me laid."

"You're so romantic," she said with a smile, snuggling in closer. "Earlier today, I thought it would be fun to go out to dinner. But something happened at school, and now I only want to stay home and have you hold me."

"Oh, baby, I'm sorry. What happened?"

"Would you mind taking a few chicken thighs out of the freezer and putting them in the microwave for five minutes on *defrost*? We can talk after I get out of these clothes." She gently pushed me away. "And you can get me a beer, too."

When she returned, I handed her a Sam Adams. After taking a few sips, she took the chicken out of the microwave and put them in the oven. Taking my hand, she led me into the living room.

"I could get used to this," she said as we sat on the sofa, her head on my shoulder and bare feet curled up under her. "I'm glad we've got some time before dinner is ready."

"Me, too." I took her hand. "Tell me what's so important. What happened at school? You weren't attacked by a student, I hope?"

"No, nothing like that." She hesitated. I could tell she was searching for the right words. "You've been around the children I teach, right?"

"Not this particular class, but yeah, in general."

She took a sip of beer, put it down on the coffee table and then laid her head back on my shoulder. "So, you know most of them are from lower-income families." I nodded, thinking to myself how fortunate she was. If she'd been hired to teach in the elementary school two miles south of her, it would have been a hell of a lot worse. Not only was the neighborhood poorer, it was seriously gang-infested. Two, three guys a week got capped in that section of the city. At least she didn't have to deal with that kind of crap.

"A lot of my kids come from single-parent homes," she added. "It's so sad. There are no dads around, which means the moms have to work. And a working mom often translates into a lot of my students going home after school to an empty house or, closer to reality, an empty apartment. It tears me up, hon. My little

42

guys are second graders. Seven and eight-year-olds. They're still babies, for goodness sake."

"Yeah, sad." I knew it sounded lame, but what the hell else was there to say?

"It's worse than sad. It's such a helpless feeling. I want to do something to help them."

"Come on, babe. Believe me, I understand. But neither of us can do much of anything to help their situations. You and I both know only to worry about things you can control." I paused and pulled her closer to me. "You help these kids in so many ways. Immeasurable ways. Ways that'll stay with them a lifetime. You teach them to read and write. Teach them morals. Teach them to look out for one another. What you're doing changes their lives in ways you'll never see or know about unless they come back to visit you when they're adults. Hopefully, they'll have made better choices than their parents did."

"Thanks, darling. I know you're right. Most of us go into teaching believing we're going to have an effect on the lives of the kids we teach. But since we hardly ever get to see the change in real time, we never really know. Oh, I get to see their reading and math scores go up. Stuff like that. But do we have a real effect on their lives? I honestly don't know the answer to that."

She sat in silence for a few minutes. "I'll give you an example of something that happened today. Darn depressing. There's a boy in my class named Edwin. Edwin Cosgrove. Just turned eight years old. One of the younger kids in the class. He's not a great student, but he tries. You'd like him. Same as a lot of the children in my class, he lives in a single parent home. He and his mom. She came to a few of the parent-teacher nights, so I know she's at least interested in her child. Problem is, she's twenty-three years old. Edwin is almost eight. Do the math. She's from Louisiana. Had very little formal education, and consequently her skill-set is severely limited.

"I left the classroom today around four this afternoon. Was walking to the car when I saw Edwin sitting on the curb in front of the school. I walked over and asked if he was all right. He said he was waiting for his mom and then he started to cry. Turned out he'd been sitting there for over an hour. His mom never came to get him.

"My heart broke when he told me that, so I offered him a ride home. The mother, thank god, was there by the time we arrived. When she opened the door, her red eyes told me she'd been crying, too. She told me she lost her job today. She works, or worked, as a maid in that creepy motel over on Naples Street. She told me she spent the afternoon looking for a new job. She didn't even score an interview, poor thing."

Becky's eyes now sparkled with tears. I reached for my hankie and gave it to her.

"I was at a loss for what to do or say," she said. "I had thirty bucks on me. I gave it to her. Wished it was a hundred. Told her to keep looking for a job. One would turn up. A pep talk, for god's sake. I felt so silly, but what else could I say or do?"

"You did all that could be expected, babe." I put my arm around her. "I'm proud of what you did. You have a wonderful heart. And we can afford to give the mom a hundred bucks or so. At least it'll keep her going for a few days."

"You remember our school is playing in a baseball game tomorrow afternoon at five, right?" she said out of the blue.

I nodded. "I can tell you for sure I'm gonna be there."

"At Crocker-Amazon? Oh, that's so great. You can meet Edwin in person."

"You're bringing him to the game with you? Hope you told his mom."

"Yes. I told her. In fact, got her written permission. Believe me, I'm aware of the law. They drill it into you in the classes you take for a teaching credential. Her letter is in my purse. I'll show it to you."

She started to stand, but I took her arm and gently pulled her back to the sofa. "I believe you, babe. No need to show me."

"Thanks," she said, leaning over and giving me a kiss. "I'm taking him to the game and then home after the game. You're going to like him a lot. He loves baseball, by the way. You can take him to a Giants game."

"Whoa. Hold on." I leaned back into the cushion. "Repeat what you just said?"

"About the baseball game?"

"No. Come on, you know what I mean."

"About Edwin? I said I was bringing him home tomorrow after the game."

"You mean to his own home, right?"

"Unfortunately, no. Not unless his mom found a new job."

"Now wait a minute. You mean if she hasn't found a job by tomorrow afternoon, you're bringing the kid here?"

"That's what I mean, yes."

"I want to get this straight. Tell me you're only talking about bringing him here for dinner, and after dinner you'll take him back to his house."

"He can't go back to his house, Reg. Not unless his mom is there. And who knows when that'll be? Come on, don't be an old grump. This is a big house. We could put him up for as long as it takes his mother to find a job. Might be a day or two. Might be a week. A slight possibility it could be longer. Hard to tell."

"An eight-year-old? What the hell we gonna do with an eight-year-old?"

"Take him to school and back. Give him breakfast and lunch, feed him dinner. Give him books to read. Say his prayers with

45

him. Take him to our softball games." She burrowed into me. "We have one tomorrow night though I'm pretty sure you're not going to be able to play." I nodded but remained silent. "Anyway, we can put him to bed. Give him a kiss goodnight. Things he needs in his life. He's only eight."

"Does he say prayers?"

"He does at school. You know that."

"I meant at his home."

"How would I know? If he doesn't, we can teach him while he's here so he can teach his mom." She snuggled in closer to me. "I've been thinking about this for a while, my darling. It's a wonderful thing to do. Could make the difference between Edwin living a productive life or you arresting him for gang-banging when he's sixteen."

"Or even before he's sixteen."

She squeezed my arm lightly. "Come on, Reg. You know what I mean." She put her head on my shoulder. "When we got married, we wanted children, remember? We tried and tried. Nothing worked. We talked a lot about adopting, but never found the right child. Please take a look at Edwin. We could really help him." She put her hand on my cheek and turned my face toward hers. "And this will give me a chance to find out if I could be a good mom. Real on-the-job-training."

"Babe, I agree this is an important matter, a big decision. But do me a favor, okay? If you want to be a mom, let's go back through the right channels. I'll be fine with Jim, or Justin, or whatever the heck his name is."

"Edwin."

I nodded. "I'll be fine with Edwin. But only for a few days, okay? I don't think it's a good idea to bring home a child who's in your class for all kinds or reasons. First of all, the paperwork involved to bring a kid into our house to live, even for a day or two, has been monstrous. You'll be dealing with child protective services, you know. They're a no-nonsense agency, in case you didn't know."

"I know, Reg. But just for a day or two. We can do at least that." She put her head on my shoulder again. "Just let him stay with us for two or three days. I'm sure his mom would sign whatever papers needed. It would give her a chance to find a job. Then she could take him back."

"I'll tell you what I'll do," I said. "I'll agree to have him here for three days. Not one day more. Conditional on his mother writing up a hold-harmless paper protecting us from being sued if something happens to Edwin while in our care." I paused. "You okay with that?"

She nodded into my shoulder. "Oh thanks, baby. This is a good thing to do. To help out a mom like this. You'll see."

"Tell you what else I'll do. I'll check at the office tomorrow to see if anyone is aware of a job opening for Edwin's mom. What's her name?"

"Edwina."

I looked at her as if she'd cracked a joke. She hadn't. "Edwin and Edwina." I sighed. "Perfect."

CHAPTER 8

A fter dinner, Becky left to make our house suitable for the new roomie. I figured I had two choices—work the Garcia case or watch television by myself.

I didn't particularly want to go back to work on the Poppy Garcia matter, but the alternative, to watch television the next few hours by myself, was an easy *no thank you.*

I walked back to the kitchen and sat, trying to piece together a plan that would solve both of my Poppy Garcia problems: Bobby's questions and concerns about her case not being well handled in the first place and the accusations made by this Twitter dude.

On one level, the Twitter guy had legit reasons to complain. It was becoming clear that Egan didn't give a rat's ass about solving the case. But dammit, our whole Unit shouldn't be slammed because Egan was an inept asshole. If and when I ever meet this Twitter jerk, I'm gonna slap him upside the head and tell him just that.

And how do I handle Bobby? I'll gave him credit—he played me just right. His video affected me exactly as he intended, transforming me from a neutral observer to an involved advocate. The first lesson they taught us going through the Academy was never become emotionally invested in a case. Clouds your judgement. Over my decade and a half as a police officer, I've lived by that rule. With Bobby counting on me to bring Poppy Garcia's killer to justice, I could feel the distinction between *better judgement* and *emotionally involved* starting to intersect.

Sitting at the table, I decided to re-read the damn murder book again. I needed to find something to convince Bristow to give me the time needed to do justice to Poppy's memory.

Opening the book, I thumbed to the Conclusion - Open Case tab. *Poppy Garcia has been waiting a long time for justice,* I thought. *If somebody's going to find the son-of-a-bitch who shot her, might as well be me.*

Section one of the 'C-OC' began with the standard questionnaire. I scanned it.

Crime of domestic violence: NO
Hate crime: NO
Burglary: NO
Sexual assault: NO
Kidnapping: NO
Gang-related: YES

I scribbled a note on my legal pad: "What's the evidence for being gang-related????"

I thumbed to 'Section Two: ACCESS TO ENTRY'. In it, Egan wrote only two entries. The first said there was no damage to the front door; the second said that the lock showed no evidence of being picked.

From those two entries, Egan drew two probable conclusions: a) Poppy Garcia knew the perp(s) or, b) they tricked her into opening the door. For reasons he never explained, Egan opted for the former, that she knew the perp or perps and welcomed them into her home.

I shook my head. Either Egan was a bigger idiot than I imagined, or this was his way of closing down the investigation. I was convinced it was the latter.

I wrote in my notebook: "*Access to Entry* conclusion iffy at best. Could've been a ton of people who Garcia would've let into her flat. Friends. Co-workers. A delivery man. Her priest or rabbi. A cop. Her mother."

I went back to the murder book and flipped open the tab labeled "Interviews." The section opened with a note from the coroner's office establishing Poppy's probable time of death as sometime between the hours of nine and eleven the morning of June 26th.

Of the twenty-seven people Egan interviewed in depth, Poppy's mother, Maria Garcia and her female friend, Lydia McNamara, who stayed with her the night of the 27th, garnered the most attention. Both women left the flat the morning of the murder at seven and took the N-Judah streetcar downtown. Egan references his interview with the conductor of the streetcar who identified a photo of Mrs. Garcia and her friend as being on his car that morning. Next, Egan established the two women ate breakfast at the El Dorado Restaurant on Powell Street between eight-thirty and nine-forty by introducing a Master Card receipt for $34.42, signed by Mrs. Garcia and time-stamped at 9:37 a.m. the morning of the 28th. Egan spent the next few pages retracing the two women's steps between the time they left the restaurant and 11:30 that morning when Mrs. Garcia made a phone call to her daughter. The daughter didn't answer, so Mrs. Garcia left a message. Both Mrs. Garcia's cell phone provider and the actual recording on the daughter's answering machine corroborated the time of the call.

The interview went on for another six pages, focusing on her story of wandering around the city with her friend. It ended with a paragraph summarizing Mrs. Garcia's day. The final sentence read: "Mrs. Garcia's whereabouts the day of the murder make it impossible for her to have committed the crime."

I shook my head in disbelief. Every cop knows not being present when a crime is committed doesn't eliminate you from being a suspect. What if the person knew the murderer or, better yet, had prior knowledge the murder was being planned? In legal jargon, they'd at least have been an "accomplice." Egan obviously knew that. What made him so eager to shield the mother?

I closed the murder book and wrote in my legal pad: "Egan claims the mother's whereabouts the day of the murder made it impossible for her to have committed the crime, failing to mention she could have been an accomplice." I wrote: "Sloppy! Sloppy! Sloppy!"

I started wondering if Egan ever called the mother back. I was willing to bet if he hadn't returned the mother's email to the murder book, then he hadn't called her back either. I leaned forward in the chair, the scabs on my leg starting to itch. I patted my trouser leg, willing the itch would go away. It didn't. I got up and hobbled to the bathroom. Found the bottle of aspirin on the top shelf. Becky heard me and met me in the hallway.

"You doing okay? Want me to take a look?"

"Thanks, babe. Just itchy. I'm practicing self-control." I plopped two aspirin in my hand, dry swallowed them and hobbled back to the kitchen.

CHAPTER 9

The clock on the stove read eight-fifty as I poured another cup of coffee. I could hear Becky moving furniture. She had gone back to remodeling the spare bedroom for Edmund, or Edwin, or whatever the hell the kid's name was. I sat at the table, my itchy leg outstretched beneath it, and reopened the murder book, flipping to the section marked 'Summary'.

"Last chance, Poppy," I whispered to myself. "Wherever you are, say a prayer I find something."

"Poppy Garcia: Victim of a Gang-Related Shooting," blared Egan's Summary headline. In case the reader might conclude he made it all up, he added this sub-headline for authenticity: "This conclusion fits the facts as investigated by Lead Homicide Inspector Barry Egan."

** *Victim: Poppy Garcia; Female. Age 25. Shot, execution style, while standing in her kitchen facing away from the killer.*

**Weapon: 9mm "silenced" handgun.*

**Coroner Report: Victim not sexually assaulted.*

**Interviews with employees of firm where victim worked confirmed no known enemies.*

**Victim was never married. Friends confirmed she did not date much, which ruled out jealous husband or boyfriend.*

**Victim's mother had ironclad alibi the day of the murder.*

She has been ruled out as suspect.

I starred that line and wrote in my notebook: "mother's alibi not sufficient," and then continued reading.

**Victim born out of wedlock. Mother states she didn't know the father's name, only that he was a man she met in a bar and made the mistake of sleeping with him without protection.*

**Hospital birth records confirm "Father Unknown."*

**Evidence did not point to robbery as none of the rooms in the house produced alien fingerprints.*

**None of the rooms were disturbed.*

**A quarter kilo of uncut cocaine was found in the victim's bedroom dresser drawer.*

**Lead Inspector believes the evidence shows murder was motivated by some perceived insult to a gang or gang member, rather than robbery motivated. Lead Inspector is led to this conclusion because if robbery was the motive, cocaine in bedroom dresser drawer would have been found and taken.*

Conclusion: *Since there was no evidence of forced entry, Lead Inspector concludes the following:*

** *The victim knew the killer(s) and was not coerced into letting shooter into her flat.*

** *The killer(s) were in the house only long enough to assassinate the victim and leave.*

** *Cocaine in bedroom leads to the conclusion this was not a home invasion burglary, but rather a gang-retaliation murder.*

I stopped reading and leaned back in the chair. It was evident to me from Egan's conclusions he'd given up on this case from the get-go. But why? *Sloppy,* I wrote in my notes, knowing full well Egan's report was more than just "sloppy." Much more. His conclusions felt purposeful to me. I wondered what could possibly have motivated him to advance this theory; in essence, to cook the murder book! I tried to put myself in his place. Since Morales wasn't going to join him, Egan knew he'd be in the house alone for over an hour while waiting for the coroner. I shook my head and started to think through the different scenarios when it hit me.

Son-of-a-bitch! "What if ...?"

Leaning forward, I put my elbows on the table and opened the murder book to the section tabbed 'Evidence'. Since everything at a crime scene is considered potential evidence, murder books must include a listing of every item found, no matter how insignificant. I'd already gone through a number of these pages earlier but spent time only on the ones that seemed germane to the case. I'd already perused pages on uncompromised locks, the lack of identifiable fingerprints anywhere in the house, the ballistics of the weapon used, things of that nature. Now I was after a different kind of information. Something relevant to the case before me.

This time, I opened the sub-tab marked "Kitchen."

The number of pages listing kitchen items didn't surprise me. Every knife, fork, and spoon had to be listed, as did every cup and saucer, every glass, every pot and pan, every electric machine, every coffee pot, toaster, and blender. I thumbed through those pages quickly, eager to read what Egan had to say about the money on the kitchen table.

I read through his report twice in case I'd missed it. But I hadn't missed it. The money Graser told me he saw on the kitchen table didn't make the murder book. Nor did the laptop computer. Ditto the cell phone and large camera bag. A smile creased my lips as I sat back in the chair and gazed at the ceiling, "You're a weaselly son-of-a-bitch, Egan," I mumbled aloud. "I'm gonna enjoy arresting your sorry ass."

It took me thirty minutes to finish my brief. Only one other 'evidence' issue needed to be clarified: the quarter kilo bag of cocaine supposedly found by Inspector Egan in Garcia's dresser drawer. I've been around illegal drugs my entire career but would never classify myself as an expert, especially where it concerned the thought process of addicts or dealers. But I knew someone who did.

CHAPTER 10

Pulling out my cell, I walked into the living room and dialed a number. When no one answered by the fourth ring, I was thinking maybe I'd made a mistake. At the sixth ring, I was just about to disconnect when a cranky voice growled at me through the ether. "Why the hell you calling me at this ungodly hour, Decker? This better be good."

Walt Kincaid was the Special Agent in Charge of the FBI Drug Task Force based in San Francisco. The Drug Task Force's job was to find ways to keep the Mexican cartels from flooding the country with narcotics. I was introduced to him years ago by my old partner Tom McGuire, and we've been friends ever since.

"Yeah, Walt, and I love you too, you grouchy old bastard. Hell, in the old days . . ."

"And don't even start on how it was in the old days. This ain't the old days. Hell, in the old days, I was young, and you hadn't even been born. These days, I'm old and need my sleep. And you should be in bed with that pretty young wife of yours." I heard him chuckle. Then he said to me, "And I see you've been taking some hits from the Twitter crowd. What's up with that?"

"That's partly what I'm calling about, Walt. You got a minute?"

"Absolutely. Go for it."

"Twitter people are a strange breed, if you ask me, Walt. My nephew happens to be a big Twitter fan and has been listening to that nonsense about the SFPD being a bunch of homophobic racists. He called me yesterday asking if what he was hearing was true."

"And you told him the truth, I hope."

"Well, that's the rub, Walt. I started nosing around the murder book today looking at the way the case was originally handled, and I'm starting to think those Twitter jerks may be on to something." I told Walt the backstory, from my nephew's phone call to reading through the murder book myself. "It's the conclusion of the Inspector assigned to the case that the vic was killed by gangbangers. Therefore, Q.E.D, it was a gang-related murder."

"And how'd he come to that conclusion?"

"He said he saw no evidence of forced entry and concluded, therefore, the killer, or killers, had to be someone she knew. And, oh yeah, one more thing. They found a bag of coke in her bedroom. A quarter kilo. Uncut."

"Whoa. You're telling me whoever did the girl didn't take the cocaine? Are you kidding me?"

"I wish," I replied. "And because the coke happened to be miraculously left behind, the Homicide Inspector concluded her murder couldn't have been drug related. I admit it sounds strange, but in his mind, it goes something like this: If she were done in by druggies, they would have ransacked the house for drugs. But they didn't. Ergo, she didn't steal the coke from them. Once that was ruled out, there is no motive except, presto, a gang-related hit.'"

"For god's sake, Decker. You know as well as I do that's a distinction without a difference. Who is this bozo? He working in your section?"

"At one time, he did, yeah. But no longer. For the past eight or nine years, he's been working in Sacramento. Our old chief, the one who went to work as the Governor's Chief of Staff, hired him for the Capitol Security office."

"Scary."

"But to be fair to him, Walt, this murder took place thirteen years ago. At a time when it seemed almost every murder was drug or gang-related."

"Come on, Decker, everybody knows drugs, gangs, and murders are synonymous. But still . . ." He went silent. I visualized him trying to see the murder scene in his mind. "How long after the murder was the body discovered?"

"According to the coroner, the woman was killed between nine and eleven in the morning. Body wasn't found until sometime after nine that night. So, ten to twelve hours, minimum."

"If this 'gang' had known no one would be over to see the vic that day, why would they be in such a hurry to leave? They could've spent the whole damn day there. Had a party, for god's sake, and no one would have been the wiser. Until, of course, the body was found. And this guy Egan is telling you they left without checking to see if there was anything of value to steal?"

"You're right. And if they knew the Garcia woman, they would have known she worked at night, and therefore slept most of the daylight hours. Wouldn't have had any visitors. I deal with gang members all the time. Ransacking the house would've been the first thing they did. And, if they found the dope, it would've been party time the rest of the day."

"Makes sense to me," Kincaid replied. "I mean, even your Lead didn't think it was a random hit. Seems to me your suspicions are right-on. Doesn't make any sense they didn't find the coke and take it. In the real world, in our world, that coke woulda been long gone."

"That's exactly how I figured it, too, Walt. Thanks for helping me sort this out. I'm feeling a lot more confident about seeing Bristow tomorrow to request the case be reopened."

"If you need reinforcements, have him call me."

I laughed. "Yeah, that'll go over big-time. Bristow taking suggestions from the FBI on how to do his job."

"Well, you tell him from me the original lead inspector must have been sniffing the stuff he found in the vic's drawer."

"Brilliant, Walt. I'll tell him first thing tomorrow morning." We both had a chuckle over that one.

"You do that." He hesitated for a moment and then said, "Hey, as long as I have you on the phone, you up for a Giants game anytime soon? It's been a while."

"You're right, my man. We need to go. Too damn long." I'd always thought of myself as a Giants fanatic, but when it came to "fanatic," Walt was me on steroids. He'd played college ball at William & Mary, and as a senior, was drafted by the Phillies. Had a cup-of-coffee in the minors before being let go. Got himself a job at the FBI soon thereafter. "But let me take a rain check until I get this Garcia thing settled, okay? Even if the Deputy Chief lets me keep the case open, it shouldn't take too long. In the meantime, though, if you want to scratch your baseball itch, Becky's school is having a game over at Crocker-Amazon tomorrow at five. Wanna come? A titanic struggle between her school's sixth graders and some other elementary school."

Kincaid took a deep breath, then said slowly, "Uhh, thanks, Decker, but I think I'll wait for a Giants game if you don't mind." He paused. "And how is Becky doing, by the way? Looking forward to the summer?"

"Well, we got kind of a problem here."

"Uh oh."

"Yeah. It's not real serious, at least not yet. She's bringing a student from her class to come live with us. I'm not too thrilled about it, tell you the truth."

"Don't blame you. What's gotten into her? Next thing you

know, she'll be wanting to have a kid of her own."

I laughed. "That's what scares me the most, Walt, and I don't know what to do about it."

"I'm afraid it's too late at night for me to wrap my mind around that problem, my friend. But listen, anytime you want an ear, you got mine. Just give me a call." He paused and then said with a laugh, "Preferably before eleven at night."

"Thanks, Walt. You're a good friend. I'm hopin' to be done with this case sooner rather than later. The Twitter thing is a two-edged sword. It got us to reopen the case. That's the good thing. But it's also showering the department with really bad pub, and that ain't good. In any case, thanks for listening. We'll get to a game soon, I promise."

CHAPTER 11

I sat back on the sofa at the same time Becky closed the spare bedroom door.

"How's it going?" she asked, as she sat down next to me.

I smiled and squeezed her thigh. "Unbelievably well." I filled her in on my conversation with Kincaid and the notes Graser took that confirmed Egan stole items from the murder victim's house. "I can't wait to nail the son-of- . . . ." I caught myself in time. ". . . to nail the jerk."

Becky smiled, and then said, "Oh, how gross of him. How do you think your DC will react?"

"Bristow? I think he'll be relieved. He's told me over and over how much he disliked Egan. Always thought he was out for himself. And he sure as hell didn't appreciate the effect Egan had on some of his fellow officers."

"Didn't you tell me he was Manny's partner for a few years?"

"Yeah. But I don't think they were obsessively tight. At least from how he talks about him now."

"How's it going with the Twitter person? Is he still attacking the department?"

"I haven't looked at it since early afternoon. Not sure I want to see. Just makes me angrier. But that dude's next on my radar. I think I can neutralize him, but for that to happen Bristow has to let me freelance for a few more days. Can you imagine the crap hitting the fan when the Twitter crowd hears what Egan did?"

"Come on, hon," she said with a hint of annoyance. "I know you're trying, but we have a little guy here now. You've got to watch the language."

"Oh, stop," I said in a jocular voice even though I could feel the anger bubbling up behind it. "I hardly cuss at all these days thanks to you. And I'll bet he probably uses a lot worse language than just the word crap."

"He won't if he wants to live here. So, please, watch what you say around him. Kids are so absorbent. He hears you swearing, and he'll imitate that."

"Okay, okay." Now I was thoroughly miffed. "Can you imagine . . ." I paused for effect, "the *poo-poo* hitting the fan when . . ." I stopped and looked over at her. "You satisfied?"

She looked at me as though I were a recalcitrant student of hers, which, in a way, I guess I was. Discretion being the better part of valor, I quickly changed topics. "Have you got everything ready for Edwin?"

"I think for the most part I kid-proofed the house." She laid her head on my shoulder. "You okay now with having the child with us?"

"Anything is possible over another beer or two," I said, the temperature in the room returning to near normal. I gave her a kiss on the cheek and walked to kitchen and brought back two open bottles. We both took a sip. "Can we talk for a few minutes?"

"Absolutely." She took a sip. "Go for it."

"I want you to know I'm still feelin' twitchy about this kid staying here. For me, the first issue is the firearms in the bedroom. We've got to think through how to establish a kid-free zone in our house, because as of now, the kid can't go anywhere near our bedroom."

"Same thing crossed my mind," she replied. "What about a gun safe?"

"Damn, babe. You know how much one of those puppies' costs?" I felt myself getting cranky again. "Anywhere from a couple hundred bucks to well over a thousand. If this kid were ours, a gun safe would be here tomorrow, cost be damned. But he's not ours. I'm having enough trouble with him even being here let alone spending a fortune so we can change our entire way of life. Please tell me he won't be here long enough to force us to buy a gun safe. Or a safety gate on the damn basement steps. I can just see the lawsuits."

"You're so funny, sweetheart," she said with a laugh as she took another sip of beer. "He's not a toddler. He's eight years old, for goodness sake. At least from what I've observed of him on the playground, he's pretty athletic for his age. He won't be falling down the basement stairs. Honest."

"The issue for us is *could he* fall down the steps! It's a *probability* issue wrapped in an expensive outcome. And it's not just the steps. He could trip and bang his head or choke on a piece of meat. Whatever bad happens to him while he's staying at our house, we're liable. We could be sued up the ying-yang."

"Our insurance covers all that, Reg," she countered.

"You sure of that?"

"I am. I called our agent today." She paused, put her beer on the table, and said, "Okay, let's stop dancing around the issue. Tell me what's really bothering you."

I took a deep breath, slumped back into the sofa and stared at the ceiling. "You know, to tell you the truth I'm not sure. My gut's telling me to be careful, filling me with unease about the kid being here. I can't really explain it." I sat up straighter and took another hit on the beer. After a polite burp, I slumped back again. "Or maybe it's because I'm jealous."

"Jealous? Jealous of what? An eight-year-old kid? You're kidding, right?"

"I know it sounds odd, even to me when I say it out loud. But I began to think of all the things we share together. Things just between you and me."

"Like?"

"Like the two of us eating dinner together and talking about our day. Like getting your opinion on life, liberty and the pursuit of happiness. Our happiness. Like watching TV after we finish up on office work and lesson plans. Hopping in the sack to make whoopee."

"Come on, babe. We'll still be able to do all those things. Especially the whoopee ones." She put her arm around my shoulder. "That'll never change. First of all, he's not going to be here that long. A few days, maybe. A week, max." She put her mouth next to my ear and whispered, "No matter how long he stays, he won't break us apart. I promise you."

I finished the beer, thinking that in cases like this the best play is to just keep your mouth shut. But stupid me didn't pay attention to *in cases like this*. I went that proverbial *Bridge Too Far*, and suffered the consequences. "Babe, let's chalk it up to me being jealous. That's all. And I'm embarrassed about feeling this way. Like . . . if I were a real man, I wouldn't care. You would do your thing and I would do mine. Be nothing more than roommates."

"Oh, Reggie, stop!" she said, her voice dripping with irritation. "Roommates? You've got to be out of your mind." She pushed herself off the sofa. "I'm going to bed. When you decide to be a grown up, you're welcome to come back."

It took me an hour and another beer—six today but who's counting—before deciding to be a grown up. When I got to the bedroom, she was already asleep. I was going to awaken her and apologize, but didn't. Knowing I had to be at the Hall early in the morning, I wrote her an apologetic note mentioning I would see her at her ballgame that afternoon. Leaving it on her dresser, I climbed quietly into bed and fell asleep.

CHAPTER 12

C arolyn Knecht was always the first to arrive at the office. I left the house early the next morning hoping to coincide my arrival with hers. It worked. I parked in the lot, rode the elevator to Homicide and found her alone in the breakroom making coffee.

"Well, this is a surprise, Inspector Decker. What brings you in so early?"

"Wanted to return this," I told her, handing her the murder book.

She took it and placed it on the table next to her desk. "Thanks. I'll show it logged in as of last evening at five thirty-five."

"You're a good lady, CK. I appreciate it. Got a question, though."

"Fire away," she said, pouring herself a cup of coffee.

"Let's go back to my desk. Don't want too many eyes seeing you and me together. They'll wonder if we got something going."

"Wouldn't want that to happen," she replied with a smile. "Ruin my reputation." Upon reaching my desk, she sat. "Your question?"

"About a note you put in the book a year after the murder. It said you'd received an email from Poppy Garcia's mother and were leaving a copy of it in the book."

"Yeah. Long time ago, but I remember writing the note. So?"

"The book was checked out by Egan a few days later. Out and

back in a few hours."

"Get to the punch line, Decker. What's the problem?"

"The email isn't in the book."

Her brows stitched together. "Can't be," she said through the frown. "I put it in there myself."

"Let's go back and take a look. I leafed through every plastic sleeve in the damn book last night and couldn't find it. Only thing I could think of was Egan took it."

When we got back to her desk, she retrieved the murder book and put it on her desk. She checked her handwritten note and then leafed through all the plastic sleeves. I could hear her foot tapping an impatient rhythm under the desk.

I kept silent, letting her be as thorough as she needed to be. After what seemed like a swim through Jell-O, she came up for air. Shrugging her shoulders, she said, "Don't know what to say."

"Nothing to say. For whatever reason, Egan removed it from the file. Could have been possible that he took it home and forgot about it when he moved up to Sacramento."

"Well, except for the shock of having something gone missing, it doesn't mean much. I archive all my electronic correspondence. Give me a few minutes. I'll retrieve the copy I made."

"CK, you're the best. I can testify to the fact that at least some of the terrible things people say about you aren't true.

She laughed. "Decker, if you didn't have that sweet lady at home, I'd be having some lascivious thoughts about you right about now."

"Lascivious is all good," I replied, with a chuckle. "Have as many of them as you want. By the way, you expect Bristow today? If so, I need an appointment."

"How much time would you need?"

"I'm guessing thirty minutes max."

"He's got a pretty thick schedule today, Deck. Could get you in at, say, ten. I can only give you about twenty minutes. Will that work? He's got a lunch in North Beach. Told me it might last all afternoon." She winked conspiratorially.

I nodded my head, and smiled. "Far be it from me to interrupt an important all-day lunch meeting." I paused. "Yeah, ten will work. I promise I'll be in and out in fifteen minutes. Would it be possible for you to retrieve the email by then?"

"You'll have it in half an hour."

I thanked her and went back to my desk. Gloves was already there, his face buried in his computer.

"You look so high tech," I kidded him as I slowly sat down.

"Compared to you, I'm a high-tech wizard. In fact, compared to you, everyone in this room is a high-tech wizard."

"Wouldn't want it any other way."

"By the way, how's the leg?"

"Still a little leaky. Doesn't hurt much, though. More an annoyance than anything else. And before I forget, do you happen to know of any jobs available for a woman who works hard but lacks a set of definable skills?"

"I thought you said Becky had a job."

"Ha-ha. Good one, Manny. But I'm serious. Becky has a student whose mom lost her job. Husband's nowhere in sight. Becky offered to keep her student at our place until the mom found another job."

"Going to keep the kid at your place? You're kidding, right?"

"I wish. He's eight years old, so, you can see how desperate I am to get his mother a paying job."

"I can imagine. Poor bastard." He paused for effect, then said, "Not you, Deck, the kid."

I nodded politely at his joke, then continued, "She had a job as a maid in that seedy motel over on Naples. You remember, the one a few years back that housed the prostitution ring?"

"Wouldn't know," he said with a laugh.

"Yeah, right! You were probably their best customer. Anyway, they, the motel not the hookers, closed up. No explanation. Poor lady's out of a job and I'm the poor dude stuck at home with an eight-year-old kid until we find his mother suitable work. I'm sure she could do a lot of things. So, it would be helpful if you knew a place that could employ her."

"I'll keep an eye out, Deck, and also put out the word. We'll find something."

CHAPTER 13

No sooner had I made it back to my desk than CK handed me a plastic sleeve. Nestled in the sleeve was a single piece of paper.

"Thought it better to wait for you to get back to your desk before I brought you this." She tilted her head toward Morales in a way that said *can't be too careful*. "Thank god for electronic files." She placed Maria Garcia's missing email on my desk. I quickly scanned it. "Notice she addressed Egan by name, wondering if he'd made any progress in finding her daughter's killer. Plus, she left a phone number." CK pointed to the country code. +52. "Mrs. Garcia moved back to Mexico about a year after her daughter died." Underneath the country code I noticed the area code. 618. My quizzical look was enough for CK to continue. "That's the area code for Durango, a State in the Northwest sector of the country." I nodded, trying to see the location in my mind, while wondering if Egan ever called her back.

"What about da man?" I asked, pointing to Bristow's office. "We still on for ten?"

"Oh, sorry," she said. "He changed the time to ten-thirty. Best I could do. Will that still work for you?"

"No problem." I picked up the plastic sleeve. "Thanks, CK. I'll show Matt this, too, if you don't mind."

She gave me a short nod and walked away. Ten minutes later, I walked back to Morales' desk.

"Got a minute?" I asked.

"Absolutely." He sat back in his chair. "But before you start, I wanted to ask if you found what you needed on the Garcia homicide in the murder book?"

"Unfortunately, no. Still a few things I need to clear up. That's why I need to talk to you."

"Fire away, but remember, the Garcia case was Egan's baby from the beginning."

"Understood. But what I still can't get my head around is the feel for the scene. Were you called to the house with Egan?"

"No, Deck. Come on, you know how it's done. Same as it is now. If your team catches a case, the one who's the least busy gets the call. The Garcia case was no different. Egan happened to be on his way back to the Hall when the call came in. I was out on another case. In fact, I thought about all this yesterday after we talked. The day Garcia got popped, I didn't make it home from my case until three the next morning. Hell, there was a murder epidemic afoot, and we all were caught up in it. Egan went to Garcia's residence by himself. I joined him the next day. About noon, as I remember. We took a run through the house together. Went room by room talking over the evidence he and the coroner's crew had bagged and tagged the night before."

"From what I've read in the murder book, I'm glad you didn't have much to do with that case, partner."

"Hey, Deck, you can't even begin to imagine what a bitch those two years were. In all the years I've been in Homicide, I've never experienced anything even close to what we faced in '07 and '08."

"I hear you, Manny. But as the guy just now familiarizing himself with the case, the question I have is did you, Manny Morales, ever read the murder book? Your name is on it, you know."

"I know it is, but that was just pro-forma. All the cases we handled were filed under both our names, even if one of us had nothing to do with the case. But to answer your question, I can't say for sure whether I read the Garcia book or not, but the odds are I didn't." He tilted his chair back and stared at the ceiling. The look on his face was hard to read. "I'm not trying to deflect blame," he finally said. "I know my name is on the damn report, but this was Egan's case from the get-go."

"And you didn't have any say in the investigation itself?"

"You just can't imagine how bad things were back then. All those murders. Egan and I were catching four to five at a time. I remember how exhausted I was. We divvied them up as best we could. Mostly just split them down the middle.

"Garcia got herself capped in late June, if I remember correctly. We already had five cases that month. An odd number. Egan had two, I had three. He volunteered to take the Garcia case, and I was only too happy to let him." A sad smile flashed across his face. "By the time I arrived the next day, Egan had his mind made up the hit was a gang deal. Started . . ."

"Wait. Hold on a minute. Did he ever explain to you why he thought it was a gang hit? I read through the murder book line by line and can't for the life of me figure out how he came to that conclusion. Did you ever ask him?"

"Never directly, no! We talked about the case, of course, along with his other two cases and my two open cases. We had a standing engagement. Daily. Six-thirty at a bar on New Montgomery. You'll remember the one. It's still in operation. We met there so many times, I was sure by the end of the year we'd both be alcoholics."

"Yeah, yeah," I said, waving my hand dismissively. I saw the anger float across his face. "Wait, Manny. I didn't mean to get impatient. It's just that I scheduled a meeting with the DC. He gave me fifteen minutes and then he's out the door." I looked at my watch. "Gotta be there in exactly eight minutes."

"I understand. No need to apologize. I'll be quick. As I was saying, Egan filled me in on the progress every day during our bar time. He told me from the get-go it was a nothing case. Couldn't find a motive. No forced entry. Blah, blah, blah. But looking back on it now, I'm embarrassed. Do I think I could've done more and, in fact, probably should've done more? Yeah, I do. But even now, I feel badly turning on him like this."

"Don't be silly, Manny. You're not turning on him. Egan quit on you, and on the Department, when he adios'd for Sacramento."

"I appreciate your saying that, Deck. Have to tell you, though, the whole situation back then still grates on me. Nothing but turmoil. Nowak quits. Then Egan." He interlaced his fingers behind his head and leaned back in his chair. "When Egan took off for the Sacramento job, I'm thinkin' all kinds of conspiratorial things. You weren't there so can't appreciate what I'm talkin' about. In early two thousand and ten, a whole raft of people deserted the Department, including Egan and the then Chief Nowak. Maybe they were all in cahoots with one another. Hell, I don't know. In any case, I was thoroughly pissed off, probably because I was jealous." He smiled. "But I'm cool with it now." He brought his chair down to level, looked me in the eye, and said, "The fact is Egan's now nothin' but a rent-a-cop. The kind of guy they hire when they need security at the county fair. He's way down the totem pole. Serves the prick right."

"All the political intrigue in Sacramento is way beyond my pay-grade, Manny. Screw 'em all. Right now I'm only worried about the Garcia case. I understand you weren't with Egan every step of the way, so weren't aware why he did things the way he did. Tell me one thing, though. In your estimation, did he do a credible job?"

"Honestly, Deck, the only thing Egan ever said to me about

76

the Garcia murder was it was a loser from the get-go. You know what I mean, right? It wasn't a glamorous case. There was no clear motive. The victim herself was inconsequential. Crazy stuff like that."

"Inconsequential victim? Geez, Manny. You should've reported the guy then and there. Or at least kicked his ass. I just hope, because her last name happened to be Garcia and not Jones, that Egan didn't think her life was inconsequential?"

"Hell, Deck, between you and me? Being Hispanic myself and having the son-of-a-bitch as a partner for five years? Yeah, I wouldn't be surprised if her last name influenced his disinterest." He took the last sip of coffee from his cup. "Geez, why do I torture myself drinking this stuff?" he asked, making a face and tossing the cup in the waste can by his feet.

"Anyway, Deck, my suggestion? Even if it was a botched case, it's now an *old* botched case. Even worse, it's an old botched *cold* case. And you and I are both aware that the odds of turning a cold case into an arrest are virtually nil." He leaned forward on his desk. "Bottom line is you're going to work your ass ragged and end up not finding anything that wasn't gone over and examined in the original investigation. If I were you, I'd save myself a ton of aggravation chasing a lot of dead ends. Just chalk it up to sloppy police work by a guy who no longer works here and call it a day."

"What am I supposed to tell the Twitter guy?"

"Tell him to go 'F' himself."

"Problem is, the more I dig into this case, the more I sympathize with the bastard."

CHAPTER 14

I knocked on Bristow's door and stepped into his office. He was at his desk, head down, writing something on a memo pad. "You available, DC?"

He glanced at his watch. "Yeah. Come on in." He pointed to a chair. "Sit," he commanded. "CK said you needed to see me. Want you to know I don't have a lot of time. Is this about the murder we talked about yesterday?" He didn't wait for an answer. "What did you find?"

"Well, you said I could take a look, but also that I should talk to Egan and Morales so as not to eat up a lot of time chasing rainbows."

A trace of a smile settled on his lips. "So, what'd you find?"

"I talked to Morales, of course. He said because Egan had the lead, he didn't know much about Garcia's murder because the caseloads were so staggering in those years. He told me he'd been full up with his own caseload and couldn't give any time to Egan's. Told me after I checked out the murder book to come talk to him."

"Did you?"

"Yeah. I read the murder book cover to cover and a few minutes ago had a good conversation with him."

"Perfect. So, it's wrapped up. That's great news. After you contact that Twitter idiot and tell him to cease and desist maligning our department, you can move on to what you're being paid to do." He smiled. "Thanks, Deck."

"I didn't wrap it up, Matt."

Bristow, who by this time was halfway out of his chair, pivoted toward me so violently I thought he would fall over. He started to say something, but I put out my hand. "Hey, listen to me for a minute, Matt. There are a number of things wrong with this case. Egan's murder book is wacko. In fact, I'm thinking now the Twitter dude might be on to something. At least as far as what Egan did with the case. I don't want to engage the online community having no facts, and I'm telling you if we went to the jury of public opinion with what we have, we'd be laughed out of the courtroom. It's crystal clear Egan cooked the murder book to make the case come out with the conclusion he wanted—that it was a gang hit. Unfortunately, he couldn't find any clues as to what gang and why they wanted to kill Poppy Garcia. As far as he was concerned, it was *case closed*! Please turn out the lights on your way out the door."

Bristow sat back down, gazed at me with a bored expression and sighed. "Tell me, why would he want to do that?"

"I talked to Manny about the case just now. Asked the same question. His answer surprised me. He agreed Egan shut the case down early. Told me Egan was pissed because he caught the lead on what he thought was a 'nothing' case, and because it was a 'nothing' case, wanted to shut down as soon as possible."

"And why would he think it was a nothing case?"

"According to Manny, Egan's justice meter didn't function well when Hispanics were involved. Especially Hispanic females."

"Morales said that? He actually corroborated the Twitter guy's theory? I'm gonna have to talk to him. If that stuff gets out, the department's in for a world of hurt."

"You don't have to talk to him, Matt. Manny's on board.

80

Given his ethnicity, he had his doubts about Egan, too."

"You're sure, though, Egan made up stuff? Or worse, suppressed evidence just to close the case? And both you and Morales agree racial prejudice was a factor with him closing it up?"

"Looks that way to me. Let me handle the Twitter guy, though. I promise I'll be at my diplomatic best before I kick his ass and get him off our back."

He laughed. "You do that, Deck." He looked at his watch. "Okay, got to go to my meeting."

"Hold on, okay? Got one more thing to talk to you about. And it's serious stuff."

"You're a bundle of fun this morning, Decker. Okay, give it to me quickly. I really do have to run."

"You remember Max Graser, right? I think I mentioned to you that he was the first officer at the scene that night. Babysat until Egan showed. I talked to him on the phone yesterday. He told me what he saw at the scene."

"Dead body. Hysterical mother. We know all that. What else. Come on, hurry up. I'm gonna be late."

"Slow down just a minute, Matt," I said, my temper flaring just a tad. "What I'm about to tell you is infinitely more important than your meeting. This is a young woman's murder we're talking about, for god's sake."

I halfway expected Bristow to pull my file for a reprimand, but instead he sat back with his hands extended in a the-floor's-all-yours gesture. I nodded my thanks.

"Poppy Garcia was counting tip money from her previous night's cab fares when she was killed. Graser told me there was probably two or three hundred dollars on the kitchen table. Most in paper, but some coins, too."

"And why is this worth missing my meeting? Come on, Deck, what else you got?"

"I got money on the table that didn't make the murder book, Matt. Neither did the vic's cell phone Graser saw on the table. Nor her Dell computer into which she was entering the night's take. Nor a large leather case loaded with expensive camera equipment." I paused for effect and then said again, "None of those made the murder book."

"You're sure of all this?"

I nodded. "Read the book twice, cover to cover."

Bristow sat back in his chair and looked at the ceiling while clicking and unclicking the ball point pen clasped tightly in his hand. I could tell he was trying to fit the pieces together. Finally, he sat upright, picked up his phone and instructed CK to call City Hall and tell them he'd be a few minutes late. Turning to me he said, "So we're dealing with not only a racist son-of-a-bitch, but a thief son-of-a-bitch as well."

"A two-fer, Matt."

"Have any great ideas on what to do next?"

"I've given it some thought, yeah. But first there's an anomaly I found while going through the evidence." I paused, then said, "And it's a puzzler. She was murdered in her kitchen. You knew that, right." Bristow nodded. "By a nine-millimeter auto, not a revolver, right?"

"I'll take your word for it."

"Hey, I'm just quoting the murder book," I said with a touch of annoyance in my voice. "But Matt, no shell casing was found. You and I've been around the block a few times, wouldn't you say? You ever hear of a gang or drug hit where the perps cleaned up their brass? Brass is only picked up by people who don't want their gun identified by the shell casing leading back to them."

Bristow shook his head but didn't say anything—just sat there clicking his pen.

"Exactly," I said, reading his body language. "If a gang

capped Garcia, the gun would be living with the crabs under the Bay Bridge or carried by some gangbanger in South Central. In either case, the last thing those guys would worry about is their weapon being traced back to them. So why take the brass?"

Bristow remained silent for a few moments, then replied, "Good question, Deck. And I don't have an answer. But when you really think about it, so what? The missing brass doesn't tell us what to do with Egan."

"Unless he was the one who pulled the trigger."

"Oh, come on, Deck. Don't be going around spreading those kinds of rumors. That's beneath you." For appearances sake, I held up my hands in an apologetic fashion. Bristow nodded, acknowledging my acquiescence. "And remember," he continued, "this case doesn't only raise legal questions, but public relation ones as well. We have to satisfy both."

"You're talkin' about City Hall, of course."

"Of course." He sighed, then continued. "We're dealing with a thirteen-year-old cold case that's already in the national news thanks to the asshole tweeter. They weren't fond of how we handled it back then, so let's not give them any new ammunition for the present. If we reopen the case, they're going to be ultra-sensitive about how we proceed."

"I understand, Matt. If Egan's arrested as the perp, we're going to be in the spotlight. What if I went to Sacramento and arrested his ass in private? I'd bring him back in my car and sweat him in jail for a few days until he answered our questions. Then we could formally charge him."

"Perfect. Our own personal *Gitmo* in San Francisco." He chuckled. "I can see you didn't get a law degree, Inspector. Also, I'm assuming you weren't serious."

"Of course, I wasn't serious, Matt. But I have to tell you, if you ordered me to do it just that way, I wouldn't have argued."

He looked at me quizzically, then smiled. "Let me tell you how we're going to play this, then. First of all, Egan is no dummy. He'll know he's in deep manure as soon as he's arrested for robbing a dead woman. The optics won't be pretty. A homicide inspector stealing items from a murdered woman while her body was still warm. A serious and gruesome charge. He'd lawyer up in a heartbeat. His attorneys would argue our evidence is all circumstantial. Unfortunately, they'd be right. All we know is there were things taken from the scene. We don't know who took them or why they took them or where they took them. Your friend Graser is going to be one of the people they'll point a finger at, saying he had the time and opportunity to steal Garcia's stuff before Egan even arrived. So, he'd also have to lawyer up, too. It won't stop there, Deck. You know that."

"So, what're we going to do, Matt? You tell me."

"Because I believe you've uncovered something that needs to be investigated properly, I'm going to reopen the Garcia murder as an active case. I want you to contact Egan and get his story." He stood and walked over to his door and gazed toward where Morales sat. Turning back to me, he said, "I'm relying on you, Deck, to be fair and impartial. I'm giving you one week from today. If your investigation hasn't shown significant progress, I'll close it down." He looked me in the eye. "We understand each other, right?" I nodded. "Good. I want you to keep me informed every step of the way."

"Will do, DC. And, thanks. You've given me all I could've ask for."

CHAPTER 15

I took a quick peek at my watch as I approached my desk. Eleven-oh-five. *Early afternoon in Durango,* I thought. *Perfect time to call Maria Garcia.*

But before I did, I moseyed over to Morales' desk. "Got any lunch plans, Gloves?"

"Just made a date with Jensen. We were thinking about the BBQ Palace. Wanna come?"

"A date with Jensen, huh? That sounds serious. Anything you want to tell your ol' partner?"

"Very funny. Got a better idea?"

"Yeah. How 'bout you and me finding some place where we can talk about partnering up on the Garcia case. Already spoke to the DC about it. He said okay as long as I don't take all your time. And only for a week." I paused. "You game?"

"Absolutely!"

"Good. Let me call Mrs. Garcia first. Not a call I'm really anxious to make, but she has to be involved. And then let's go uptown for lunch, okay? I'm buyin'."

"Gettin' to sound better all the time, partner."

~~~~~

Talking to a mother about the death of a child, no matter how old the child was or how long ago the death occurred, was not something I looked forward to. All I could hope for was the passage of time had eased the pain, making it easier for her to talk candidly with me. In any case, there was no getting around the fact that I'd be picking at the scab of a wound that never fully healed. Taking a deep breath of resignation, I dialed the number.

"Hola," a female voice answered. I closed my eyes and pushed back into the chair. It never dawned on me we might be speaking Spanish. Didn't quite know what to say. My Spanish sucked, so I stammered around in English until she rescued me. "Who is calling please." I shouldn't have been surprised she spoke English damn near as well as I did. Maybe better. After all, she lived in California for close to forty years.

"Mrs. Garcia? My name is Reginald Decker. I'm a police officer in San Francisco, California."

A delay occurred because of the distance and then her gasp rumbled into my ear, followed by a shriek. "You found my baby's killer? Oh, gracias a Dios." She started to sob.

I felt I was in a dark doorway covered with cobwebs, not wanting to go forward, but knowing I couldn't go back. "No." I said. It had no effect on the sobbing. "No," I said again, louder and more forcefully. "Mrs. Garcia. Please. Por favor." If it were possible to squeeze myself through the wires to hold her, I would have. "Mrs. Garcia, please." I took a quick peek around the office, hoping no one was listening to my crazy conversation. "I need to talk to you." The sobbing became quieter. More controlled. "I need your help, Mrs. Garcia. Please." Another delay. I heard a snort and visualized her blowing her nose into a tissue.

"Lo siento, señor." A pause, then, "Perdone. Your name again, señor?"

"Inspector Reginald Decker." Even though I could tell she spoke and understood English, I still found myself speaking slowly and pronouncing every syllable.

"From the San Francisco Police Department?" she asked, finishing my sentence. "About my daughter?" Her voice now full of hope.

"About your daughter. Yes. But before you get your hopes too high, let me tell you why I'm calling." I proceeded to tell her about my nephew Bobby, and how I became involved with her daughter's death through him. How my supervisor gave me a week to look through the case. "He assured me if I didn't find new and relevant information, he'd close the case down. I can't guarantee anything, Mrs. Garcia. My preliminary investigation may lead nowhere, but I wanted to be thorough, which is why I'm calling you."

"It is so kind of you, Inspector. I grieve for my Poppy . . ." I heard a catch in her voice ". . . every night." My heart went out to her. This conversation wasn't going to be easy on either of us.

"I can only imagine, Mrs. Garcia. From what I read in her file, she was a remarkable young woman. My nephew adored her. It's because of him I received permission to look at the case again. I'd like to ask you a few questions if you don't mind." I paused so she'd have the time to process what I was about to do. "If I'm going to move forward successfully, I'll need as much background information as you can give me. I see in the file you called our department the summer after your daughter's death requesting Detective Egan to give you an update on the murder of your child. It looks to me like he didn't call you back. Am I correct?"

"Yes, you are correct. He did not call me back."

"I'm terribly sorry about that." I paused and then said, "Have you been notified he is no longer with the Police Department?"

"No, I haven't. Where is he?"

"He retired a number of years ago." I let the magnitude of revelation sit there for a moment, then continued, "What did you think of him?" I probably shouldn't have asked the question quite so directly. Might lead her to believe he was responsible for the killers never being found. Another conspiracy theory. Just what I needed. On the other hand, it wouldn't hurt my feelings for her to say he was an incompetent son-of-a-bitch. She didn't say those exact words, but close.

"I'm not sure," she began. "I didn't think he wanted to find who murdered her. He had a loco notion it was about drugs. Why would he say that? No one who knew my daughter would say such a thing. In fact, just the opposite." Her voice started to break again.

I kept silent until she composed herself. "Are you aware they found a bag full of cocaine in her dresser drawer?"

"Mierde," she spat. I waited for her to say more. A further explanation. Nothing came. Mierde! That was her explanation. And for me it was good enough.

"Mrs. Garcia, let me apologize again for having to ask you these questions. I'm sure they must be painful. I can call back tomorrow if this is too stressful for you."

"I want my daughter's killer found. You can take every waking moment of my life if it will help find who killed her."

"Can you tell me some things about your daughter? My nephew told me she worked at a cab company."

"Yes. From the time she got out of high school. She held a number of jobs while she was still in high school. One paid her very well, but it was not good for her. I made her quit. I'm glad she decided on the cab company. It made her happy, and it made me happy for her."

"How about any boyfriends?"

She sighed. "We used to argue about that. I wanted her to get married. I wanted grandchildren. It was the way I was raised in Mexico to think those things. A woman should get married and have children."

"But you were never married, were you?"

"No, but I conceived a child so I felt fulfilled. She kept me busy." I could hear the wistfulness in her voice.

"I'm sure children have a way of doing that," I said. "If I may ask, why didn't you marry the father of Poppy?"

"You may not ask."

The abruptness of the answer threw me for a minute. "Fair enough," I said, while thinking *"for now."* I fiddled with some papers on my desk before I said, "Oh, Mrs. Garcia, before I let you go, may I ask what you what you did for work when you lived here?"

"When I first came to your country, I was a domestic worker. A maid, I think they called us."

"And?"

"And, nothing. They were nice to me. I haven't seen nor heard from them in years."

She went quiet. I knew she wasn't going to finish that train of thought so I decided to shift gears, asking about Poppy's boy-friends.

She waited a few beats, then said, "My daughter had many male friends, but none appealed to her. At least in a boyfriend way. She had many girlfriends, too. When she went out, it was mostly with them. But there were times when the boys and girls also went out together." The line went silent for a few moments. I wanted to ask her a question, but before I could voice it, she spoke again. "Poppy did not drink much. She didn't frequent bars like a lot of young women her age. I am thankful I did not have to worry about her. What she liked to do was people-watch. She loved taking pictures of people. Did you get a chance to glance through her collection?"

"Of pictures?'

"Yes. She filled many albums. Well, I shouldn't say albums.

That is so old fashioned. More like my generation." She gave a soft laugh, then said, "She had them on her computer. Or on those little sticks you put into the side of a computer."

"I'm glad you're telling me this. I never saw any of her pictures, Mrs. Garcia. And there's no record of any flash drives being found. That's what we call those sticks, flash drives." I paused. *This will surprise her*, I thought. "We also aren't in possession of any camera she might have used. Do you know anything about her camera?"

"Of course, I do. I bought her the camera."

"Can you tell me about it? Make and model, that sort of thing?"

"They never found her camera? That is so strange. I not only bought it for her, I also bought all different shapes and sizes of lenses for her. The ones you screw on, you know? She was my only child. I bought her the best. Detective Egan took them from Poppy's home. He told me they were part of his investigation and would return them as soon as the investigation was complete. It was one of the reasons I contacted him a year or so after she died. To see if anything new had come up about my Poppy's murder, and to get her property back. He never called me back."

"Do you still have a list of that property?"

"Of course."

"Can you email me that list? The makes and model numbers, along with the costs? And the receipts of the purchases if you have them."

"How soon do you need it?"

"As quickly as possible."

"I know where they are. I'll take pictures on my phone and send them to your email."

"Perfect." I gave her my email address. "Before you go, may I ask you one more question? Just a matter of curiosity on my

90

part. Where did the name Poppy come from?"

I could hear her sigh. "The poppy flower had a special meaning to me. And she was my flower, so I gave her that name at birth."

I waited for her to say more. She didn't, so I said, "I'll look forward to receiving your receipts."

I hung up, uncurled myself from my desk and waved to get Morales' attention. I pointed at my watch and then flashed him ten fingers. Ten minutes. He nodded. I walked to CK's desk and asked, "Is Garcia's murder book still around? I need to confirm something." Then I leaned over and, in a whisper, said, "Is it possible to take it home again tonight? I promise I won't say a word to anyone."

"Your lucky day, cowboy," she said with a smile while pointing to the carton on top of her filing cabinet. "I'll get it for you. Rest the leg. How's it going, by the way."

"Hey, it's healing. And thanks for letting me prowl around the murder book again. Promise I'll treat it with kid gloves."

"Just get it back here tomorrow morning as early as you can or I'll tell everyone you stole it."

I blew her a kiss, took the book back to my desk and opened to the evidence section. Went through every page of items found in the house. No camera. No lenses. No computer. No flash drives. No cell phone. No money. The sudden spike of adrenaline coursing through my veins was electric.

Egan, you son-of-a-bitch, I thought. *You stole everything from that girl. I'm gonna put your ass away for good.*

I motioned to Morales that I was ready to go.

Ten minutes later, we were in his car headed for Johnny Foley's Irish House. As soon as he cleared the lot, I pulled the murder book from my briefcase and showed it to him. "You know the drill. Anybody asks, you never saw this. Has to be back on CK's desk early tomorrow morning."

CHAPTER 16

We arrived at Foley's at one-thirty. Just enough past the noon hour rush to find a table. I'd been a frequent visitor to Johnny Foley's Irish House since I arrived back home from my military duty. Great food and, if you're Irish or want to be Irish, a great bar. Because we were still on-duty, we had to forego the bar and just eat food. Circumventing the letter of the law, I ordered a plate of mussels cooked in Irish whiskey.

"I'm glad we're getting a chance to talk about this case," Morales said. "As I've told you, I'm not at all proud about having been involved in it."

"Wait 'til I tell you about my conversation with Poppy's mother. But as to your involvement, I understand where you are coming from, and I don't blame you. At the front end, I didn't think it was fair to involve you in a case where you might be required to interrogate and maybe arrest your old partner."

He snorted. "Yeah, right."

"No, hear me out." I went through the inconsistencies in the murder book, along with the personal items Graser saw in the house that suspiciously never even made the murder book. "I just talked to Mrs. Garcia and she told me about all the stuff she bought her kid. Expensive items, like cameras and computers that were never returned to her. She told me she asked Egan personally to send back those personal items. Wanna guess what he told her?"

"I can only imagine. He probably said they were evidence in a murder case."

"Exactly. She never heard from him again. After a few years, she gave up. He essentially just stole them."

"So, what specifically do you want me to do? You know the Deputy Chief is gonna be on my ass to clear this Morrison case."

"I know, but Bristow gave me permission to ask you to help out in, what he called, 'your off hours'."

"Sure," Gloves said with a laugh. "Sounds just like him. *In my off hours*."

"Well, as you know, reopening any case is dicey, at best. Everyone who had a hand in it, no matter how small, will be asking why a fellow officer is nosing around in their business. Especially since it was never solved. And even more especially, one that's been classified as cold. Because you were the partner of the guy who caught the case, your involvement in its reopening will be helpful. Even so, we still have to be sensitive to everybody's feelings."

"Yeah, and to complicate matters, we also have to answer that Twitter crap."

"Precisely," I replied. "The Twitter crap is the only reason we reopened the case in the first place. Unfortunately, our reopening it is just gonna lend gravitas to the Twitter jerks' accusations." I sat there for a moment, then continued, "Knowing the load you carried back then, I appreciate your being upfront with me. No matter what, I don't want you to be tied in knots about what the hell Egan may have done."

"Thanks, Deck. I appreciate the vote of confidence. As you know, partnerships are like marriages. It's possible to get divorced and still maintain a friendship. Doesn't happen often, but it happens. Egan's been gone for over nine years now, and we don't see each other but once a year or so, but we still call each other friends."

"I hear you, Manny. Hell, you and I are partners, and we'll be friends until we shuffle off this mortal coil. That's because I trust you, and I hope you trust me."

"I do, brother, I do. So, tell me how I can be of help."

"I thought you could legitimately follow the thread I uncovered. Trying to find the items that went missing from Garcia's house."

"And how do you suggest I do that without people who were on the original investigation, in this case Egan himself, finding out I'm poking around?"

"I wouldn't worry about that. All we need to do is tell whoever asks that there's new evidence suggesting Garcia was robbed, and Homicide is doing a quick check to see if any of the stolen items surfaced in the past number of years. You won't get pushback from that story. And I'd suggest you begin with any pawn shop contacts you have, or even had back in the day. As you know, these cold cases are a bitch because everything happened so long ago. We shouldn't expect much from this part of the investigation, so don't feel bad if you come up empty."

"I still have contact with quite a few pawn shop owners. I'll start there."

"Perfect! And just to let you know, more as a heads-up than anything else, I'm calling Egan this afternoon. What the hell, he wrote the damn murder book, for god's sake. Let's ask him why some of the items we know were in the house never got listed in his damn book."

Morales snickered. "Good luck with that."

"Yeah. It's going to be interesting to see how he tries to weasel his way out of this."

"Okay, now I have a question for you. Been wondering how'd you get away with taking the murder book offsite? We both know it's not allowed to leave the premises."

I laughed. "Well, first off, you have to have friends in high places."

"You talkin' about CK, no doubt. I have to start romancing that girl."

"I'll put in a good word for you."

"Gee, thanks." He smiled. "By the way, since the items we're looking for never showed up in the murder book, how am I to know what the hell we're looking for?"

"Because you're sittin' here with Mr. Lucky," I said, reaching into my coat pocket and pulling out a small notebook. "Thank you, Max Graser. Thank you, Maria Garcia." I opened the notebook and pushed it over to Manny. "Graser just happened to write down all the pieces he saw in the house that night. I ran them by Mrs. Garcia just an hour ago. She's also sending me a list of the property that went missing. And her list comes complete with receipts." I ran my finger down the items. "Take a look. Those missing items were expensive. Pawn shops, here we come."

Manny and I were back in the office by two-thirty. With all those unanswered questions about Egan, it had been a weird day, and was about to get even weirder. I had no sooner sat down at my desk than my cell phone rang. Didn't recognize the number, but as was my wont, I answered anyway. Glad I did. A voice from my past. The long-ago past. Before I was even on the force, *past*.

"Reggie Decker?" the voice asked. "Richard Sherman."

I paused for a few seconds before the name rang a bell. And what a ring it was. "Oh . . . my . . . god!" I said with deserved exaggeration. "Richard Sherman. What the hell, man?" I was so flummoxed, I didn't quite know what to say. "Where the hell are you?"

"I'm in San Francisco on a short in-and-out trip and remembered you were here and thought I'd get in touch. I know it's short notice, but was hoping you had a few minutes this afternoon for a drink or something before I have to take off again. You got some time?"

"For you, Sherm? Well, hell yes I have the time. How 'bout this afternoon at, say, three-thirty. That good for you? I'll buy you a drink somewhere."

"Perfect. You're still at The Hall, right? I'll pick you up out front. Three-thirty. I'll give you a call when I'm close."

I hung up, pumped my fist in the air, gave a soft *whoop* and walked over to CK's desk.

"So, what can I do for you, cowboy?"

When I asked for Barry Egan's phone number, her whole demeanor changed. "Whoa, you're getting serious about this case, huh?" she asked, with a detectable edge to her voice. "You sure you want to call him?"

"It's your boss who wants me to call him. He's reopened the Poppy Garcia murder in light of some new allegations, and asked me to give it a look-see. Told me I had a week. I figured there was no better time than now to get some answers. And since more than a few questions center around how he handled the damn case, I'm gonna have to talk to him directly."

"About what exactly, if I may ask?"

"Like how come some of the vic's possessions were not included in the murder book. That's a good one for starters. I'm gonna give him the benefit of the doubt. Maybe he has a perfectly logical answer. Only way I know to get answers is to ask him directly."

"You might be kicking over a hornet's nest, you know, questioning a fellow officer's honesty."

"Oh, come on, CK," I said. "For one, he's not a 'fellow officer.' If I'm doing the math correctly, nine years ago the bastard walked out on all his 'fellow officers.' As far as I'm concerned, nobody in this building, most of all me, owes him *squat*."

"Between the two of us, I hope you screw the son-of-a-bitch." She bent over her desk and rummaged through a pile of papers. Finding what she wanted, she turned and handed me an index card. "This is both his cell and office number." She smiled. "I hope you get the son-of-a-bitch. Good luck."

"Thanks, CK. Have a feeling I'm gonna need that luck."

Egan's phone rang six times before going to voice mail. His answering machine told me to leave a message at the beep, and he'd return my call. As instructed, when I heard the beep, I left a message to call me as soon as he was able. Then I called his cell. Same thing. Not available. Leave a message. This time I was not in the mood to be polite and made it strictly a business call. A serious business call, at that. I told him I've been tasked to look into a murder he worked back in '07 and needed some information. I gave him my phone number and asked he call me back asap. Short and sweet.

I looked at my watch. Still had some time before Sherman showed up. I picked up the phone.

"Kincaid," the voice said.

"Hey, Walt. Decker here. Hope I'm not bothering you. Got a few minutes?"

"Only a few, my friend. What's up?"

"You know the case we spoke about last night? Well, I talked to the mother of the vic this morning. Strange conversation. She's hiding something from me, and I need your help. I told you, I think, that Egan exonerated her back in the day because she was nowhere near the house the day of the murder."

"And you and I both know that doesn't mean she wasn't involved." Kincaid said.

"Precisely. And that's the reason I'm calling. If I can't clear the mother, the person closest to the victim, I'm whistling in the dark."

"And you need me why?"

"The only way I can think to find out if she were involved as an accessory would be to go through her financial records. To eliminate her from my suspect list, all I'd need is some financial corroboration she didn't pay for the hit. But she won't cooperate with me. And to compound the problem, she won't tell me the name of the man who fathered her child. I'm not trying to pry into her past life. I really could care less who the Father was. All I want to do is eliminate his sorry ass as a suspect. She claims she never knew his name. A one-night stand in some bar. To get his name would take a court order, and I don't have the time. Bristow is allowing me only a few days to wrap this up. But you . . ."

"Uh oh. I can hear the other shoe about to drop."

I laughed. "You know me too well, Walt. But, after all, you *are* the FBI, and we both know the FBI is favored with certain, shall I say, *sub rosa* perks. At least that's what us low level law enforcement types have been led to believe."

"Nothing but jealousy and sour grapes."

"No doubt." I laughed again. "In any case, I was wondering if you could bring some of your magic to bear on this one."

"Give me a thumbnail. Can't promise you anything, though."

"Thanks, Walt." I opened a file on my desk. "I've done some digging on Poppy Garcia. I found out, for example, how old she was when she died. Twenty-five. Subtracting that number from the year she died, I get the year she was born. Nineteen eighty-two.

"Gee, why didn't I think of that," Kincaid said sarcastically.

"I know you don't like to be shown up, Walt. But I'm a genius. What can I say?"

"Yeah! Yeah!" he laughed. "Get on with it. I haven't got all day."

"I accessed the Bay Area birth records for the year 1982. The paperwork showed what we all knew. Her mother's name was Maria Garcia, an immigrant from Mexico. Came to the United States a year before her daughter was conceived. She got employment as a domestic worker. Back in the day, as you know, domestic worker was the euphemism for maid. No address or references listed. On the birth certificate, where the name of the father should be listed, it says Unknown."

"Then you're SOL, my friend. There'd be no way for us to

find the father's name. At least through legal channels."

"That's what I figured, too. Oh well, not sure the paternity issue has anything to do with the case, but what I do know is the mother was giving money to her daughter. Quite a lot of money, actually. Had to come from somewhere. I want to know the 'somewhere.' The mom put her daughter through school, paying the usual expenses you would expect. Clothes, food, lodging. And speaking of lodging, the mom and her daughter lived in a duplex out on Kirkham. Where the daughter got whacked. As you know, Walt, that property is not cheap. I'm guessing the mother didn't own the property. It would be really helpful if you could find out who did. In any case, as the child got older, the mother bought her all the stuff a modern teenager would need or at least want. Cell phone, computer, camera, just to name a few. Could be a lot more for all I know. But she was giving her damn expensive toys for someone with no visible means of support."

"That you know of."

"*That I know of.* Correct! Oh, would also be good to know what bank the mother used. Maybe you could find that out, too?"

"You said the woman and her daughter lived in a duplex in the Sunset? You could get that data yourself, you know."

"I know. But you, Walt, could get it a lot faster. Like I said before, you are the mighty FBI."

"Yeah, yeah." He breathed an exaggerated sigh and then said, "Send everything to me in writing and I'll see what I can do. Again, no promises."

"Hey, Walt, you're a good friend. Thanks a heap."

CHAPTER 18

I sent Kincaid every shred of information I had on Maria Garcia and then packed up my things as I waited for Sherm to show up. As if on cue, my phone buzzed. "Your chauffer has arrived," he said with a chuckle. "No street parking here. I'll make another loop of the block and pick you up out front."

"Be right down."

"God, Sherm, it's good to see you again," I said, grabbing his proffered hand and giving him a bear hug. "You haven't changed a bit. I've been trying to think how long it's been since we've seen each other."

"Many a moon, pardner. Many a moon," he answered, moving into traffic.

"How familiar are you with the City?" I asked. "I mean do you get here enough to have a favorite place to eat or drink?"

"Tell you what," he answered. "I don't get here all that often, but I do have a favorite place to hang. The O'Brien House. I'm taking you there."

"The O'Brien House? Derek Cora's O'Brien House? Hey, man, you don't have to do that. It's way too pricy."

"Well, if I had to foot the bill, we'd be eating at McDonald's." He patted me paternally on the leg. "But fortunately, I'm not footing the bill. I got lucky. You got out of the Army when, '03?"

"Earlier. '01."

"I stayed in until '05."

"You were in the 10th SFG the whole time?"

"I did. It's how I met Derek Cora."

"Cora was in the military?" I asked.

"No. Just a rich guy who needed some protection."

"So you actually worked for Cora?"

"Yep. But haven't for a long time. When I worked for him, he had me running all over the freaking world. I ended up leaving Cora's world to work for his old girlfriend, a woman named Brigitte Le Pendu. Believe me, she's a lot nicer boss that Cora. The downside is I don't get here very often. When I do, I'm only here, at max, half a day. Maybe an eight o'clock breakfast meeting and then I'm back on an airplane for my next meeting. Could be a thousand miles away. I may not get back for months. There have been times in the past when I didn't step a foot into the Bay Area for an entire year. But the time sequence when I'm here is generally the same, in and out! But not today, thank goodness. Today, I'm on my own. And because of that, I get to see you. We're almost at the O'Brien House. I'll explain it all to you then."

"You got a good gig going here, Sherm. Tell me what the hell you did for Derek Cora? How'd you meet the guy?"

"Long story, Reg." He laughed. "We're here. You ever been to O'Brien House before?"

"Oh, yeah. All the time. Even come here for breakfast most days."

Sherman smiled. "You're going to like it, my friend. Follow me."

"Right this way, Mr. Sherman," the maître d' said as we walked in the front door. Sherm had obviously called ahead. We were seated and ordered drinks.

"So, tell me again how you got this gig. Are you still tight with Cora? Damn, man, as a cop I'm gonna tell you to stay away from that dude. He has a poisonous reputation. Supposedly traffics in underage girls which he procures for the rich and famous. Even a few ex-Presidents have been named as clients of his."

"Well, he's certainly got friends in high places, that's for sure," Sherm replied. "But that stuff about the underage girls? I was with him for two years and never saw anything like that."

"So how did you get mixed up with him?"

"I was fortunate, really. For obvious reasons, a lot of us ex-special forces guys get recruited for bodyguard work. I had a reputation as a good soldier and was fortunate to meet a Senator who was impressed enough to introduce me to Mr. Cora." The drinks arrived and Sherm paused to make a toast. "Here's to good friends being reunited. May we always be brothers-in-arms." We clinked glasses.

"Now, back to how I came to work for the infamous Derek Cora," Sherman said. "Get this. The Senator introduced me to Cora on a Tuesday. The next day, I was flying with Cora on his private jet to an island in the Caribbean. It's not just any island, mind you. It's his personal island. He owns the freaking thing. Gotta tell you, Reg, I had a hard time getting my head around that one." He laughed and said, "I spent the next three days there answering questions about the best way to establish personal security for his family and friends. He must have been satisfied with my answers because he hired me."

"When did this all take place? What years are we talking about here?"

"I interviewed with him in the fall of '06. Officially, I went to work for him in February of 2007. Just six months after I got out of the service. You, my friend, were already a member of the SFPD by then, right?"

"You've done your homework, I see. Don't tell me you're thinking of offering me a job," I said with a laugh.

"Well, truth be told, the thought has crossed my mind, Deck. But not, of course, for Mr. Cora. There were things about him I really didn't like. He was way too much of an ass bandit."

"Ass bandit? God, Sherm, I hadn't heard that one since I left high school."

He laughed. "Yeah, I keep 'em all. Or maybe it's that I'm getting older and starting to remember my youth more fondly." He paused and then said, "In any case, I think you'd like working for Brigitte Le Pendu. Like I said, she's Cora's ex, a French lady in her early forties who is very bright and whose family is filthy rich. I've worked for her these past twelve years."

The waiter came and Sherm ordered appetizers. While we waited, he said, "Don't feel awkward about the talk of a job with Le Pendu. I know you love what you're doing. And I'm happy for you. In the future, though, it might be something worth looking at. Right now, in the *Le Pendu circles*, you've got a friend in high places." He laughed and raised his glass in a toast. "To good friends."

As we munched on smoked trout fillet, bay shrimp cocktails and a marinated calamari salad, we reminisced about old times. Sometime during the conversation, I looked at my watch.

"Damn, Sherm," I said. "We probably should be taking off soon. I've got to get back to the Hall to get my car. I'll need it after the game to get home. I really do want you to meet Becky, so would it be possible for you to get someone to pick up your car at the Hall and drive it to Crocker-Amazon Park?"

"That wouldn't be a problem at all. I'll call my guy and tell him to pick me up at your Park." He smiled. "But just so you know, the only reason I'm coming is to meet your squeeze."

"You'll like her, Sherm. She's a good lady."

CHAPTER 19

On the way to Crocker-Amazon, I asked what it was like to work for Cora.

"Well, at the beginning it was a little weird. Shortly after I started, he assigned me to be his *fixer*."

"Fixer? God, Sherm, that's right out of *The Godfather*."

"Hey, tell me about it! Let's just say Derek Cora's impulsiveness got, and still gets him, him in a lot of trouble. For me, it was embarrassing, to tell you the truth. He had certain impulses he either couldn't or didn't want to control. They pulled him down all the wrong paths. My job was to keep him on the straight and narrow if I could. It was doubly hard because he not only was a rich and famous dude in his own right, he spent all his time hanging out with other rich and famous dudes. And, to top it all off, he never had good instincts regarding women. Even Brigitte, the perfect woman for him, got fed up and left him about a year after I came on board. I was glad she liked me enough to hire me. Best thing that ever happened to me."

"Well, if and when you see the guy again, be sure to thank him for the great meal, okay?" I laughed. "No way I could ever afford eating or drinking there on my salary."

"All the more reason for me to get you a job with Ms. Le Pendu."

"What, so I could eat and drink at fancy restaurants?"

"Well, that's not something to spit at, you know."

"Hey, Sherm, I appreciate your even thinking about me. I really do. But I love what I'm doing."

"I can see that," he said with a smile. "I'm just waiting to meet the brains of your marriage, Deck." He elbowed me in the ribs. "Maybe I'll be able to convince her that you should come aboard with us. You'll be in a safer environment and make a hell of a lot more money. That'll get her."

I laughed. "I seriously doubt it, my friend, but, hey, go for it."

We drove in silence for a few minutes before I said, "We're meeting Becky at the sports complex where I spent my youth playing little league ball. Every time I go there, it's a trip down memory lane. And just so you'll be able to tell your grandkids where Uncle Reggie grew up, I'm gonna take you through some of the mean streets of San Francisco on the way."

He looked over and said with a laugh, "Can't think of anything I'd rather do."

I drove south on the freeway and turned off near the Cow Palace. "Welcome to Visitation Valley. I grew up three blocks from here."

"The mean streets," I said.

I watched Sherm in my peripheral vision. His eyes were never at rest. Obviously, his military training was kicking in, carefully weighing the environment around him. Adapting to it. I half expected him to start sniffing the wind like a feral animal. Wary. Looking for avenues of escape even when there was no visible sign of danger. If I hadn't already known Sherman had 'been there, done that' in Iraq with the Special Forces, his reactions to the environment through which we were traveling certainly would have told me.

"By the way," I continued, "Cora lives in a place called Pacific Heights. As the crow flies, no more than four miles from here. But, in terms of wealth, lifestyle and power? Hey, might as well be a thousand miles." I slowed and pointed out a bunch of kids loitering on the street corner in front of a liquor store. "See those dudes over there? What do you think their chances are of getting out of this hood in one piece? How many are there? What, twelve?"

Sherm's eyes narrowed as he took in the scene. I could hear his mind working on the problem of twelve. Not the problem I posed, but thinking how many he could he take down if attacked. How many weapons they had and what caliber. Sherm may not have been a lot of fun at a party, but he was just the kind of guy you'd want on your side if you were alone in the bush.

"Of those twelve?" I continued. "From my experience, four will be dead before the year's out. Killed on these very same streets. Of the remaining eight, at least one will be in jail for murder; another five will have serious drug problems and will probably end up in jail for robbery or assault. One, maybe two, may make it out in one piece. Not a fun future to contemplate if you were them."

"They've got choices, same as everyone," Sherm said quietly.

"True enough," I replied, "but growing up in grinding poverty like this? Knowing that the chances of you getting from here to the neighborhood where Cora lives is virtually nil? Hey, just might tend to make you wanna give up."

"Come-on, Deck. These kids ain't seen poverty. They don't know what real poverty is. Come on, Deck, you were there. Iraqis in Sadr City? Hell, they'd see this neighborhood and take off all the explosives strapped to their skinny-assed bodies and get on their knees to thank Allah for delivering them. Take 'em to Najaf. Even the nice places there are nothing compared to where these kids live. The real problem those guys standing over there have is they've been fed that *woe-is-me* victim garbage for too long."

I could see this conversation was going nowhere, so I didn't

109

reply. Sherm pushed back in his seat and, for all I knew, started calculating fields of fire.

"Not to change topics, or anything . . ." I looked over at Sherm, "but we're at the Park." He smiled. Good. No hard feelings. I found a parking spot close to the entrance and we walked into the complex together.

"This where you played as a kid?" Sherm asked.

"Yep. Every time I walk through these gates, I get a chill. Even though the park has gone through a ton of renovations since I last played ball here, I still love the feel of it. During the time I was away, they reduced the number of baseball diamonds here from ten to six, using the new real-estate to build two soccer fields. And since I've returned, of those six diamonds, only four remain. And those four are forced to share their space with tennis, basketball and bocce courts." I shrugged, then said, "No big deal, really. Just reflects the demographic changes in the neighborhood."

Games were being played on all four of the diamonds. Not many spectators, though. About what you'd expect this time of day. At Becky's game, there were only three dads and a handful of mothers present, most with young children on their laps. *A shame,* I thought, remembering when I was a kid how much I appreciated having my mom, and hopefully my dad, at the game. I also knew from being a cop that the kids whose parents paid attention to them by coming to something as simple as their baseball games, stood a hell of a lot better chance of never having to see the inside of 850 Bryant Street.

Becky's team was on Diamond Three. Sherm and I sauntered slowly over and found her sitting in the first row with a child by her side. I guessed I was about to meet Edwin, so I put on my happy face, waved and joined them

Hi sweetheart," she said, flashing me her sweet smile. No hint of residual anger from last night. "I'm glad you could come to meet Edwin." She turned toward Sherman, put out her hand and said, "And this must be the infamous Richard Sherman. I've heard so much about you these past couple of days, I'm glad to finally meet you." Sherm took her proffered hand, shook it and said, "The feeling is mutual. I spent the afternoon with your husband who spoke about nothing but you. I simply had to come here to see if he was not making you up. Obviously, he wasn't."

She looked over at me and said, "He's a smooth one, Reg. You could learn a lot from him." She laughed, took hold of Edwin's hand, and said, "Edwin, this is my husband, Reggie. He is a policeman."

I moved half a step to Becky's left so I could be in front of the boy. At the same time, he moved ever so subtly to close the space between himself and Becky. He had no intention of letting me get close to her. I'd seen the same reaction dozens of times from children protecting their single moms from strange men. I smiled inwardly, thinking the protection thing in kids was pretty cool.

"Edwin," I said, leaning over and putting out my hand. "I'm happy to meet you. Your teacher has told me a lot about you. I'm happy you're coming over our house tonight."

For a moment, Edwin didn't move. Then, he reached out and

took my hand. I clutched his and gave it an exaggerated shake. A shadow of a smile creased little Eddie's lips. I'd won round one. I wondered how many rounds there'd be in this tussle, and how many of them I'd have to win.

"Sit down, you guys," Becky said, motioning to the empty seats beside her. "How's your leg, babe? Feeling better?"

"Doing better, for sure. Don't feel or see any discharge. That's a good sign."

"I'm glad. We'll just have to keep Edwin from bumping into you." She smiled.

"I'm hoping him bumping into my leg won't be a problem, either. And I don't think he likes me enough yet to sit on my lap or wrestle around on the living room floor."

Don't take it personally," she whispered as I sat. "He's shy. Been through a lot these past few months. He misses his mom." She turned to Sherm and said, "Sorry. Didn't mean to leave you out of the discussion. Family stuff."

"No problem." he replied. "I know exactly how that is."

"Sherm took me out to cocktails today. At O'Brien's."

"The O'Brien House? The one on Nob Hill?"

"The one and only. Sherm used to work for the owner. And, no, not as the chef."

"And what exactly do you do, Mr. Sherman?" she asked.

"Sherm," he replied. "Please, call me Sherm." He paused, and then said, "I offered your husband a job."

Becky cocked her head, looked at me and said, "Seriously?"

"No, he's pulling your chain."

"No, I'm not!" Sherm said emphatically. "I work for a Ms. Brigette Le Pendu. The reason I wanted to meet you this afternoon was to tell you that she would love to have your husband and you in the fold. Brigitte respects people like your husband; people with the wisdom to lead employees through the land mines of modern life. He would be invaluable to her." He looked at me, smiled and then turned back to Becky. "And you, too, Becky. Brigitte would love you. Want to stay home and start a business? Brigitte would know just how to do that. Want to stay in teaching? Brigitte has loads of friends in the school business, be it in children's education or higher education. Reg tells me you played collegiate baseball. You want to become a women's softball coach at a major university, Brigitte could probably arrange such things."

"Okay, Sherm," I interrupted. "Enough! You've given her the spiel. Best to give it a rest for now, okay? Plenty of time for her to think about it later."

"Absolutely, Deck. Just know it's an open-ended offer. One extended by Brigitte herself."

"I have one question. . ." Becky began, before a buzz from inside Sherman's coat caused him to raise his hand like a stop sign. "Hold onto that thought," he said as he reached for his phone. He lips pursed together as he listened intently. He nodded his head once and then put the phone back in his coat pocket.

"My apologies," he said. "Duty calls. My driver is out front waiting. I'd love to continue this conversation in the near future, though. I'll give you a call, Deck." He took Becky's hand, gave her a nod of his head and said, "it was a delight to meet you. I'm glad for Deck. He found the right woman."

CHAPTER 21

"Y ou sure that Sherman guy is legit?" Becky asked as she lifted Edwin into the back seat of the car.

"He means well, babe. We go back a long way. He comes off as a bit pushy, but that's just Sherm. You'll get used to him."

"I don't know. All that blather about hiring people who could lead his people through the land mines of modern life? Where the heck did that come from? And, while I'm at it, I didn't like the idea of him bribing me with that softball shtick. I hope I'm wrong, but there's something about him that makes me uncomfortable."

"I hear you, baby. He's a little rough around the edges, but I still think we should give him a chance."

~~~~~

When we got to the house, Becky took Eddie inside while I unpacked the car. The kid had one ratty suitcase and a Nike gym bag, along with a shoebox full of school supplies. It looked as if he didn't plan on staying long. I could only hope.

I went to change while Becky showed Eddie around the house. She spent a long time in his room helping him unpack. It was hard to believe he had so many clothes packed in those two small cases. Now he had me worried.

After getting comfortable in sweats and a t-shirt, I walked to the kitchen, grabbed a beer and went to find out how our house guest was liking his new digs. I stood in the doorway watching Becky read to him. He was sitting on the bed next to her wearing Nike sweats. I flashed back to when I was this age thinking I never had gear that expensive. It made the cop in me wonder where his mom got all this stuff.

When Becky finished reading, I told the kid his sweats were pretty cool. He rewarded me with a half-smile. "Did your mom buy those for you?" I asked. He slowly shook his head back and forth, "My mom's friend."

"That was nice of him."

He shook his head again. "He hit my mom."

"Oh, Edwin, how terrible," Becky said, instantly putting her arms around him. *A mom in waiting*, I thought. "I'm so sorry. Did he hurt her?"

Nodding, he said in a soft voice, "He made her cry."

Becky hugged him tighter. I walked over and sat beside him. "If someone ever hits your mother again, you tell your teacher. Do you understand?" He didn't respond, so I asked again, this time with my cop voice. He stared at me, his eyes narrowing a tick. Only then did he nod.

Becky leaned in closer to him. "A man should never, ever hit a woman or a girl," she said softly. "The man who hit your mother was a bad, bad man. If you ever see anyone hit your mother again, you tell me at school. Mr. Decker is a policeman. He will put the man who hit your mother in jail."

Eddie squirmed out of Becky's hold, turned to me and asked, "Are you a real policeman?"

I nodded. "Yes, I am."

"Sometimes policeman comes to my house. My mom never lets me see him. She puts me in my room and closes the door. Sometimes my mom has to take me to a friend's house to stay overnight."

I knew where this was headed and didn't want to go there, so I said, "Hey, are you hungry? I think we're having hot dogs tonight." I gazed at Becky. She nodded. "And chips. What say we go eat?"

He peeked at me through glassy brown eyes, and a ghost of a smile framed his lips. I acknowledged his acceptance, and the three of us walked to the kitchen.

Eddie sat quietly as Becky fixed a dinner of hot dogs and chips. I smiled. I guess she hadn't promised the mom we'd feed him only healthy food.

"She fixes a super dinner, doesn't she?" The kid nodded, his cheeks puffed out with food. He may be shy, but when it came to eating, the kid was anything but shy. "You're a fan of hot dogs, huh?" His head bobbed up and down while his hands were at work re-stuffing his mouth. Eating hot dogs reminded me of baseball which in turn reminded me I had two tickets for Wednesday night's game at Oracle.

"Slow down, Edwin," cautioned Becky. "You'll make yourself sick. If you do, you won't be able to go to school tomorrow and your Uncle Reggie will have to stay home with you."

"Fat chance," I said with a smile. Turning to Eddie, "Do you know who the Giants are?" His eyes brightened, and his head bobbed up and down. He tried to speak through his food-filled mouth, so I held up my hand and said, "You can only talk after you finish chewing."

His eyes narrowed, obviously not liking to be told what to do. The next instant, though, they relaxed, and he nodded. *Good. He's learning*, I thought. Accepting he has rules to follow.

"I saw them on television" he said through his last swallow. "Over at my friend's house."

"Who's your favorite Giant?" I asked, hoping the male-bonding-through-sports routine worked as well on eight-year-olds as it

117

did on forty-year-olds.

His face lit up. "Madison Bumgarter." He mispronounced Bumgarner, but what the hell, close enough. I knew right away this kid and I were going to get along. At least baseball-wise. Bumgarner had been the horse of the Giants staff for years. Unfortunately, he was traded in the off-season, so I guessed I was going to have to be the guy who gave him the bad news. Poor Eddie was going to have to figure out another Giant to root for.

"Do you play baseball?" He acknowledged my query with a nod. "Did you bring your mitt with you?" He shook his head in the negative. "No problem." I tousled his hair. "We have two or three mitts in the basement. You can borrow one of them. Tomorrow or the next day we'll go over to the park and throw the baseball around. And while we're talking about baseball, we have tickets to the Giants game. Would you like to come with us?"

A smile overtook his face, and his head bobbed up and down. "When can we go?" he shouted.

"I think we have a fan here." I said to Becky. "And guess what? I actually have two tickets to the game on Wednesday night. Bristow gave them to me. Think he'd want to go?"

"If you can get one more," she said, taking hold of my hand, "I could come, too. He might be too much for you to handle alone."

"Well, I wasn't thinking of going without you, babe. And I'm not sure we'll need an extra ticket. You remember my friend Jerry, the guy in charge of ticket sales at the ballpark? I'll call him tomorrow afternoon. I'm sure he'll be able to get us another ticket. One where we can all sit together. Even if he can't, I'm sure we could put Eddie on our lap. Not ideal, but doable. Besides, he'll no doubt be asleep by the third inning."

"With his energy, don't bet on it. And I'll call his mom tomorrow to get permission."

I leaned over and whispered in her ear, "Be sure not to get us in a position where she thinks we're her son's way out. You don't want to give her an excuse to split, knowing her kid's in capable hands."

"Better than capable, Reg," she responded somewhat defensively.

"Come on, you know what I mean. The difference is our 'capable hands' have a shelf life. And a short shelf life at that."

Becky frowned, took a quick peek at her watch, and said, "Time for bed, Edwin." When he didn't react, she clapped her hands. "Let's go."

"I'm sure glad I don't have you as a teacher," I said with a laugh. "You're one tough lady."

Taking Eddie by the hand, she turned to me and smiled. "You ain't seen nothing yet."

No sooner had I finished putting the plates in the dishwasher than I heard the bath being run. The kid was getting the full monty on his first night at the Decker hotel. I wondered how he was going to enjoy the stay. I secretly hoped it wouldn't be long enough for him to either enjoy, or not enjoy, it.

I unloaded my briefcase on the kitchen table and had settled down to work when Becky came out and asked if I'd help tuck Edwin into bed. How could I refuse? As we walked back to the bedroom, she asked if I knew any prayers we could say.

"Did you ask him what he says at home? Maybe we could say those."

"He didn't know any prayers."

"Then I guess his mom ain't too religious, huh? You sure you want to introduce prayers into his life?"

"Of course. What prayers did you say when you were growing up?"

"Our family had a great routine," I told her. "Took about ten

119

minutes each night. You want to do them?"

She shook her head. "I'm guessing ten minutes the first night might be too much. Can you do a simple one?"

We walked together back to his room. Becky had him climb under the covers as I sat beside him and rubbed his head.

"We are going to say a prayer with you before you go to sleep," I said. He stared at me with no readable expression. "Do you know what a prayer is?" Again, the blank face. I wasn't up to giving him a class in theology, so I said, "A prayer is something to help you go to sleep. I'll say it first. After I finish, you and Mrs. Decker will say it again. Are you ready?" He looked at both of us before nodding. "Now I lay me down to sleep," I began. Becky coaxed him to repeat the words back with her.

So far, so good, I thought. "I pray the Lord my soul to keep."

Along with Becky, he again repeated the words. "If I should die before I wake, I pray the Lord my soul to take." It took both of them a while to get through that last full sentence. Upon finishing, I stood and gave him a kiss goodnight. Becky did the same. Leaving a night light on, we both walked out, closing the door behind us.

"I know the dude didn't understand a word of that prayer," I whispered to Becky. "But we did the right thing."

"Yeah. If nothing else, it made us feel better," She smiled, adding "But what he told us tonight? About his home life? As a teacher, it gives me a whole different perspective as to what some of my kids' home are like."

"Before he goes back, maybe you could get him help through the school district."

"Unlikely, but I'll see what I can do."

CHAPTER 22

Three important events occurred that night. First, Manny saying he had great news for me.

"Thank god!" I uttered.

"Whoa, that doesn't sound good. What's up?"

"Nothing bad. Becky brought the kid home today. Just a different vibe around here. Something I'm going to have to get used to. So, that's my sad tale. Please tell me your great news is you got a hit on our stolen property."

"You're a mind reader, Deck. That's precisely what I got."

"Praise the lord and pass the ammunition," I said, pumping my fist in the air. "Tell me."

"Place called New Liberty Pawn Shop in Brisbane. I sent a text to all my contacts this afternoon. This came back about twenty minutes ago. The Dell computer. Purchased in September of 2009. The owner has a copy of the payment receipt to the guy who brought it in. How do you want me to handle it? Want them to send us the receipt record?"

"Nah. I'd rather talk to him in person."

"Figured you'd say that, so I arranged a meeting with the owner at eight tomorrow morning. Can you make that? I can pick you up if you want."

"That's great news and great work, Gloves. Since the shop's in Brisbane, be easier if I picked you up. Will seven give us enough time?"

"As you know only too well, it just depends on traffic. The owner is great guy. He doesn't normally open until ten so if we show up a wee bit after eight, our presence won't hurt his business."

"Thanks for doing that Manny. I owe you."

The second event was that Becky and I found the prayer thing with Eddie didn't work. Could have been we said the wrong prayer. Or maybe we should have been the ones praying, and let the kid go to sleep. In either case, we had a crisis on our hands within an hour of closing his door.

After I'd finished watching the Giants game, I walked down the hallway to check how Becky was doing on her lesson plans. I stopped when I noticed the kid's door slightly ajar. I remember closing it when we put him to bed, so I peeked in. No Edwin. I checked the hall bathroom. Empty. I went down the hall and opened the door to Becky's office.

"Do you know where Eddie is?"

"He's not in his bed?" I shook my head. "Did you check the bathroom?"

"He's not there. I checked. The door is open."

"Where do you think he could be?" she asked, rising from her chair.

"Only place he could be is in our room. Maybe he was afraid in his new surroundings and came looking for us. Wanted to feel safe."

We walked into our room together, both expecting him to be curled up in our bed. Instead, a sliver of light emanated from under the closed closet door.

"Son-of-a- . . .". I started to say the B-word, but knowing Becky would call me out, I quickly turned to ". . . gun". Which made me think of the guns I kept in the closet. Two quick steps brought me to the door which I quickly jerked open. In hindsight, a bad move. Even though chances of him learning how to jack a round into the chamber of my Sig and then releasing the safety were remote, it was still a theoretical possibility. So, me bursting in on him as I did was not a very prudent move. But I lucked out. Eddie wasn't after weapons; he was after solitude. We found him sitting cross-legged on the floor counting money from the box of loose change I kept on the top of my dresser.

"And what do you think you're doing in here, young man?" I asked angrily as I took a step toward him. Becky grabbed my arm, thinking I was going to swat him or something. She didn't have to worry. I was so relieved he hadn't found the guns that I would have picked him up and kissed him, not hit him.

"I . . . I," he stammered. "I couldn't sleep."

"So, you came in here and sneaked into our closet?"

His eyes narrowed and he glared at me with something just this side of hate. I'd seen the same stare in hundreds of gangbangers I'd rousted over the years. If Eddie was on that track, I felt sorry for him.

"I couldn't sleep," he reiterated, hoping the excuse would suffice.

"Don't worry, honey," Becky said as she stepped around me and sat next to him on the closet floor. Putting her arm around him, she said, "I know this isn't your home, and I know it's all new to you. Your mom's not here and you miss her. We understand that, and feel sorry for you, sweetheart." She gave him a hug "It won't last long. Before you know it, you'll be back home with your mother. But while you are here, you must do what we tell you. When we put you to bed, you have to stay in bed. Do you understand?" He looked at the floor and then slowly nodded. "You can only get out of bed if you have to go to the bathroom. Okay?" He nodded again. "We do the same thing. When we come to our room at night, we stay in our room until the morning. You have to do that too, okay?"

I smiled at how rationally Becky laid out the rules for him living here, as if his eight-year old mind would easily grasp the logic. She was trying to make tonight's episode nothing more than a monstrous misunderstanding. I desperately wanted her to be right—that love and rational thought conquered all. Since the world I lived in was not quite like that, I was none too hopeful.

All this brought about the third important event.

Once we got him settled in his own bed and watched as he fell asleep, we went back to our room and climbed into our own bed. Becky cuddled up next to me. "I'm sorry about all this. It will get better, I promise. He's just got to learn our rules."

"And how long do you think it will take for him to learn 'our' rules?"

"He's only eight, Reg. Give him a chance. And, in the meantime, give me a chance to give him a chance, okay?"

"I know this probably sounds selfish, but I'll say it anyway. I'm worried about the 'in the meantime' part of this."

"I don't understand what you mean."

"Well, it's not hard to understand. I'm starting to think, *in the meantime*, what happens to me? *In the meantime*, what happens to us? Look at tonight for an example. You spent a few hours with him before he went to bed, hours that used to be spent on your lesson plans for the next day. After that it was 'us' time. But not tonight. Tonight was 'the closet episode.' Because of that, you didn't finish your lesson plans so you were closed up in your room. And now we're in bed about to go to sleep. Did I miss something here? Oh, wait! Now I remember. We used to spend time *together* at night. Just the two of us getting reacquainted after our eight, ten, twelve-hour days."

"I know, darling. I'm sorry. I really am. I'm just not sure what to do. Edwin needs us right now."

"Needs you."

"No, needs both of us, hon. Most especially you, a man in his life. Neither of us have been a parent . . . yet. Look at this as on the job training in case I get pregnant." She laughed. "This is only going to last for a week or two, sweetheart. I promise. Please tell me you can handle that, okay?"

Her plea had its intended effect. "Okay, babe. I'm willing to give it a try as long as we establish that Edwin's stay here has an end date." I thought for a minute, then said, "How many days are left in the school year?"

"Eight. Three days this week and five next. A week from this Friday is the last day."

"Let's agree, then, barring any unusual circumstances, that we'll keep him until the last day of school. No matter what has happened in the meantime, the next day he goes back to his own home, whether his mother is employed, in jail, or whatever. You tight with that?"

She raised up on her elbow and gave me a kiss. "You're such a good man, Inspector Decker. Thanks."

"And what has it cost us? A little over a week of our lives and a thousand-dollar gun safe." I laughed. "And it should get me laid more often."

"You keep this up, and it will," she whispered as she snuggled closer. Not quite what I had in mind but, in the bigger picture, it was a victory of sorts.

CHAPTER 23

I picked Manny up at seven-fifteen and hit the 101 Freeway in the middle of the morning commute.

"As long as we've got some time," I said, looking at a sea of red lights in front of us, "tell me what you thought of the murder book."

"Glad you reminded me. It's in my trunk, so don't let me forget it."

"I won't. What did you make of it?"

"Well, have to admit, I'd be embarrassed if it was my work."

"That's exactly how I felt, too."

"He was my partner, dammit. I should have counseled him to take a refresher course. 'All hat, no cattle' as the saying goes."

I laughed. "Doesn't convict him of a crime though; only incompetency."

"I saw in the murder book, he interviewed two of Poppy's girlfriends. As long as we're looking into his handling of the case, with your permission, I'd like to try to reconnect with them. Get their impressions of Egan."

"Been such a long time I'm not sure it would do any good, but hell, no reason not to try."

"Thanks. I will. And what about the Twitter crazies?"

"The deluge has slowed to a trickle, but they still have over three-quarter of a million re-tweets. Most of them unfavorable. I'd still like to get my hands on the instigator of these Tweets, but first things first. We gotta deal with Egan."

We pulled off the freeway a few minutes after eight and arrived at the New Liberty Pawn Shop fifteen minutes later.

~~~~~~

Manny introduced me to Mr. Nguyen Pham, the sixty-something owner of the pawn shop. "He's from South Vietnam, Deck. Escaped with his family on a boat a few days before Saigon fell." Pham shook my hand and bowed respectfully with his head. "He told me his father was a colonel in the 1st Infantry Division, killed in action during the Hue-Da Nang Campaign."

"A brave man," I said to Pham, returning the bow. "My father served two tours in Vietnam. From 1970 to 1972. By '75, everyone knew the war was lost. But your father did his duty and fought on." I returned the bow. "I honor him." I paused for a moment, then said, "And forgive us for being late."

"Not a problem," Pham replied with barely a trace of an accent. "Shall we?" he said, ushering in the door. As soon as we were inside, he closed the door, made sure the "CLOSED" sign faced outward and pulled the inner security gate shut. "I'm sorry," he said, somehow feeling the need to apologize for closing the shop. "There are valuable items in our store. And the neighborhood . . ." He shrugged. I appreciated the irony. It was probably safer in Saigon now than in San Francisco. "Can I give you a quick tour?"

I nodded and said we'd be honored. Had to admit I was surprised at how well-designed Pham's shop was. Except for the row of power tools hanging on the back wall near the check-out counter, the interior reminded me more of a mall-style jewelry store than a hard-to-find pawn shop in the outer reaches of San Francisco. Four rows of well-lit glass display cases filled the floor space. The cases on the far wall featured watches, rings, antique coins and assorted jewelry. The cases in the two middle aisles localized the household items such as dishes, silverware, crystal and decorative table displays. On the wall closest to me were all things electronic, including cameras and computers. I guess I didn't do an adequate job of hiding my surprise from Pham.

"We consider ourselves an upscale shop that buys and sells upscale merchandise," he proclaimed with pride as we strolled to the rear of the shop. Nodding toward Morales, he said, "This officer asked about a particular computer we may have purchased between December of 2007 and December of 2009. Dell, I think it was." He looked at Morales for confirmation. "Unlike some shops," he continued after receiving Manny's nod, "we keep good records. We have nothing to hide, Inspector." He turned and pushed a button under the main counter. A medium-sized file drawer opened behind him.

Obviously prepared for our visit, he bent and picked up the top file folder. Laying the contents on the surface of the nearest counter, he gestured with a sweep of his hand. "It's all yours, Inspector."

The file contained three pieces of paper. The first was a copy of a 2008 receipt from New Liberty Pawn Shop made out to someone named Octavio Godines for one Dell computer. The purchase price was listed at two hundred twenty-five dollars. I reached inside my coat pocket and pulled out the receipt Maria Garcia emailed me to compare her serial number with the one printed on Nguyen Pham receipt. They matched.

"Let me take a photocopy of this receipt for our files," Mr. Pham said. "You can have the original."

I turned to Morales and said, "Now we have to hope there is a dude named Octavio Godines somewhere in our data base."

~~~~~~

Before we left the shop that day, thanks to Pham's memory and record keeping, we knew Octavio Godines was a real person and by tomorrow would even have an address for him.

"Mr. Godines was a small, muscular man," Pham told us. "I remember because the back shelf there . . ." he turned and pointed, "the one near the back of the office . . ." he paused so we could locate the exact spot he was referring to, "is exactly five feet, ten inches high. Mr. Godines walked under it without having to duck his head."

"How old?" I asked.

"His driver's license said he was twenty-six."

"He showed you a driver's license?"

"Of course. Our customers know *no identification, no sale.* Take it or leave it. And by identification, we mean a driver's license with a picture." He reached into his file folder and pulled out a photocopy of Godines' driver's license.

"While processing the items I was buying from him, I had one of my workers check with Sacramento to see if his license was legit and current. It was on both counts. No outstanding arrest warrants on file. As you know inspector, these kinds of checks aren't thorough, but they do give us enough of a background to proceed."

~~~~~~

"Got to say, Pham's got some cojones," Manny said as we exited the store. "I'm sure Godines told him in no uncertain terms what would happen to him if he ever showed that receipt to the Federales."

"No doubt about it," I said. "But coming out of Vietnam at the time he did, he'd already faced a lot tougher hombres than this Godines dude. Now we have to track this guy down? No doubt a gang member. Maybe Egan was right after all. This was a gang hit."

Manny laughed. "Don't go all soft on me now, Decker."

"Yeah, right. So, what's the address on the license?"

"Cotter Street. In San Jose. I'll bet it's a phony, but I'll also bet if he's still in the Bay Area, that address will be close to where he hangs out. These bad-ass dudes are none too bright. I've got friends in the San Jose PD. I'll give 'em a call tomorrow. Pham had an employee check out his license through Sacramento, so we know Godines was his real name. If it weren't, the guy would have played hell getting the damn check cashed, and Pham assured us it was cashed. In any case, I'll call down to San Jose to see if anyone's heard of our boy Octavio."

"Perfect. But make that call away from the Hall, okay? Better no one but Bristow knows you're hooked up with me on this."

CHAPTER 24

I'd been at my desk no more than a minute or two when CK called wanting her murder book back. I walked it over to her.

"You sure you're through with this?"

"Yeah. Thanks. But remember, it's now officially an active case so don't go puttin' it back where no one could ever find it again."

She looked at me as if I was from a different planet, took it and placed it on top of her filing cabinet. "I hear you've just adopted a kid. Congratulations."

"Who the hell told you that?"

"You can't hide anything in this department, Decker. You know that. How long have you and your lovely wife been with child?"

"One lousy freaking day. It's an eight-year-old student of hers. The boy's mother lost her job." Mentioning the mom reminded me to run a sheet on her. I held up my left hand while I wrote myself a quick note. "Okay. Sorry. Becky wants us to 'adopt him' until his mother finds work. I'm guessing it's a hormone thing."

"Oh, stop!"

"I know. I'm partly kidding, but I do think it plays a role. First night he's with us, he sneaks into our closet while Becky is doing lesson plans and I'm in the living room. Bad news for all of us since the closet is where I stash my guns."

"Damn, Deck, you of all people should've thought of that. You've got to buy yourself a gun case at least."

"I know. I know. I'll stop at Dick's Sporting Goods on the way home and see what they got."

"How many weapons do you have besides the ones the department issues?"

"I've got three rifles, a shotgun, a .40 Caliber Sig and a 9mm Taurus G2c for Becky."

"You're going to need more than a case, my friend. You're gonna need a gun safe for all that hardware."

"I hear you," I said with a touch of annoyance in my voice. "Just thinkin', though, price-wise it's gonna be a bitch."

"How's Becky with all this?"

"I feel sorry for her. Not only is she dead tired, she now has a student in her class as tired as she is." I took a sip of my coffee. "Not what you'd call the perfect mix."

"I feel for you, Deck. And Becky, too. I had three kids. At my age now, there's no way I could handle an eight-year-old. I wish you luck." She hesitated. "Becky's never had children, right?"

"Right. That's why I mentioned the hormone thing. She's thirty-three, and her biological clock is ticking. You know what I mean."

CK laughed and shook her head. "You're living in the dark ages, Inspector Decker."

"Well, you may be right," I said, "but that's my explanation and I'm stickin' to it."

"You do that, John Wayne." She smiled and patted me on the back. "And good luck."

As I got up to leave, she put her hand out to stop me. "Oh wait. Morales called and wanted me to tell you to call him ASAP."

"Thanks," I said, "for everything." I patted her on the shoulder, walked back to my desk and called Morales.

~~~~~

"Thanks for calling back, Deck. Our new friend Octavio Godines? Turns out to be one wicked hombre. MS-13 dude. That's probably why Mr. Pham couldn't read his tats."

"Do your friends know where he is? And please don't tell me he's dead."

"No, not dead. On the contrary. At this exact minute he's locked up in the Santa Clara County Jail awaiting trial. A 'strike two' trial, at that. Maybe that'll give you some leverage."

I felt the adrenaline rush. "You have a contact I can call? Maybe make an appointment to see the guy?" I wrote down the name and phone number he gave me. "It would be ideal if they'd let me see him today. Any chance you could arrange that? I'd hate for them to let the guy skate before I talked to him."

"I'll try. But you know how the law and lawyers work. I'll call you back within thirty minutes."

Didn't hear from him for a whole hour. "Sorry I'm late getting back to you, Deck. Long story. First off, I got you a meeting with Godines at nine tomorrow morning at the Santa Clara County Jail. Can you do that?"

"Well, hell yah, I can do that," I said with a whoop, pumping my fist in the air. From the number of colleagues who looked at me with a scowl, I'm guessing my yelp of enthusiasm was not well received. "Thanks Manny. Good work."

"Wait! Before you hang up, I got other news. What I'd classify as good news. You ready for this?"

"Depends what you classify as 'good' news."

"How 'bout Egan calling me thirty minutes ago?"

"You're kidding! Egan? What did he say?"

"Well, to tell you the truth, he's got nothing good to say about you, Deck." He laughed.

"That's strange! He doesn't even know me. I probably met him all of three times in the years before he quit."

"Well, I tried to tell him what a charmer you were." He paused for effect, and then added "But that boy didn't buy a word of it."

"Yeah, well, that *boy* was not the most reliable family member we ever had. More like the brother who ran away from home, and, in the process, took all your valuables with him on the way out the door."

"I hear you."

"You talk to him again, tell him I'm not after his scalp. I'm only trying to close a few loopholes in this Garcia case."

"He told me he'd meet you in Sacramento on Friday. Wants you to call him tomorrow evening at 8:30 sharp and he'll tell you where and when to meet. Here's the phone number he gave me."

"Good work, Manny. Thanks." I gathered my papers together. "You're on a roll." I paused. "Think you can engineer a Giants win tonight?"

"Piece of cake. Have a good time."

CHAPTER 25

I left the Hall in the early afternoon. CK was right. If Becky insisted on having Eddie live with us, even for a few days, I had to be a responsible adult and store my weapons in a secure place. I ended up buying a standing steel case with a kid-proof locking system at Dick's in Daly City. They promised delivery by tomorrow afternoon. My birthday. *Something wrong with this picture*, I thought ruefully. *I was just forced to buy an eight-hundred-dollar birthday present for myself.*

I got home a few minutes before four, surprised to find Becky's car in the garage. Since we still had a few hours before trekking off to the Giants game, I thought I'd give Becky a break and take the kid over to the park and throw the baseball around, hoping the exercise wouldn't break open any of the scabs dotting my leg.

I opened the front door to the sound of Eddie yelling. "No - I - Am - Not - Tired! Stop saying that." I followed the sound to his bedroom. Becky was sitting on the bed. The kid was standing by the closet. His back to her.

"What's the problem here?" At the sound of my voice, they both jumped.

"Edwin and I were having a talk."

"She kept telling me to do my homework," he stammered in a peevish voice, his eyes staring at the floor. "And then she got mad at me and said I must be tired." That was accompanied by an exasperated breath. "I am not tired." He emphasized the word "not" with a stomp of his foot.

I glanced over at Becky and arched an eyebrow. "I think I came in somewhere around the foot stomp, if I'm not mistaken." She nodded, a bemused expression on her face.

I turned back to Eddie. "Did your teacher tell you to do your homework before we went to the Giants game?" He took his time, but finally nodded his head. "So, when are you going to do it? We have to leave for the game in a few hours." He still had his back to us. "Eddie," I said in my most authoritative voice, "turn around when I'm talking to you." He hesitated, but turned, his head still bowed forward, his eyes still on the floor. "Let me ask again. When are you going to do your homework?"

"He wanted . . ." Becky began, but I put my out hand to stop her.

"Hold on. Let him answer the question." I took a step closer and knelt gingerly in front of him. "I'm going to ask you one more time, and this time you'd better answer me. When are you going to do your homework?"

"I was going to do it." He pouted, still staring at the floor. His foot tracing circles in the carpet only he could see. "I don't know. I . . ." he paused and then said, "I just don't want to do it now."

"Wrong answer, Eddie."

"And my name's not Eddie," he yelled, looking up at me sharply, accompanied by another foot stomp. "Don't call me that anymore. My name is Edwin."

I remained silent for a minute and then replied, "Okay. I'll make you a deal. I'll call you Edwin from now on, but you must do something for me." I paused, waiting for an answer. The kid was not about to make the bargain so quickly. I had to hand it to him. He was already learning the art of the deal.

He thought about it for what he considered an appropriate

amount of time and then nodded his head. I nodded back. "So, here's what you can do for me. Did you bring a mitt with you when you came to our house?" He cast a glance my way for the first time, his eyes still dark and squinty, but happier now the conversation had turned away from doing his homework. He slowly shook his head. "Well, no problem because I have an extra mitt just your size in the basement. Let's you and me and Mrs. Decker go to the park down the street and throw the baseball around for a while. When we get back, you are going to finish all your homework, and then we'll go to the Giants game." I stopped, letting my words sink in. I could tell they had some effect because when he looked up at me, I could see light in his eyes. "Do we have a deal?" I asked. Slowly, his head bobbed up and down. "Well, then, come over here and shake my hand and we'll get going. I want to see how awesome a ball player you are. You might even be playing for the Giants when you get older."

Becky helped me stand. "How's the leg?" she asked. "Still bothering you?"

"A little. It's getting better, though. I was on my feet a lot today, so it's bothering me probably more than it would normally."

"Good. You change while I go the basement to find that old mitt of yours. And I'll do most of the throwing and catching today, too. Don't want you to aggravate your wounds." On our way to the park, I told Becky about the gun safe. She did a double take at the price, but told me I'd done the right thing. Her praise made me feel better.

She nodded at Eddie, now known as Edwin, as he hop-skipped into the park. "You know, he's really a good kid, Reg. A little high strung, but that's because he misses his mother."

"Probably not nearly as much as I do," I chuckled. "Have you talked to her?"

She shook her head. "Not yet. I was going to call after dinner but forgot we're going to the game. Sometime I've got to ask her what's going on in her life. I know you don't want to hear this, but I do enjoy having Edwin here." I shook my head, thinking about my conversation with CK about hormones.

We played catch in the park for a little under an hour. Truth be told, Edwin and Becky played catch. I mostly watched. I was impressed with the kid. He turned out to be a pretty good little ball player for his age. As I remembered, kids in his age bracket threw the ball in an arc, their arms not quite strong enough to overcome gravity. Not this kid, though. His throws were ropes. Straight and hard. I was impressed. I told Becky on the way home I should stay close to him. Could be his agent when he's of age. She patted me on the butt and smiled. "You go for it, champ."

CHAPTER 26

I looked at my watch. "Come on, guys," I said through the kitchen door. "Time's a-wastin'."

"Hold on, Reg, we're coming," From somewhere in the back of the house, I heard the toilet flush. A minute later Becky walked into the kitchen hand-in-hand with Edwin. "How do we look?" She proudly brought Edwin forward and spun him in a circle. "Pretty cool, huh?"

"Very cool, indeed," I acknowledged. She'd dressed him in Giants colors: an orange t-shirt, jeans with the pant legs rolled up two or three turns, and a Giants baseball hat. "Hey, little man, where'd you get the new hat?" I bent in front of him and pulled the brim down over his eyes.

He stepped backward and took hold of Becky's hand as he re-seated the hat back on his head. Looking at her with nothing short of adoration, he said in his high-pitched, squeaky voice, "Teacher gave it to me."

"Then I guess you're all set to go, huh?" His face lit up and his head bobbed like a float in water. I looked at Becky. "I think that means he's ready?" She gave me a thumbs up.

The Giants were only four games out of first place, and on a modest three game winning streak. Even though they had a lot of turnover in the off season, they were still drawing pretty well as evidence by the three-quarter full ballpark. Since I was in no shape to drive, park and walk a mile or so to the stadium, especially with an eight-year-old in tow, we took an Uber.

The driver dropped us on the Third Street side of a crowded Willie Mays Plaza. I called my friend Jerry, and five minutes later he was exchanging my two tickets for his three. I couldn't help but smile. Being a cop had its perks.

On the way to our seats, we stopped at one of the booths that sold player gear. Since there were so many new players on the team, I bought him a Joey Bart jersey, thinking this was a young player whose jersey shouldn't go out of style in the majors for a long time. I helped him put it on and was rewarded with my first ever hug. It felt awesome. I began thinking this kid and I could coexist after all.

As we continued up the ramp to our seats, Becky took my arm and pulled on it so my ear was close to her mouth. "Be careful," she whispered, "He can become habit forming."

I nodded, smiled and whispered back, "Edwin? Not a chance. But his teacher sure could." I patted her fanny for emphasis.

By the time we reached the seats, we'd added a large bag of peanuts and a swirl of cotton candy. "Remember our first time here?"

"Oh, Reg," she said. "You ask me that every time we come to a game." She nudged me with her shoulder. "A girl always remembers her first date, especially if she ends up marrying the guy." She swung her upper body around and, with her free hand, pointed to some seats on the level above us. "Right up there if I remember correctly."

"Just checking." I squeezed her thigh and kissed her on the cheek. "When we get back to the house let's re-enact what happened when I took you home that night after the game."

"You better hope he sleeps soundly then," she said. "As I remember that night, we were a wee bit noisy. Wouldn't want to wake him up." She laughed as I put my hands in a prayerful position.

"How many games do you think we've been to since that night?" I asked.

"Too many to count. And you'd be here every game if you could."

"But I would always only want you to come with me," I said diplomatically.

She laughed. "You're only trying to get laid tonight."

"Didn't think I was that transparent," I replied with a smile while squeezing her upper thigh.

Turned out to be an excellent ball game. No score going into the bottom of the third. The first two games of this series were split, so this game was a must-win for the Giants. By the bottom of the fourth, Edwin was squirming in his seat. By the bottom of the sixth, we were in a cab and on our way home.

Becky put Edwin to bed so I could watch the rest of the game on TV. Giants ended up winning 4 – 1, which brought our record to 16 - 22. Not as good a start as I expected at the beginning of the season, but it was still early June. No way was I about to stop believing'. This was going to be our year. I could feel it.

Becky resurfaced about thirty minutes later. "Got him to say his prayers again," she said as she snuggled into me on the sofa. I turned off the TV and put my arm around her. I was about to ask if she wanted to go fool around when the house phone rang in the back bedroom. We both looked at our watches. Almost eleven.

"Let it go," I said. "Nothing good ever comes from an eleven o'clock phone call."

She arched her eyebrows. "Sorry," she said, pushing herself off the sofa. "You never know. Could be an emergency."

"From who?" I answered, but by that time she'd already answered it.

"No, it's a large house," were her last words before she closed the bedroom door. That surprised me and I was debating whether to go back and find out who the hell was on the phone when I heard the bedroom door open.

"Who was that, pray tell?" I asked, none too pleasantly.

She didn't answer until she reseated herself next to me.

"That was Edwin's mother. She's missing him."

My anger turned to joy. "Well, halleluiah," I cried. "I'm glad she finally came to her senses. Is she on her way here to pick him up?"

"Yes and no. She wants to come over tomorrow. but not to get him."

"What the hell does that mean? She's just coming to visit? Goes to show you no good deed goes unpunished."

"Not to visit, Reg. She said she wants to come live with him at our house."

I looked at her like she had grown two horns and was wearing a nose ring.

She caught my expression, and shook her head. "She wasn't kidding, Reg. She wants to come here to live."

"There's no way in hell that's happening," I said angrily. She grimaced at my choice of words. "Sorry, babe, but that's just the way it is. Under no circumstances is she coming here to live. You know that, don't you?"

"She's without a job, Reg. She can't stay where she's living now. She owes two month's back rent. What's she going to do, live in some homeless encampment on the street? Or a tent in Golden Gate Park? With Edwin? I couldn't live with myself."

"There are a ton of public assistance agencies in this damn— excuse me—darn city. Someone will help her."

"It's not fair, Reg. We have so much and she has so little."

"The world isn't fair, Becky. You and I both know that." I was in no mood to fool with this any longer. "Let me tell you how we're going to handle this. At least in the short term. You call her back and tell her we'll pay the overdue rent plus we'll give her money to cover her rent for a third month. That'll take her to the beginning of July. We'll keep Edwin here like we agreed. To the day school's out. After that, she takes her child back home and she's on her own. Not our problem." I brought my hands together as if I were washing them. "And that's the end of it. Just to make myself clear, she is not coming to live with us. Not tomorrow, not the next day, not ever. Period."

"I understand. Honest I do. Let's just get through this final week and we can revaluate. Maybe his mom will surprise us. Maybe she'll have a job by then. Maybe I won't be so tired."

"Maybe. Maybe. Maybe," I said.

"Yeah, maybe!"

CHAPTER 27

I was up early the next morning and walked into the kitchen to find Becky and the kid already having breakfast. Becky, always the teacher, was reading Edwin the story of Horton the Elephant. Damn if I don't remember my mom reading me that book at breakfast same as she was doing with Edwin. Spooky.

When she finished, I asked Edwin if he liked the Giants game last night. He beamed and nodded his head. "The Giants won that game after we left. Isn't that great?"

He nodded and then went back to looking at the Dr. Seuss book. Too bad. I was hoping he'd be a bigger sports fan than that. Disappointing. Another reason his mother should just come and get him."

"It's not that he doesn't like baseball, Reg. He does. But Dr. Seuss holds a sway over every young child. As he should. Children love Dr. Seuss." I looked over at Edwin paging though the book looking at pictures.

"Well, all I can say is 'I meant what I said, and said what I meant. An elephant's faithful, one hundred percent.'"

Becky laughed. "See what I mean? You remember that from being a kid." She paused and then said "You have to be at the office early today?"

"Yeah, I do. Manny found the guy who pawned Garcia's computer," I poured myself some cereal. "He's in the Santa Clara County jail. I'll be leaving here in a few minutes to go down and interview him."

"Ok, but don't be late. We're having your birthday party tonight. Edwin is really looking forward to it."

"I'll be back no later than two.

I retreated to the bedroom so I could call Morales' jail contact without Eddie making a lot of noise. I told the guy I wanted to confirm my visit with Octavio Godines at ten o'clock. He said I was on the calendar.

I called Manny to let him know that I had confirmed the appointment. He wished me luck and said I could tell him all about it at my party tonight. I groaned.

"Hey," he said. "I'm honored I got invited. It'll be fun. Wait 'till you see your kick-ass present."

"You already know what it is?"

"Becky told me about it so I kicked in a few bucks. Not much. Come on, it's not like I know you all that well. We've only been together for what, three—looonnng—years?" He laughed.

"Finally," I said with an exasperated sigh. "I'm getting the recognition I deserve."

~~~~~

I arrived at the Santa Clara County Jail at twenty minutes after ten. I'd visited this jail probably thirty times in the past twenty years, so I wasn't a complete stranger to its visitor protocol. I walked up to the blackened glass window and deposited my badge, gun and ID into the tray. Through the speaker phone, I told the deputy I had a prisoner interview at ten forty-five. The voice behind the glass directed me to a door on my right. I pushed the buzzer, and the door clicked open.

I gave the deputy the leather portfolio containing my notes on how I was going to deal with Godines. He'd already placed my gun in a small, soft-sided lockable case which he put in a safe near his feet. The deputy gave me a receipt for the firearm and sent me and my portfolio through an airport style X-ray machine. Once through, my badge and identification were returned, and I was escorted to another doorway and asked which prisoner I was there to see. I told him Octavio Godines and gave him Godines' "Personal File Number." Every prisoner housed in the Santa Clara jail was issued a PFN. If you didn't know it, you had an exactly zero chance of seeing the prisoner.

The deputy looked over his sheet and told me my interview was scheduled on the seventh floor, Pod *B*. As I remembered it, the pod designated which corridor you traversed once you exited the elevator. Pod *B* was the middle corridor, the one where violent prisoners were housed. Octavio Godines was obviously thought of as a very bad hombre.

The deputy took me to the elevator, held up both hands and flashed a seven with his fingers to a barely visible camera housed above the elevator door. Even though I'd heard the speech a dozen of times over the years, it was his job to tell me how the system worked, and true to his calling, he did. "There are no buttons for the rider to push. The elevator will only go where our control tells it to go. In your case, to floor seven." He waited until the car arrived and watched as I entered. After a short ten second upward flight, the doors opened on floor seven.

I walked the few steps to the desk at the entrance of the cell-block and told the deputy my name and who I was meeting. "Sureños," the deputy said, identifying Godines as a gang member from Southern California. "Bad dude." He took me down the hallway and deposited me in a ten by ten interrogation room. In the middle of the room was a metal half-desk with circular seats on opposite sides. I sat. A moment later the prisoner door opened and in walked Octavio Godines flanked by two burly Correctional

Officers.

Godines looked a lot like Pham described him, but older. A short, thick Hispanic, he wore prison-issue red pants and a lime green short-sleeve shirt. The green shirt identified him as Sureños. The red pants as violent. The tree-trunk sized arms protruding from the sleeves identified him as a guy who had spent long hours in prison weight rooms. I was relieved to see those arms secured to a waist chain which the security guards attached to a bolt in the floor beneath his seat. They hooked the chain to the floor in such a way that prevented Godines from sitting upright. The guards could have given him more slack, but chose not to. Another reminder of who was in control. They tugged at the chains a few times to make sure they were secure and left.

Godines and I sat in silence for a few moments, each sizing the other up. Finally, I said, "My name is Reginald Decker. I'm a San Francisco Police Department Homicide Inspector." At the word "homicide" I could see him flinch ever so slightly. Excellent. I wanted him to know this wasn't going to be a friendly meet and greet. That a lot was at stake. I tapped the portfolio I'd laid on the table. "And you're in big-time trouble."

His face was passive, but his eyes radiated hate. I studied him for a moment. He was older than I first thought. The lines around his eyes more pronounced. I pegged him to be in his early forties. He was bald, but his head and face were heavily tattooed. The tats told me he'd been a gang member for a long time. Fifteen to twenty years ago, tats were used as an identifier, a form of intimidation saying you were not to be messed with. Smart gang members nowadays didn't want identifiers. They saw a certain wisdom in being less visible, especially as they started moving into more white-collar type crimes. It was a purely pragmatic decision. Violence was still their calling card.

I stood and slowly strolled around him, another way to

establish who's in charge. That I was free to move and he wasn't. His eyes followed me as far as they could before he was forced to turn to pick me up as I came around his back side. But I didn't come around his back side. Instead, I stopped directly behind him. Another subtle message.

"Been in the gangs a while, I see." The elaborate MS-13 tattoo that ran across his upper neck from earlobe to earlobe was a dead giveaway. "You must be a real looser. Intelligent MS guys I've met are, unlike you, making a lot of money and managing to stay out of jail." I let that comment sit for a minute and then said, "They don't need fancy ink to show they're real men." By this time, Godines gave up on my stroll and faced forward. "You're probably asking yourself right this minute—who the heck is this guy and what does he want with me." I was now showing my friendly side. Being a buddy. *Just you and me, pal.* "Well, Octavio, I can answer all your questions. All you have to do is ask."

"I don't care who you are or why you're here. You can talk all you want 'cause I ain't sayin' a word to you."

"Well, the dead man wakes," I said with a snort. Getting the bad guys to talk is the toughest part in any jailhouse negotiation. Once you got them talking though, you've won the battle. Even though we were only in round one, I felt like taking a victory lap. From now on, I knew it was simply a matter of time. "Let me get right to my question," I said. "You pawned a computer at the New Liberty Pawn Shop in Brisbane about eleven, maybe twelve, years ago. Do you remember that?" He smirked but didn't respond. "I know it was a long time ago so it's understandable you can't remember." I paused "But I've got just the cure for that poor memory of yours. I've got a receipt with your name on it." He didn't bother turning his head. His ass was mine, and he knew it. The jailhouse code, however, was never to cooperate with the enemy, unless, of course, you were offered something in return. And

I had that something to offer. It was time to play my ace card. I completed the circle and sat across from him. Couldn't tell if he was pleased to see me or not, but I couldn't have cared less. We were about to get down to business.

CHAPTER 28

I opened the portfolio, laid the papers on the table and leafed through them slowly. Godines feigned disinterest. Slumping forward in the chair, he looked at the floor or studied the tattoos on the back of his hand. One time, though, I caught him peeking to see what I was up to. *Gotcha*, I thought.

"Ah, here it is," I said with great flourish as I pulled the receipt from the papers strewn in front of me. I placed it on the table so it faced him and in slow motion pushed it forward. "This is the receipt you signed when you received the payment for a computer you brought to the pawn shop. This is your signature, isn't it?" I pointed to the bottom of the receipt. He looked at it through hooded eyes, then went back to studying the floor. "Well, no big deal. We can have an expert testify in court that it's your handwriting. And the owner of the shop remembers you, too. He told me he could pick you out of a lineup, if you let it get that far." I paused. "I'm assuming, of course, you're not that stupid."

Again, no response. I took the receipt and placed it at the bottom of my stack. I then pulled out a packet of official court documents, holding them up so Godines could see the seal. "Recognize these?" I pushed the top paper toward him. "Lookie here," I said, pointing to his name. "Court documents. With your name on them." He flinched, no longer so disinterested.

I pulled a page from the stack, put it on the table and slid it over to him. "Says here, Octavio, that you already got a strike on you." I sat back and stared at him. His eyes held mine, the hatred now replaced by a hint of fear. "Says in these court documents that you're incarcerated on a burglary charge. That you broke into a business owned by some rival gang. Norteños, no doubt. Took off with what? Six hundred bucks?" I looked at him for confirmation. He didn't say anything, but his body language told me to continue, obviously curious as to where I was taking this. "I've been a cop for a long time, Octavio. And you? You've been a two-bit criminal for a long time. You know the robbery you committed is a felony. That should scare the hell out of you. Another felony means you'd be a two-striker. Put you away for a long, long time. But you and I both know the law. Since the burglary happened after business hours, and no one got hurt, it's not a felony that's gonna get you that second strike. Hell, you and I both know that not much will happen to you. You're for sure gonna get convicted. I'm guessin' maybe four years. I'm also guessing that right at this moment you're thinkin' you'll be out in two. No big deal, huh? Hey, you're golden." This time he nodded. I was making progress.

"But just so you know, compadre, the computer you fenced at the pawn shop is a horse of a different color. It was stolen from a residence. And you know what that means, right?" I could see in his eyes he knew, but I wanted him to hear it from my lips. "A residential burglary is a different animal from a business burglary. Residential burglaries are taken more seriously because there's a greater risk that innocent people might be hurt. They are, as you know so well, classified as 'strike' worthy. In your case, 'strike two' worthy." He knew where I was taking this. He closed his eyes, and his head slumped lower. "So, my friend, instead of you looking at a four-year sentence which statistically would put you back on the street in two, you're facing a term of twenty-five to life." His chains rattled as he adjusted his position.

"That ain't true. You're making all this up," he said.

"It ain't true, huh? It gets worse, Octavio. Much worse. Not only was this computer stolen in a residential burglary, but the owner of this computer was shot dead." I let that sink in and then said, "If you don't help me on this, I'm gonna get you a freaking life sentence with no parole."

Octavio Godines sat slumped over for a long time, his eyes staring at the floor. Not only did I not speak, I tried not to even move. Didn't want to interrupt what was by now traveling through his brain like a freight train.

Finally, he straightened as best he could, looked me in the eye and said, "What do you want from me, homey?"

"Now you're getting smart, Octavio. I want to know how this computer ended up in your hands. If you don't tell me, or if you give me a line of crap, I'm gonna leave here and pin your ass to the wall."

There was silence as Godines weighed his options. He didn't have many.

"It was a long time ago."

"Sorry. That answer doesn't fly." I got up and made a show of straightening my papers in preparation for leaving. "See you at sentencing."

"No wait." He paused. "Somebody gave it to me."

"Gave it to you? You're gonna have to do better than that, Octavio, or I'm going to hook your ass on a murder one."

"It was a cop." My heart did a backward flip.

"Name. What's his name?"

"I don't know his name. Never saw him before."

"Don't give me that slop." I started putting the papers back in my portfolio. "I gave you a chance, Octavio. Have fun on Death Row."

"No, wait," he pleaded. "The guy was a cop. I met him at a

party fifteen or so years ago. He knew who I was. He asked if I wanted to do business with him. Minor things, like laundering stolen property. He brought me stuff, and I'd launder it through my contacts. And no one's hurt."

"Name, Octavio. I'm not leaving without a name."

He sighed and shook his head back and forth. "I haven't seen him in years."

"Name, Octavio."

Silence, and then, "Egan. His name was Barry Egan."

I immediately pushed the "come get me" button located on the underside of the table. Within seconds, the door opened and both guards appeared. I held up my hand. "Sorry to bother you guys, but I need a stenographer here immediately."

CHAPTER 29

I retrieved my gun and phone and limped out the front door of the Santa Clara County Jail at ten past one. If I hurried, I could still catch Becky on her lunch break. I sat in the car and texted that I was out and on my way home.

She replied with the picture of a birthday cake strewn with candles. In case I missed the message, she typed "Happy Birthday," followed by "How'd it go today?"

"WAY BETTER THAN I EXPECTED," my text shouted back. She replied with a happy face and a message saying she had to get back to class.

I signed off with "Come home as soon as you can." I was rewarded with another happy face and the message "Be on our way home as soon as school's out. See you 4:30-ish."

~~~~~~

I got lucky on the drive back to the city. Traffic was lighter than expected, allowing me to use cruise control most of the way. I called CK to see if she could schedule me a thirty-minute meeting with Bristow sometime after two-thirty. She called back saying he'd give me thirty minutes if I got there by two-thirty. I told her to book it.

I placed a quick call to Godines' attorney and then called Manny.

"Hey, partner. Glad you called. Dyin' to hear what happened today."

"I'm on my way back now. You at the Hall?"

"Yeah, but don't have to be. I was invited over to your house for birthday dinner. Happy birthday, by the way.

"Thanks. I'm coming back to the Hall. Got a meeting scheduled with Matt. Wait there for me and we can talk." I paused. "Then you can follow me home."

"Sounds good. While I have you, tell me how it went with Godines."

"It was interesting to say the least. Let me give you the condensed version. Say slowly after me; B-A-R-R-Y-E-G-A-N."

He gave a short whistle. "He fingered Egan straight out? Damn. Good for you."

"Had to blackmail the SOB by holding a second strike against him. I'll tell you what, though, after my mentioning his second-strike, it was like the Red Sea parting. He just somehow started to remember things."

Manny laughed. "Yeah. Funny how you quickly capture their hearts and minds when you're holding 'em by the balls."

"Amen to that. Turned out it wasn't Godines' first goat rodeo. He knew the territory. He'd been blackmailed before."

"Not surprising," Manny said with a chuckle. "I've used the same tactic myself. And you know what? I don't feel at all bad about it. It's for a higher cause." He laughed.

"Not always, unfortunately. The cop who first blackmailed Godines was our friend Egan. And certainly not for a 'higher cause.' He just wanted to get noticed by the brass so he could move up in the food chain. But bottom line, we got Godines testimony signed and sealed by the jailhouse stenographer"

"How long was he in bed with Egan?"

"Over thirteen years. Told me he started doing business with him in the late nineties."

"Dang, man. A long freaking time ago. Egan came to Homicide in the early part of this century. In the nineties, he worked Robbery. The son-of-a-bitch musta been fencing stuff through Godines for years."

"Yeah," I said. "And that he kept him on the payroll, so to speak, was a testimony to Godines' effectiveness. But when I asked Godines if he'd like to spend the next twenty or thirty years in jail and then get his sorry ass deported back to El Salvador, he started to sing like a canary. He knew exactly what he'd be looking at if he picked up that second strike."

"And I'll bet Egan told him his chances of picking up that strike was not a matter of if, but when.

"His exact words, as a matter of fact. Egan told him he could fix it so Godines would never be charged with an offense that would merit the second strike. All he had to do was what Egan told him to do. And, as you can imagine, Godines signed up for that bargain *muy pronto*."

"I'll bet!"

"Not only that, but Egan made it easy for him. At the front end, the only thing he wanted was information on Norteños gangs. Easy stuff, like members' names, where they hung out—that kinda crap."

"I can see where this is going. The ol' bait and switch."

"Right again," I said. "Not long afterward, however, Egan ratchets up the ante. Like you said, bait and switch. Just standard operating procedure, baby."

"You know, I'm starting to feel sorry for the poor bastard. Didn't he realize he was being played with? You just know Egan taped every damn encounter with him to ensure his loyalty."

The traffic was getting heavier, forcing me to turn off cruise control and sit up straighter. My leg didn't appreciate that maneuver and barked at me. I must have made a sound because Manny asked if I was all right.

"I'm okay. Just my leg acting up. I'm already at the off-ramp. What you said a few minutes ago about feeling sorry for Godines? Don't waste your time. He's a bad dude who'd cut your heart out without blinking an eye."

"I know, I know. And if it were a zero-sum game, I'd wish them both consumed by the fires of hell. But if push did come to shove, I'd vote to save Godines before that prick Egan."

I laughed. "Put that way, I'd agree. Especially when he has the evidence to put Egan away for a long, long time."

"I hope you're right about that. It'll come down to how believable he is in court. Egan will get a gaggle of attorneys who will paint poor ol' Godines as nothing less than the second coming of Attila the Hun."

"Well, the prosecution's got a damn strong case, too. The miracle of Egan rising through the ranks on info supplied to him by Godines is one for the record books. And when he finally gets the plum Homicide job he was after, he keeps Godines on the string to fence items he picks up at murder scenes. And it's not all that tough to do when he's the one writing the inventories at the scene. According to Godines, Egan made an extra ten to fifteen grand a year fencing stolen items."

"You sure about all that? Sounds like con speak to me."

"No, I'm not sure, but it turns out our friend Godines was not too trusting of his pal, Egan. He kept a list of all the items Egan gave him and, even better, a list of where he himself fenced 'em. Said he knew he couldn't trust the prick, so what does he do? He photocopies every freaking receipt he received from a pawn shop. Dates, times, merchandise. When I asked him where he kept that list, he told me his attorney had it. I spoke to the attorney right before I called you and asked him to email the information to me tomorrow morning before nine. Guess we'll see then."

CHAPTER 30

"Okay, you two, remember, no shop talk," Becky said as we walked through the front door. "This is a birthday party." We both looked at each other and raised our eyebrows, like, fat chance. "Oh, by the way, your gun safe was delivered about an hour ago. It's in the garage. Happy birthday." She laughed.

"A gun safe?" Manny exclaimed. "You bought a gun safe? Good for you."

"Was the only choice I had. Couldn't let the kid get close to my weapons. We'll go check it out after dinner."

While the living room had a few streamers across the ceiling, the dining room featured an array of ribbons, streamers and balloons that would make even Macy's jealous. Becky had been busy.

The table was set with paper plates, festive napkins, a bottle of champagne in an ice bucket and a large sheet cake next to which was a gaily-wrapped present. At the far end of the table sat Edwin, dressed in a long-sleeve patterned shirt and dark khaki pants.

Pointing at him, I said, "Looks like someone took you shopping today." He flashed a small grin and then, just as quickly, unflashed it. In the blink of an eye the happy face vanished, and he retreated back into himself. Being on the force for so long, I'd seen this kind of behavior way too often. Mostly from young teenagers, though I knew from experience the 'tude started at a younger age. It was at this moment, however, I realized what "younger" meant. In any case, I wasn't about to let Edwin get away with it.

"Did your teacher tell you where I went today?" He glanced at me sullenly at first, and then quizzically. I smiled inwardly. A win for the good guys. "I went to a jail. Do you know what a jail is?" The quizzical look was replaced by a wary one as he nodded his head slowly up and down. "Have you ever been to a jail?" This time he shook his head vigorously. "When the birthday party is over, would you like me to tell you about it?" His eyes softened as he again moved his head in the affirmative. "Can you say 'hi' to Inspector Morales? He works with me. He's a policeman, also." I sneaked a quick look at Becky. She smiled and nodded her head.

"Nice to meet you," Manny said, reaching across the table to shake Edwin's hand.

Becky looked at Edwin and asked, "Can we sing Happy Birthday to Uncle Reggie?" She flashed me a smile and began a robust round of Happy Birthday. Once finished, she cut the cake and passed a piece to each of us. To me, she said, "You can open the present after we eat the cake."

"And drinking the champagne," Manny insisted, popping the cork and filling our glasses. "You get just one," he said. "You gotta be at the top of your game with Egan." After Becky poured Edwin a glass of carbonated grape juice, they gave me a toast. I took a small sip and then placed the glass on the table. After finishing the cake, Becky said, "Okay, you can open your present now."

I reached for the brightly wrapped present and ripped off the paper. Inside, I found myself starring at an iPhone 11. It's not often that I'm surprised enough to be speechless, but this was one of those times.

"Happy birthday, Sweetheart. Pretty cool, huh?"

I waited a few moments before I found the words. Pulling her to me, I said, "My fellow officers are gonna be jealous as hell. Ain't that right, Manny?"

"Count me in that jealous group," Manny said with a smile. "Hey, pass that puppy over here so I can take a look."

"Not until I get to play with it first," I said. I gave Becky a big kiss. "Thanks, my love. I really appreciate this."

"I've always known what an 'early adopter' you were," Becky said with a laugh. "Just that you never got around to the actual 'adopting.'"

"Tell you what. When I show this off to the guys in the office, I'll be the envy of the entire fifth floor."

Morales smiled. "Maybe we can play around with the phone later, huh? I can recommend some good apps for you."

"Thanks. You guys are too good to me. Once I master this new technology, watch out." I laughed.

"Speaking of watching out," Manny said. "This phone has its own tracking device. Bristow's gonna be able to find you wherever you are."

"Dang, just what I need."

Manny gazed at his watch. "I hate to break this wonderful party up," he said, "but it's getting close to witching hour."

I nodded and stood. "Babe, we have to go to work. Can you take Edwin into the back bedroom and keep him there? I'm gonna call Egan from the kitchen. Under no circumstances is he to come back out here. When I'm finished, I'll come get you. Shouldn't be long, maybe ten minutes, but you never know."

"No problem." She gave me a hug. "Good luck. Hope it all works out."

Manny and I walked into the kitchen and poured some coffee. "You have any idea how this is going to play out?" he asked.

"Not really. Just that I'm gonna be as accommodating as possible. He's already agreed to meet. I won't do anything to jeopardize that."

We sat in silence watching the big hand on the clock slowly creep to the top of the hour. At exactly seven fifty-nine and forty seconds, I began dialing Egan's number. He answered on the third ring. In the most non-threatening voice I could muster, I said, "Hi Barry. It's Reg Decker from San Francisco."

"I know who it is, Decker. Don't blow smoke at me."

I scowled and flipped him off, remembering what a first-class prick he was. Manny smiled. "Wouldn't think of it, Barry," I lied. "Listen, we need to talk. I just got a few questions I need to ask you about this cold case I'm working on. One that you caught back in '07. I'm thinking it would be better if we met in person. You have some time tomorrow? I'd be happy to come to your neck of the woods."

"The way you been slammin' my name around, Decker, why would I want to talk to you?"

"Well, first of all, I haven't been slamming your name around. This all started with some numb-nut's tweet. Originally, we were just trying to shut the dude down before it got out of hand." I knew Egan wasn't buying any of this, even though most of what I told him was true. "Thought that since you got the case, we might be able to talk through some of the issues. Like how to get this Twitter dude off our ass."

"Hey, Decker, go to hell. I don't need to take any of this from you." I guess I didn't fool him.

"You're right, Barry. And I'm not pullin' your chain." I paused and then said in my best conciliatory voice, "Listen, all I want to do is talk in person. Man-to-man. About some things I heard about you and this damn case that I haven't shared with anyone, and, truthfully, that I don't believe. Wanted to give you a chance to respond. This is totally between you and me. No one else has to know." I wanted him to think he could work with me and, if push-came-to shove, he might even be able to buy me off. "I haven't said a word to anyone about this, not even Morales. What say we hook up tomorrow early-to-mid afternoon? I'll meet you anywhere you want, and we can talk this thing through."

A silence followed. I could almost hear him calculating the odds. "Okay," he finally said. "I'll meet you tomorrow, but this is how it's gonna work. Number one, you come alone. If I even get so much as a sniff that you have someone with you or following you, I'll be gone."

"I'm okay with that," I said. What else could I say?

"Number two. To ensure you come alone, I want you in Sacramento at ten."

"Can't do that, Barry. I'm working another case. Meeting with some asshole of a lawyer. You know the drill." Hey, just two guys with a shared background shooting the bull.

There was a long pause, and then he asked, "What time *does* work for you?"

I already had this contingency worked through in my mind. I wanted him to think he was important enough that I would cut short another meeting just to see him. I was scheduled to meet with Godines' lawyer at ten. I knew for certain I'd be free no later than eleven. Factoring in a two-hour ride to Sacramento, I could comfortably be there by two. But I wanted Egan to think I was rearranging my day just for him. "Tell you what, Barry. I'll cancel my eleven and one o'clock appointments." I paused like I was calculating the drive time. "I could be there by two. That work for you?"

Silence again, and then his acceptance of a sort. "While you're driving up, I'll call you with an address. I'll be in the area, so if I see anything suspicious, a tail or even an airplane, you'll have driven up for nothin.' I'll take my chances with you in a court of law."

"Sounds like you don't trust me, Barry," I replied.

"First intelligent thing you've said," he sputtered. "I want you to know upfront, Decker, I'm not going to be a patsy or a fall guy for you."

"Understood, Barry. And no matter what you think, I'm coming up as your friend. Completely open and flexible. After all, you're family."

"Go to hell, Decker," he said, and hung up.

I turned to Manny. "And so, it begins."

CHAPTER 31

A fter telling Becky I was off the phone, Manny and I refilled our coffee cups and walked back into the dining room.

"You want some champagne?" I asked, pointing to the open bottle still in the ice bucket. "Pretty sure it still has some fizz left."

"Nah," he replied. "The coffee is fine." We sat down. "How do you envision this going down?"

"Here's my take," I said. "First of all, we know he's already spooked. He told me if I don't play it his way, he's willing to go to court. He knows I wouldn't want that to happen 'cause our ironclad case against him would be put in the hands of a jury. Egan's been around the block enough to know if you get yourself a decent attorney, there's no such thing as 'ironclad.' I think what he's hoping for is that I'll be open to a deal. I hinted as much on the phone."

"You really think Egan believes you could be bribed?"

"I have no doubt. From his warped view of human existence, hell, everyone's got a deal in him. It's why we have to play this right. And part of playing it right is for us to be circumspect about who we tell."

"Well, you know if I'm going to come with you, I've got to tell Bristow."

"I know. I'm practically in the same boat. At the very least, I have to tell him that you're my wing-man. He should go for it, but you just never know. Bristow's backed us this far, but he's susceptible to pressure from the top. We're still dealing with an ex-cop here, and no one in the higher echelons wants the public to hear about a corrupted cop, especially a homicide cop. I don't want to take a chance on anyone in-house feelin' sorry for the bastard, and blurting out that you and me are working the case together. Egan gets even a sniff of that happening, he'll be gone-baby-gone. We can't afford for that to happen."

"Understood. So, what if I went up to Sacramento tonight? Hell, I could leave right now. Get a motel and wait for you to call me in the morning after you learn the rendezvous spot."

"I thought of that, too, but the problem is Egan's going to be camped at the spot where he's planning to meet me. And that will be way before you could get there. And I don't want to take the chance you get there early and he sees you.

"No, I think you should stay here tomorrow morning, just in case Egan still has eyeballs in the Department. You and I will be interviewing Godines' attorney in plain sight. Everyone will see you, and then I'll get my stuff and leave. You come back into the office, say, a little before noon looking for me. Again, let everyone see you. Then slip away, get in your car and drive your ass up."

"That's the easy part. How the hell will I find you once I'm up there? I mean, let's say he tells you to meet him somewhere, but when you arrive, he tells you to follow him to a different location. And maybe another."

I smiled and stood. "Follow me and I'll show you." I took him down the basement stairs. "I want to show you what Kincaid sent over this afternoon." Walking over to my car, I opened the back door. Pointing to the small package on the seat, I said, "I'm going to need you to help me attach this puppy."

Manny reached in, pulled out the carton and walked it over to the worktable. "Let's see what we have here," he said, emptying the contents on the table. "Dang, man, what's this, a tracking device? Kincaid gave you an FBI tracking device?"

"Well, he wants it back, so technically he's letting me borrow it. If anything were to happen to me or the car, you've got to promise you'll get this bitch back to Kincaid."

He laughed. "Nothing is going to happen to it, my man. Or to you."

"We can only hope. But in any case, I'm so technologically challenged you're gonna have to attach the damn thing tonight and then detach it when we finish with Egan."

Manny picked up a long metal tube and unscrewed the top. "If I'm not mistaken, this houses the batteries." He tipped the cylinder and out slid what looked like a standard D cell battery. "This whole unit . . ." his hand swept over the table "is a GPS tracking device." He pointed his finger at each object. "The GPS antenna is there. The transmitter/receiver unit is there. And that's the mounting bracket that holds everything together. Only difference between this tracking device and one you or I might pick up at Best Buy is this puppy is infinitely more powerful. I'll betcha the magnets holding the device to the vehicle are strong enough to pick up a tank."

"You're telling me this whole thing attaches to the undercarriage of the car by magnet?"

"Correct."

"And it will be hard to find? I mean, if Egan suspects I have some kind of tracker, the first thing he'd do is look under the car, right?"

Manny nodded. "To bastardize a scriptural reference—*he shall seek, but shall not find*. And after I attach it? Hell, you'd actually need to put the car on a lift to find the device."

"Well, then, let's get to it."

We jacked up one side of the car, and with me holding the

lantern, Manny went to work. Thirty minutes later he was wiping the grease off his hands.

"Good work. You interested in seeing the gun safe I bought?"

"Not particularly. Seen one, you seen 'em all."

"I agree. Let's go." We walked up the basement steps together. "Remember to make a grand appearance at the office tomorrow."

"You bet. I'll be sure to be on the road by twelve-thirty and looking forward to your call."

I opened the front door. We stood quietly for a moment in the brisk night air. "Let's get this done," I said, giving him a hug. "Time to rock and roll."

As soon as he drove away, I walked back to Edwin's bedroom. The light was off so I started to close his door when he said, "I'm still awake."

"I'm surprised. Figured you'd be asleep by now. You have school tomorrow. Must be all that sugar in the birthday cake." I sat down on the edge of his bed.

"Does sugar keep you awake?" he asked.

"That's what people say. It jazzes you up. Do you know what that means?" He nodded and started to shake all over. "Very good. That's exactly what it does to you." He sat up in the bed, and I put a pillow behind his head. "How are things going in school for you? Is your teacher treating you okay? Because if she isn't, I'll spank her for you."

He giggled enough to let me know my attempt at humor had not fallen flat. "Will you tell me about the jail you went to?" he asked.

I patted him on the head. "You told me at dinner that you knew what a jail was. How do you know? Have you read about them?"

"My mom's boyfriend is in a jail."

"That's too bad. He must have done something he shouldn't have. That's why people go to jail. I visited a man in jail today." I spent the next thirty minutes telling him about Godines and how sad he was to be in jail and how terrible jail is. I hoped my message would be sufficient to keep Edwin on the straight and narrow. But I wasn't naïve. In the environment he was probably going back to, I knew the chances of that happening were not in his favor. "*But you can always hope, Decker,*" I thought to myself. If I learned one thing in life, it was if you lose hope, you ain't got nothin'.

CHAPTER 32

I got to the office at nine. Manny was already there. I walked over and asked, "What time did I say the attorney was supposed to arrive?"

"You told me ten."

"Whew. I'd forgotten. Musta been the great time I had last night." I paused. "And, hey, I really did have a good time. Glad you could make it."

"My pleasure, Deck. Thanks for inviting me."

"Okay." I looked at my watch again. "We have some time. Let's . . ." I was about to say *let's go to the meeting room and have CK bring him to us*, when I saw the dude walk in. He stopped at the first desk he came to. The officer at that desk stood, shook his hand and, turning, pointed at me. I waved and motioned the guy to join us.

He was a tall, thin, white guy dressed in blue slacks, white shirt and a tan sports coat. Not quite what I expected, but I don't have much to do with attorneys these days, thank god. He walked toward us carrying a medium-sized briefcase.

He introduced himself as Ben Cole and gave both Manny and me one of his business cards. I offered him coffee, which he accepted. As Manny went to get it, I guided him to the meeting room.

"I'm glad you got here early," I said. "We have a busy day, so getting this meeting over will help big time. Here, sit."

He nodded. "Yeah. My schedule is insane, too. I took a chance getting up here early, hoping you guys would be free to see me now."

When Manny came back with the coffee, Cole took a sip, opened his briefcase and placed a stack of manila file folders on the table. "My client, Octavio Godines, who I know you spoke with over the weekend, requested I give these to you." He swept his hand over the files. "I want to be on record as strongly disagreeing with my client giving you these folders, but he insisted."

"Duly noted," I said.

"Not sure what you told him, Inspector, but he believes in you. That you will do the right thing by him."

"What I told Mr. Godines is I will do whatever I can for him within both reason and the law. And I will. When his trial date is set, I will testify on his behalf. I'll say he was a cooperating witness in a cold case murder investigation. If I'm asked on the stand about these files I'm about to inherit, I will answer truthfully. I will be sympathetic to him because his testimony and willingness to cooperate is going to put a very bad man behind bars."

"That's what he told me, too, Inspector. I appreciate your being true to your word. Personally, though, I think he let you off too easy. But as long as it's something he feels he wants to do, I'll back him." Cole took four files from the top of the stack and fanned them out in front of us. "You'll notice each file has writing across the top . . ." And, just in case he thought we weren't familiar with file folders, he pointed with his finger and said, "chronicling the month and year. There are eleven years represented here, though not every month of every year." He paused and opened one of the folders. "Like here in the year 2002 . . ." He held it up so we could see. "There's only one entry. For the month of June."

"That's great," I said. "I think we can figure out how everything is sorted. Why don't you tell us what you brought?"

"These files contain receipted items my client sold to pawn shops, although there are a number of receipts from consignment stores, as well. All the merchandise listed in these receipts was given to him over the years by, as you know Inspector, one of your fellow police officers. The one that was bribing my client to fence stolen merchandise in return for keeping him out of serious jail time. My client contends he never received a penny from the sale of any this merchandise."

I nodded. "That's not what he told me, but right now I couldn't care less if he got rich on it."

"I'm going to leave these files with you, Inspector. But before I leave, would you have any interest in going through a file for a particular year? That way I can show you how this particular system works. Might make it easier when you go through the whole stack."

I looked over at Manny. He nodded and said, "Sure! How 'bout 2009. At least we know where some of the merchandise pawned that year came from."

Cole rummaged through his stack and pushed six files our way. The first in the stack was labeled January 2009. Inside were three receipts from three different pawn shops in and around San Francisco. All were signed off by Octavio Godines. The first, dated January 13, 2009, listed six items purchased by one of the shops for $240. I wondered what victim or victims these items belonged to. Most of it was junk. Given that he only paid $240, the pawn shop owner obviously realized the same thing. One of the items was a guitar. The shop owner bought it for fifteen bucks. I found myself hoping the new owner had bought himself a rare Gibson and ended up selling the damn thing for four grand.

The next receipt, dated April 20, listed four items purchased by a different shop for $1,596. "Son-of-a-bitch," I said to Manny, pointing to the third item on the receipt. "Ring any bells?"

"Damn. It's our Sony A900 digital camera," Manny said. "Says here the lens is missing. Wonder where that ended up? Maybe Egan gave it to someone else to pawn." He laughed and then said, "Looks like he must not have wanted all the booty he took from Poppy's house to hit the street at the same time."

"Yeah. And five months later," I said, holding up the September 6, 2009 receipt from the New Liberty Pawn Shop, "Mr. Pham is writing a check to Octavio Godines for $207 for a one-year-old Dell computer."

Cole showed us the receipts for more than fifteen separate items Egan fenced through Godines. After we located all the stolen items that belonged to Poppy Garcia, we thanked Cole and sent him on his way.

"Guess that kinda wraps it up, huh, Deck?" Morales said. "I hate to say this because he was at one time my partner, but we need to put the son-of-a-bitch's ass in jail."

"If only it was that easy. We'll be in Sacramento PD's jurisdiction and they have to be privy to what we're doing up there."

"Hey, I went to high school with two guys in the Sacramento PD," Morales said. "Why don't I call 'em on my way and tell them what we're doing? I'm sure they'll help. I'll follow you, and when I know your final location, I'll give 'em a call and they can come and make the collar."

"Sounds good. Do it."

Just then, CK walked in. "The DC wants to see you, Deck."

CHAPTER 33

"Am I in trouble?" I whispered to CK as she escorted me to Bristow's office.

"All I can say is, from the tone of his voice, I'm glad it's you and not me he wants to see." She deposited me at his door. "Good luck," she said, giving my shoulder a friendly pat. "And oh, happy birthday."

I thanked her and then rapped softly on Bristow's half-closed door. "Is that you, Deck? Come on in." He didn't sound angry. If anything, apologetic. Like he was sorry to bother me after our conversation the day before. He came around his desk as I walked in and put out his hand.

"Hey, wanted to say happy birthday. Sorry I'm a day late but didn't want to disturb you by calling your house last night."

"Thanks, Matt. Appreciate it. Let me show you what Becky got me." I fished around in my jacket pocket and pulled out my shiny new phone. "An iPhone 11."

"An iPhone 11? You're kiddin'. Let me see that." I passed it over. "I've only got an iPhone 6," Bristow said. "It's about half this size. Can I call someone?"

"Be my guest."

He looked perplexed. "Can't think of anyone to call. All my phone numbers are on my phone." He reached into his shirt pocket. "Here." He passed me his phone. "I'm gonna call my own number. Go stand by the that table."

I walked back and felt his phone vibrate in my hand. I answered.

"Talk to me," Bristow said. "I want to hear how clear the sound is."

"Hi, Matt. This is your phone speaking."

He laughed. "Funny. You say your wife got you this?

"Becky was the instigator, but Manny threw in a few bucks, too."

"I've got to get closer to your family and friends," he said with a smile. He disconnected and motioned me to sit, ironically so I thought, in the very same chair where, a mere five days before, I first brought Poppy's murder to his attention. He sat across from me.

A long pause ensued. Then he leaned forward, put his forearms on the table and said, "Deck, I hate to tell you this, but I'm gonna shut your investigation down."

I sat very still, feeling my face getting hot and my fingers beginning to tingle. All thoughts of my new phone vanished. I calmed myself, took a deep breath and said, "Shut down my murder investigation, Matt? Where the hell did that come from?" I didn't wait for him to answer. "For god's sake, Matt. I'm right on the edge of arresting the son-of-a-bitch for, at the very least theft but most likely murder, and you're pulling the rug out from under me? Your gonna let that bastard skate?"

"It's not me, Deck. It's City Hall. I got a call from the Mayor's office a little over an hour ago. The guy who phoned said the Chief had spoken to the Mayor about Egan. He . . ."

Before he could finish, I leaned forward and said, "How the hell did the Chief find about Egan, Matt?" The tone in my voice caused Bristow to walk over and shut his office door.

"I've no idea, Deck. It wasn't me if that's what you're insinuating."

180

From the edge in his voice, I could tell he was getting pissed, so I backed off a bit. "I'm not accusing you, DC, honest." I paused and then said, "So, finish telling me what the Mayor's guy said."

"The Mayor's worried about the public relations fallout if a cop, who isn't even with the Department any longer, is fingered for stealing inconsequential articles from dead people. That they'll start blaming all cops for being crooks. They want us to let sleeping dogs lie."

"Inconsequential articles, Matt? Give me a break! He stole material evidence in ongoing murder investigations. Over years, Matt."

"It's not material evidence in an ongoing investigation if the investigation is no longer ongoing," Bristow replied. I started to object, but he stopped me, saying, "I hear you, Deck, I really do. I'm not condoning what they're advocating."

I put my hands in front of me, palms out. "Enough of this crap, Matt. I still want to know who the hell told the Chief we had Egan's ass on a platter. I'm guessing Egan didn't. Neither Manny nor I did. I'm guessing you didn't. So, who? Had to be somebody on the inside, though."

"Or somebody who had been on the inside," Bristow added, lacing his fingers together at the back of his head.

I sat back in my chair, looking at him as if he had uncovered the identity of Jack the Ripper. "Nowak? You think Nowak?"

"I'm merely asking what any homicide inspector worth his salt would ask." He looked at me and winked. "Who has a motive? Seems to me at first blush, Nowak might be someone who had a motive. It wouldn't be advantageous to his reputation if his protégé, Barry Egan, was arrested for stealing from murder victims. I'm not sayin' it was Nowak, but it had to be somebody of his caliber. Someone who would catch the Mayor's attention. Or maybe it was some rich guy. A donor who gave to his campaign.

I don't know."

"Dang, Matt, you might have put your finger on exactly how it went down. Just when I was believin' you'd lost your edge, here you are thinking like a real detective." I sat back and smiled. "I swear, you might have a future in this business."

He shrugged, a smile taking over his face. "You think, huh? Well, I happen to think you're right, but, hey, that's just me." He laughed.

"Okay, tell me how we should play this. I've got Egan's ass in a wringer, and I'm scheduled to meet him in two hours. I'll be damned if I'm simply gonna walk away."

He pursed his lips. "I'll tell you what I'm gonna do. Wait, let me rephrase that. What *we're* gonna do. You keep going on as if we hadn't yet spoken. I'll take the heat in the short run, but only the short run, Deck. Just so we're clear—short run means by Monday at the latest. Capiche?" I nodded. "Wrap Egan up by the end of today if you can. If you think he's a flight risk, arrest his ass on the spot. If you need back-up, call me. I'll get Sacramento PD involved. It's their jurisdiction."

"Thanks, Matt. I appreciate the help. Just so you know, there are some loose ends still hanging out there. Manny and I are running them down. A few are just coincidences, but you know us Homicide dudes—if there are unexplained coincidences at the end of a murder investigation, you ain't done your job."

He laughed. "You are so right. Good hunting."

CHAPTER 34

I was forty-two miles into my ninety-five-mile drive to meet Egan when my cell came to life. No name was displayed, but the call had a Sacramento area code. Good enough.

"Decker," I answered.

"Put your phone on speaker so you can write down the address I'm going to give you," Egan commanded.

"Hold on," I countered, putting my new phone in its dashboard cradle and hitting the speaker button. The traffic was light so I put the car in cruise mode and grabbed a small note pad and pen from the console. "Go."

"Where are you?"

"About ten miles this side of Davis."

"You got another thirty minutes. Stay on the freeway until you get to the Natomas exit. You'll see a Regal Cinema on your right. Park by the cinema and wait for my call." With that he hung up.

"Asshole," I murmured, as I laid the note pad on the passenger seat. I expected him to give me an elaborate trail to follow. Instead, I scribbled two words—Natomas Exit. I called Manny. "You on your way?"

"Just passed the Jelly Belly factory in Fairfield. Traffic's been a bear."

"It'll clear soon. You're less than an hour and a half behind me. Just spoke with Egan. He wants me to take the Natomas exit.

You know where that is?"

"Yeah. Small town in North Sacramento."

"You got me on tracker?"

"Had you all the way from the Hall. Don't worry, Deck. Even if he takes you on a wild goose chase, I'll still be able to find you."

"You're making me feel almost safe," I said with a laugh. "From now on we're going dark. Don't call me, and I won't call you. Just follow the tracker."

Thirty-three minutes later I pulled off at the Natomas exit and drove toward the cinema which sat on the outskirts of a medium-sized shopping mall whose best days were behind it. I wondered exactly where I was supposed to park. *Screw it*, I thought. He'll find me. Probably has eyeballs on me this very minute.

Parking as close to the Regal as I could, I turned off the motor and waited for Egan. Ten minutes later, a car pulled up behind me. I glanced in my rear-view mirror and saw Egan. Reflexively, I patted the Sig on my hip for reassurance.

He sat stock still for the next five minutes. A cop's ploy designed to put fear into the heart of the hunted which I'm guessing was me. It was such a transparent maneuver that I almost got out of the car and told him to stop being such a blowhard pain in the ass. But I didn't, choosing instead to wait the SOB out. A few minutes later, I saw him put his cell phone to his ear. My phone rang in response.

"Follow me," were the only words he spoke. I obeyed and trailed him out of the mall to a perimeter road. We followed that for a quarter mile and then turned south on a two-lane highway. It was then I started logging his turns and the mileage between turns, something I'd learned early in my career from a wise old cop named Brett Hansen. Never put yourself in a situation, he told me, where you might need help but have no clue where you are. His advice had already gotten me through some pretty hairy predicaments. If push came to shove, I hoped it would here, too.

Another right-turn a mile later put us on a tree-lined lane that meandered exactly two point nine miles through the Sacramento foothills. He turned left into a cul-de-sac and pulled to the curb. Seeing the phone go to his ear, I pulled mine from the cradle.

"We're going to the house on the right. You're gonna follow me into the driveway. At some point I'm going to stop. When I do, I want you to park behind me and then get in my car." About fifty feet up the driveway, he stopped. A few minutes later I opened his passenger door and came face-to-face with Barry Egan.

It had been at least nine years since I laid eyes on him. We quietly eyeballed one another. Neither of us offered a hand to shake. Appearance-wise, he hadn't changed much. A little heavier maybe. Certainly grayer. The mustache and goatee were new, both a shade lighter than his hair. After a few moments, I slid into the front seat, giving him a small nod. With that, he put his car in gear and drove around to the back of the house.

He parked and walked to the back door. I followed. We still hadn't spoken a word to one another. Fishing from a large ring full of keys, he found the house key and unlocked the door. Standing aside, he motioned me in. I decided to break the silence.

"Comfy place," I said, walking past him into the kitchen. "Yours?"

"No." I heard the door close, and the lock being turned.

"This is really a nice place. You must have gotten to know some rich folks up here, huh?" When he didn't answer, I turned back toward him and found myself looking directly into the muzzle of his Glock. Not at all what I expected. Truthfully, it scared the crap out of me, but I couldn't let him see that. Slowly, I shook my head back and forth, like a disappointed father would do when facing his obstinate son. "This is a mistake, Barry," I said,

185

spreading my hands and giving him my most reassuring smile. "You don't have to do this."

"You forced me into this, you son-of-a-bitch," he said, his voice rising. "But I'm actually glad you did. Even from afar, I always considered you a first-class prick. And now, asshole, you're going to get what's been comin' to you." Except for the hum of the refrigerator, the room had turned deadly silent. He broke that silence by saying, "Now, bring your weapon out with your thumb and forefinger and place it on the floor. Gently. No use scratching the hardwood." Being no dummy. I did as I was told. "You and I are going for a ride in my car. I know you're not stupid and no doubt have somebody following you with some GPS rig . . ." He let that sit there, waiting for a reply. When I didn't answer, he said in a not-so-pleasant tone, "Am I right?"

When I kept silent again, he gave up. "Suit yourself. I'm sure you do. That device will bring him to this cul-de-sac. He'll see your car parked in the driveway and keep right on drivin' past. The way the SFPD is constituted these days, with the all the minorities they let in, they're just not as smart or as well trained as we were back in the day. More than likely, whoever is following you will park somewhere down the street and then hoof it back here on foot. We'd have never done it like that. Good way to get yourself shot dead, if you ask me. I wasn't going to be involved with idiots like that. Not me, baby. Not me. That's why I left."

"I haven't been in Homicide that long, so I have no frame of reference," I said in the best hostage rescue voice I could muster. "But you sound right to me." In situations like this, where lives are on the line, mine especially, we were taught to be very conciliatory. At that particular moment, I was thinking I'd probably have to use every bit of that training.

"Your backup will probably assume you're in the house," he continued, showing me who was boss. "My hope is he'll think you and I are having a heart-to-heart, come to Jesus, conversation." He smirked. "And to show him how well we're getting along, I'm gonna leave the light on in the living room so he'll think we're still hard at it, negotiating deep into the evening. Meanwhile, you and I will be tucked away in a safe-house in another county." He smiled and motioned with his gun for me to move backwards. When I didn't, he said, "I'm not messin' with you, Decker. Back away. Now!"

When I did, he picked up my Sig and put it in his waistband. "Nice piece. You guys were switching to the Sig when I left the department. You like it?"

I paid no attention to his small talk. If this was the start of the negotiation that would determine whether I lived or died, I didn't need to be giving him a sales pitch on my Sig Sauer.

"You don't have to do this, Barry. We're grown men who've been around the block a time or two. We can work something out."

"I want you to shut the hell up and do what I tell you." He motioned again with his gun, this time pointing to my right where a small table stood. "Now, empty your pockets. Put everything on the table." I did as he requested, piling my wallet, extra clip for the Sig, car keys and phone on the table.

"Can I at least keep my hankie?"

"You can keep the hankie, wise guy, but the shoes come off."

"Come on, Barry. This is ridiculous. I thought we were going to negotiate something. A deal where you don't get screwed and I get to put Poppy Garcia's murder to bed. A win-win for both of us."

"You're so full of crap, Decker." He pulled a pair of handcuffs from his back pocket and threw them to me. "After you take off your shoes, put these on." I stared at him for a minute, shook my head and took off my shoes. Straightening up, I cuffed my left wrist. As I started to cuff it to my right wrist, he said, "No, no, no. Behind your back, Decker. I want your hands cuffed behind your back." I turned around so he could see me attach the remaining cuff to my right wrist.

Egan produced a small cloth bag from his coat pocket and placed all my items that were on the table inside it. Except for my phone. He looked at it and smiled. "Dang, Decker. You've got a kick-ass phone here. New? How the hell did you score this? These puppies are expensive."

"Birthday present. My wife gave it to me a day or so ago." I shrugged my shoulders in my best I'm just an ordinary guy like you, Barry. No difference between us. We both have birthdays. Both love the newest gadgets. Just two ordinary stiffs workin' the angles. I flashed him a smile. "And please return it after we're finished here."

"We'll see," he smirked and put the phone back on the table. "No use keeping that on me so people could track us." I'll come back and pick it up later. "Okay. Back outside. You're driving."

"Where we headed?" I mumbled as he bent me face forward over the hood of the car.

"Don't get ahead of yourself, Decker. You'll find out soon enough." He took off the cuffs, opened the car door and roughly settled me into the driver's seat. Climbing into the back, he leaned forward and pushed the muzzle of the Glock forcefully into the back of my head. "Gentlemen, start your engines."

CHAPTER 35

I'd been driving twenty minutes when we passed a sign welcoming us to Yolo County. When Egan said the two of us would be hard to find because we'd be in a different county, I envisioned maybe Plumas or Lassen County in the extreme northern part of the state. The remoteness would make it hard for anyone to find us. But Yolo County? Yolo was considered part of the greater Sacramento metropolitan area. Losing the tracker was a blow, but Egan's stupidity might yet equalize my chance to live.

The county consisted mostly of agricultural land northwest of Sacramento. Its claim to fame was it hadn't as of yet surrendered to the construction lobby. On our drive through Yolo, I began planning my avenue of escape. It wouldn't be easy. Most of the land here was flat, and most of the crops were low growing, the kind that would get you shot dead in any escape attempt. Only two of the farms I saw had trees, and it was trees I needed for cover.

I must have been too transparent in my surveillance techniques or Egan was more paranoid than I imagined. "Don't even think about escaping," he said. "Or even be rescued for that matter. The guy you had with the GPS is probably still sitting by the house where we left your car. There's no escape for you, Decker. You're not leaving here alive without my say so. Better start kissing my ass, pal." He laughed.

Ten minutes later we arrived at our destination, a medium

sized farmhouse growing what looked to be a few acres of tomatoes. "Drive around back," he commanded. "Might as well park where no one will see the car."

"Is this a B & B?" I asked.

Egan laughed and shook the keys at me. "No breaking and entering here, Decker."

"B & B, Barry. Bed and breakfast. Not B & E."

"Oh, yeah. I knew that," he quickly replied, trying to downplay his faux pas. Shaking the keys at me again, he said, "As I was saying, I know the owners. They're family. Well, family two or three times removed, but who's counting? I do a few legal favors for them every now and again, in exchange, they let me use the house when they're away. They're gone the next few weeks. I bring my girlfriends up here occasionally."

"Hope you don't fancy me as a girlfriend." I said. He laughed. I laughed. Male bonding. But not as well as I would have liked.

As soon as I had the car in park, he shoved his Glock into the back of my neck. "Don't get any ideas, asshole. Do as I tell you, and you may live to see another day." He paused. "Or maybe not." He laughed and gave me the handcuffs. "Put 'em on. Behind your back again." I didn't like the 'behind my back again,' but since he had the gun, I figured I didn't have much say in the matter.

In stocking feet, I gingerly walked around the house to the front door. After unlocking it, Egan pushed me inside and switched on the light. While I'm not an expert on farmhouse design, I never expected to see one quite like this. In the entryway stood an ornate fountain that looked like it belonged at the Bellagio in Vegas.

"You like, huh? Let me fill you in on the family secret. My cousins throw the most outrageous parties. This here fountain is connected to vats of liquor in the basement. At parties, the liquor is shot up through special pipes into the fountain. Sorry, I have no time to show you how it works. We have more important things to go over. Let's you and I go sit in the dining room."

He led me into a large square room off the kitchen dominated by a dark table of indiscriminate wood, and three chairs of matching design. Egan told me where to stand while he moved one of the chairs to the back wall facing the table. The arrangement of the furniture didn't fill me with a lot of confidence. The way the third chair was placed along the back wall gave the room the aura of an execution chamber, and I had no illusions about who would be executed.

"Sit," Egan said, pointing to the lone chair.

"Looks like the Inquisition. Can you at least unlock the cuffs?"

"Sure. Come on over here." As I approached, he picked up his Glock and pointed it at my forehead. "Turn around." I did and immediately felt the pressure of the muzzle again against the back of my head. "You so much as twitch and I'll blow your head clean off." He emphasized the word "clean."

"You know, even if you did kill the Garcia woman, we can work something out."

He freed my left wrist and placed the key in my hand. "Nice try," he said, sticking his shoe in the small of my back and shoving violently. I was jolted forward, lost my balance on my tender feet and tumbled to the floor. "Undo the other cuff and flip them up here. Then sit in the chair."

I picked myself up, unlocked the other cuff and sat. "This isn't necessary, Barry. Like I said, we can work something out. Come on, you know the drill. Talk to me."

"The problem with you, Decker, is you're such a do-gooder." He shook his head as if it was the most disgusting trait anyone could possess. "You never learned when to leave well enough alone. You're more than likely going to die here today, and it didn't have to be that way."

Nothing left to lose is a hard concept to get your mind around, but oddly one that filled you with a certain freedom. When it dawned on me that I might have nothing left to lose, I thought, *screw it. No use being a wimp now.* "Did you kill her, Barry?"

"See?" he replied, again shaking his head back and forth. "Exactly what I mean. She's dead, Decker. Period. End of story. It's immaterial whether I killed her, you killed her, or the Pope killed her. She's dead. Been dead now what, twelve, thirteen years? And forgotten. In fact, she was forgotten before her body was even cold."

I thought of my nephew Bobby. "The people who loved her didn't forget, Barry."

"Yeah? And who might they be? Her mother? Hah! She was a nobody who split the freaking country two weeks after her supposedly *beloved daughter* met her maker. They were all nobodies, Decker," he paused, shook his head disgustedly, and said, "until you reopened the damn case."

"First of all, I didn't re-open the case. That was done by some asshole Twitter dude who resurrected her death as a way to embarrass the police department. My only involvement was to look at the case to prove the dude wrong."

"You made it worse, Decker. Infinitely worse. Gave the jerk reason to keep talking about her. She was a nobody troublemaker who was an embarrassment."

"A trouble-maker? I've never heard anyone say that about her. Even the Twitter dude." I paused, wondering where to take this. "Did you kill her because she was a 'trouble maker'."

"I never said I killed her. Just that she was a nobody. And a trouble-making nobody, at that." He picked up my Sig. "I really do like this weapon of yours." He pointed it in my direction. "Boom," he said, kicking his hand up imitating the recoil. He laughed. "You knew the woman was a dyke, didn't you Decker?" he said, placing my Sig back on the table.

"Barry," I said, now more aware than ever I was in a fight for my life, "what you and I are about to go through is not necessary." I reached into my back pocket for my handkerchief and used it to wipe my forehead. Showing I was nervous. Human, just like him. "You know there's no direct evidence you had anything to do with murdering that girl. Only that you conducted a sloppy investigation. Come back to the Hall with me. They might hold you on possession of some stolen baubles, bangles and beads, but a good attorney will get you off. You know that."

Egan gazed at me, a grin framing his mouth. "I want you to know, Decker, even though I hardly knew you when I was on the Force, I still never liked you. I have to tell you, though, I'm actually beginning to feel sorry for you." He took a quick glance at his watch. "I hate to have our conversation come to an end, but I'm expected to be somewhere in . . ." he peeked at his watch again. "In forty minutes. And it's at least a twenty-minute drive. So unfortunately, I don't have a lot of time."

He put his palms down flat on the table. "Do you know how long a guy like me, from my background, would last in a jail cell?" A frightening tightness formed around his mouth and eyes. "Even in a holding cell like the ones on the top floor of the Hall? Let me see now . . ." He put his hands on the side of his head, closed his eyes and pursed his lips together like he was thinking deep thoughts. Then he said "Oh, maybe half a day. Max! The janitors would come in and find my throat slit." He paused. "And you think I'm gonna let that happen? Brought down on account of some stupid spic gay female cabdriver? Not me, brother. Not me."

"But you're not going to get off by killing me. Half the department knows I'm up here with you."

"They know I'm with you in Sacramento, Decker. But not out in the boonies like this. It'll take them at least a week to find you. Enough time for me to be deep inside Mexico. I'm leaving as soon as I finish up with you. Got some influential friends down there. Rich and powerful friends. Even you would recognize their names. One of them told me he was looking for good people he could count on who knew the California scene. People with contacts. People who knew where the bodies were buried, so to speak. This particular rich dude, after doing a profile on me, called and offered me a job. Been in contact with him now for weeks. The only downside is I've got to live in Mexico. That's the price I'm paying for sending your sorry ass to hell." He leveled the Glock at me. "Sorry, Decker. Time's up. I got to get movin'. My only regret in all this is I can't take that pretty wife of yours with me. As I remember, she's a hot piece of ass, man. But you never know, maybe I can get my Mexican friends to bring her down to me." He laughed a crazy laugh and looked down at his watch again.

~~~~~

"Time's up," I heard him say. Knowing my life was about to end, my entire being suddenly became cocooned in a web of peace. But when he mentioned Becky, that feeling quickly changed. The peace I'd felt was swamped with such an anger I inwardly cried out for survival and revenge. When I saw him raise his gun, I reacted by turning slightly to my right and diving for the floor. I was barely off the chair when the bullet hit me in the chest, an inch or so below my left nipple, and twisted me further sideways.

Surprisingly, I felt no pain, just an all-consuming numbness. The floor under me was slippery with my blood. Every survival class I ever took preached if you didn't stanch the flow of blood from a puncture wound, your chances of coming out alive were slim to none. I was already having trouble breathing and felt myself slipping into unconsciousness. "Hang in there, Deck," I told myself. "You can do this." I was lying face down on the cold floor and felt the handkerchief still in my hand. With resolve born of survival, I stuffed it as best I could into my chest wound. I remember thinking all these efforts were probably for naught. I was pretty sure it would take some kind of miracle to save me.

Then the pain came. I tried not to pay attention to it at first, continuing to push the hankie into the hole in my chest. But soon the pain became too much, a screaming, crushing pain. I knew, survival class or no survival class, I was about to die. Part of me wanted to stay awake so I could consciously experience the act of dying, but the pain screamed, "Don't think about it, Decker. Just let it go. Easier that way." And I would have let go, too, except for Becky. I saw her hovering over me—crying. *No! No! Don't give up, Reg. Don't give up. I need you. You have to come back to me.*

"Well, hold on a minute, Decker," my semi-conscious mind told my body. "Don't give up so fast." I desperately wanted to reach out to her. To touch her. If even for the last time. To tell her how much I loved her. But couldn't. I was too damned tired to move. "Wait for me," I whispered as the darkness enveloped me.

CHAPTER 36

The next thing I remembered was bright light, and no pain. "Hallelujah," my groggy mind shouted, "I landed on the right side of the divide." But then I became aware of the bed under me. "Are there beds in heaven?" I asked myself inside the fog that enveloped my brain. I tried to remember if the good Jesuit padres I had in high school had tackled that particular theological paradox. While my semi-conscious mind was trying to unravel this conundrum, I turned my head ever so slightly to the right. There, sitting on a low stool next to my bed with only his head showing was Edwin. For a second my heart sank, now worried that maybe I landed on the wrong side of the divide.

Turned out I wasn't on either side of the divide. The first clue was the beeping of a machine. Regular. Like a heartbeat. Like my heartbeat. "Do you hear the beep, Edwin? That's the sound of my heart beating. You are way too young to understand, but take it from me there's no better sound in the world."

He stared at me, his dark blank eyes betraying no emotion. Suddenly, his face grew larger, like a giant balloon inflating. His once placid demeanor distorted into a menacing snarl. His eyes, fiery orbs, scared the crap out of me. I shrank back into the bed, thinking he was going to attack me. *But why?* I thought. *I'd never done anything to him. Hell, I gave him a place to stay. In my own house.* I yelled at him, "Noooo. Edwin. I'm one of the good guys."

Then, in the blink of an eye, he was gone. Replaced by his

mother. At least my drug-addled brain told me it had to be her. She came at me, a beast with fangs dripping blood. I tried to defend myself, but my arms, affixed to the bed by straps, wouldn't move. I turned my face away and screamed. Or thought I did.

When I came back to consciousness, the bright light was still there, but Edwin and his mother had vanished. I said a quick prayer of thanks. Lying back, I started to take inventory of my surroundings. I was now cognizant enough to recognize my body was attached by plastic tubing to various bags hanging on poles that surrounded the bed. The rhythmic music of my heart monitor made me feel everything was finally right with the world and seduced me into another round of sleep.

But it was a false sense of security. The next time I awakened, that son-of-a-bitch Egan was in my room. He saw I was awake and smiled that same condescending smile he gave me right before he shot me. "How the hell did you get in here?" I hissed, looking around for some kind of button I could push to alert the nurses of my danger.

"Is this what you are looking for?" he inquired, holding up the alarm call button. "Hey, don't worry. I'm not here to hurt you." He opened his coat to show me he wasn't packing.

"Forgive me if I don't believe you. You shot me, didn't you? Am I mistaken?"

"No," he said. "I shot you, all right. But you're still alive, so be thankful I'm a bad shot." He laughed loudly. I hoped one of the nurses would hear. They must not have because no one came to my rescue.

"Well, I have to go now. Only came to see how your were doing." He turned and walked out the door.

"Noooooooo," I screamed. "Noooo. Stop him! Stop him!" But no one paid any attention. The nurses couldn't have cared less as to why I was screaming. *Wait 'til I get better*, I thought. *I'll get this whole ward fired.* The exercise with Egan had so fatigued me I closed my eyes and promptly fell into another deep sleep.

~~~~~

When next I awakened, Becky was sitting by my bed, her hand through the railing holding mine. "Oh, my good god," she said when she saw my eyes flutter open. She started sobbing. Leaning over the railing, she softly kissed my lips while the tears from her eyes washed my cheeks. "Oh, baby. Oh baby. I'm so happy you came back. The doctors said they almost lost you."

Just the way her touch felt told me I was no longer hallucinating. "No need to worry," I whispered. "I'm a tough SOB." She leaned closer. I thought she was going to scold me for even whispering SOB, but instead, in a soft voice, said, "I'm having trouble hearing you, sweetheart

"Can you hear me?" I asked as she put her ear closer to my mouth.

"Barely," she replied, patting my cheek. "But with what you've been through, as far as I'm concerned you don't have to speak above a whisper for the rest of your life."

I smiled and closed my eyes. "What day is it."

"It's a little after seven on Sunday morning," she responded. "Deputy Chief Bristow called me Friday afternoon about four-thirty telling me you'd been shot and were undergoing surgery. He sent a car for me. That was so sweet of him because after telling me what had happened to you, I never could have driven here by myself. I arrived a little after seven. Manny's been with you since you were shot. He found you at that house and called the ambulance.

"The nurses have been very good to us. Put us in an empty room and brought in two beds so we could get some sleep while you were in surgery, actually *surgeries*. You've had two. But they wouldn't allow visitors 'til today. Manny and I took up residence in the nurses' office across the hall waiting for you to awaken. They're a nice group."

"You saved me," I murmured.

"No," she answered. "Manny saved you. He told me he arrived fifteen or twenty minutes after your gunfight with Egan. He called 9-1-1 and repacked your wound."

"No," I tried again. "I would've died even before Manny came. But I thought of you and how much I loved you and how I wanted to come back to you. That's what kept me alive." I paused and asked Becky for water. She lifted my head and put the glass to my lips. When she returned my head to the pillow, I motioned for her to come closer. She put her ear next to my mouth. "I almost allowed myself to die," I whispered, "but didn't because I wanted to be with you again so much."

She kissed me lightly on the lips. "That's so sweet of you to say. I love you, too. So much. But it's time for you to get some sleep. Manny's here and wants to give you a hug, too. And we'll be right here when you wake up."

"Hey, Deck," Manny said softly, taking my hand. "Anybody tell you that you look like hell?"

I motioned him to come closer. "Only honest people," I muttered through cracked lips.

He smiled. "I know you're tired so I won't keep you but a second. Wanted to tell you the department thinks you're the stud of all studs. Shooting Egan after he shot you, and then before passing out, you had the wherewithal to plug your wound to stanch the bleeding. You're a stud, man. I'm glad I'm your partner." He squeezed my hand.

I was so tired it was hard to get my mind around what he'd just said. "Wait!" I whispered. "Egan's dead? Who shot him?"

"You did, partner." I started to object, but he squeezed my hand again and said, "You got to get some sleep, and . . ."

"No, wait." I croaked. "Are you're telling me Egan was in the house dead when you arrived? How'd that happen?"

"The Forensic dudes are still doing their thing at the house, but it looks like you killed him. You don't remember?" I shook my head as vigorously as I could, which, I knew intuitively, wasn't very emphatic. "Hey, no problem. It'll all come back to you in time. Right now, you should get some sleep. Like Becky said, we'll be here when you wake up."

CHAPTER 37

They weren't there when I woke up. Not because they didn't want to be, but because at 6:30 a.m. the next morning the hospital staff decided they needed the Intensive Care suite for some other poor bastard, and pronounced me sufficiently "recovered" to be moved to the Recovery Room.

As they wheeled me to my new digs, I heard a commotion in the outer hallway. I looked quizzically at one of the staff members pushing my bed. He noticed and, leaning closer, said, "You be da man, Inspector. The noise you hear is the press wanting to get a crack at you." I groaned. One of the nurses took my hand and said, "Don't worry, hon. We're not going to let them anywhere near you." I squeezed her hand in reply.

As I was pushed into Recovery, the staff all gathered around to greet me. I felt like some kind of celebrity. Straps held my hands to the bed, otherwise I would've fist-bumped 'em all. The high of thinking I was a celeb lasted all of five minutes. By the time they got me comfortable in my new room, I was asleep.

The next thing I remember is being shaken by a nurse. "Wake up, sleeping beauty," she said. "Doctor's here to talk to you."

I reflexively tried to raise my arm to check out the time, but restraints still held both arms to the bed. I scanned the walls of the room. No clocks anywhere. "Can you tell me the time?" I asked the nurse who awakened me.

"Half past two," she replied.

"In the afternoon?" I asked incredulously.

"In the afternoon, Sugar," she responded. "Time flies when you're havin' fun, doesn't it? Oh, your wife and your friend left a while ago. They said if you woke up, I was to tell you they'd be back in an hour or so."

"They've been here the whole time?"

"Sittin' right in those chairs. But you just kept on a snorin'." I heard a noise to my left. "Well, here's your doctor now. I'll let you two be alone for a while."

The doctor introduced himself as Chief Surgeon Mark Golden and plopped himself down on the bed near my feet.

"Been a long night. How are you feeling?" My weak smile gave him his answer. "Pretty much to be expected," he said, glancing through the charts the nurse had given him. "I was the doctor in the OR when they brought you in. Given the seriousness of your wound, coupled with the elapsed time between being wounded and getting you into the OR, you're fortunate to be here talking with me. And your good fortune, as I was led to understand, is mostly attributable to your actions after being shot. Your colleagues out there . . ." he nodded to the doorway, "are talking about you as being some sort of super cop."

"The press?" I croaked. "Believe me, they are not my colleagues." I emphasized the word *not*. "They would like nothing better than to put me through the wringer and then hang me out to dry."

He acknowledged my testiness with a smile. "How are you feeling?" he asked again.

"Better than I would have expected given what I think happened to me. Is that the drugs talking?"

"To a certain extent. We'll reduce the amount tonight."

"When do you think I can go home?"

"Five or six days I'm guessing. You'll be in rehab for a while, but you can do that at home. You were very lucky, Inspector. The *bullet with your name on it*, as they say in the movies, passed through you without hitting any vital organs. That doesn't happen often. It's the reason you were able to stay conscious long enough to administer first aid to yourself before the cavalry arrived. If you hadn't, the cavalry would have found you dead."

"Funny, but I don't remember much of anything."

"Not unusual. Tell me what you do remember."

"I was sitting in a chair about fifteen feet from a psycho ex-cop. He had disarmed me about an hour before. In fact, he had my gun sitting on a table next to him. He told me he had to get going. Even apologized for what he was about to do. When he raised his gun, I remember thinking I'm a dead man. But then thought *what the hell, Decker, at least make him earn it*. I waited a beat and then launched myself sideways out of the chair." I gave a tired smile. "It wasn't much of a launch. I didn't get very far before he fired. I felt the bullet hit me. The only thing I remember after that was laying on the floor packing the wound with my hankie, which thankfully I had in my hand. All those survival school training classes I took finally helped." I chuckled and was immediately kicked in the ribs with a stab of intense pain.

"Oh, yeah," the doc said with a grin. "I would discourage you from laughing for the next few days if you don't want to get a hit again like you just did."

"Thanks. I'll remember your advice."

"You're a lucky man, Inspector. That dive, and you packing your wound, saved your life. The slight movement you made was the difference between the bullet hitting you straight on, smashing through your sternum on its way into your heart or, as it actually did, entering your chest on a downward path a few inches to the left of your sternum. That little move of yours caused the bullet to strike your third rib which, no surprise, broke on impact."

He paused, and then said, "As I'm sure you know, bullets do strange things when they hit hard surfaces. In your case, the bullet hit your rib at such an angle it was deflected into a downward trajectory. On the way down, it grazed your fourth rib, causing the angle of deflection to increase even further. It then grazed the anterior portion of your ilium, which in layman's terms is your hip bone, and stopped dead, no pun intended, in your left buttock. None of your vital organs were hit. You'd already been through your second surgery when we decided to leave the bullet where it was—in your butt cheek. The only interior damage was caused by two bone fragments from your rib that slightly punctured your lung. Do you remember having trouble breathing?"

"I do. Yes."

"If the puncture had been larger, it would itself would have necessitated an operation. But as it was, we found the puncture to be small enough to be able to heal on its own within a week or two. I'd recommend you don't play any basketball for a while." He smiled and patted my thigh. "Tell you what, though, it was a miracle you stayed conscious long enough not only to shoot and kill your assailant, but also pack your wound enough to stop from bleeding out."

"I didn't shoot anyone, Doc. Couldn't have. Someone is making that up."

"Well, that's not what your partner told me. He said there were two people shot in that room and only one lived to tell the tale. And you only lived because you had the wherewithal to stuff a hankie in the entrance wound to minimize the bleeding. Only after doing that did you lose consciousness. An unbelievable story, Inspector. It wouldn't surprise me if your colleagues begin thinking of you as the second man in history to walk on water."

"I remember packing my wound, but I'm telling you, Doc, I didn't shoot anyone. How could something like that happen

206

without me remembering?"

"Hmmm," the Doc said. "Can't help you there. I'm nothing more than a lowly trauma surgeon, not a shrink."

CHAPTER 38

Five minutes after the doc left, the nurse arrived and released my arms from the torture straps that secured them to the mattress. Two minutes later, she allowed Becky and Manny back into the room. I wanted them to stay as long as I could keep my eyes open. I never guessed being among the living could be so enjoyable.

I knew some powerful drugs had been introduced into my system, and thankfully felt their hold on me sliding away. Their withdrawal, however, produced two effects, one beneficial and one not so much. The beneficial one allowed my mind to became considerably less foggy. For example, I knew now for certain neither Edwin nor Egan had visited me. Nothing more than drug induced hallucinations bordering on nightmares. The not so beneficial effect of the withdrawal was the reintroduction of pain now slip-sliding back into my body.

Becky came over to the bed, took my newly liberated hands to her lips and kissed them. She bent over and did the same to my lips. To someone who had cheated death, Becky's kiss was the taste of heaven.

"How's Edwin," I asked. "You guys doing okay?"

"Oh, Reg. When the Deputy Chief Bristow called to tell me what happened to you, I alerted the Child Protective Services immediately. They came and picked him up later in the afternoon."

"I'm sorry, baby."

"No, Reg. Best thing for both of us. I told the CPS people if you hadn't been hurt, we would have tried to keep him for the summer. They have an alternative spot for him. A place called Stornetta Ranch. Up north in Mendocino County. I'd never heard of it, but the people I talked to at CPS raved about it."

I nodded weakly. "Perfect for him," I whispered. "You did the right thing."

She smiled and squeezed my hand. "I hope so"

Manny waited until Becky and I shared some quiet moments together before he took my other hand and gave it a squeeze, commanding my attention. "Deck," he said, "you and the big guy," he pointed skyward "must be on pretty good terms. No other way to explain what happened to you at the farmhouse. You feel strong enough to tell me how it went down? You've got a lot of friends at the Hall, and not only in Homicide, been calling me wondering what juju you been using. They want some."

A sharp pain in my chest short-circuited my laugh. "Nice of them to ask," I remarked through pursed lips. "Tell 'em the secret's gonna cost 'em." I shifted in bed to relieve some of the pain. Becky helped me turn onto my right side, both of us careful not to disturb the wound's dressing. Once situated, I said, "I'm still wondering myself about what the heck happened in the farmhouse. I can't remember anything." I felt Becky squeeze my hand. I squeezed back and whispered, "Sorry."

"Don't worry." She smiled at me. "You're trying, I know. I'll chalk it up to the drugs." She smiled.

"You're sweet," I responded. I turned to Manny and asked how he found me.

"I'll tell you, but then you owe me a detailed report as to what happened there before I arrived." I acknowledged my debt with a slight bob of my head. "Well, first of all, I tracked you to the first house in Sacramento. When I arrived, I saw your car parked in the driveway, so I drove down the cross-street and waited."

"Not your fault," I muttered as another stab of pain bolted through my chest. "It's what Egan hoped you'd do. He suspected there'd be a tracking device on my car, so he purposely left it in the driveway hoping whoever was tracking me would assume we were in the house 'negotiating'." I stopped, shifted in the bed and said, "Egan hoped the tracker would sit passively in the car while he took me to the farmhouse and took care of business."

"Gotta give the son-of-a-bitch credit," Manny said. "I read it exactly that way. Both of you inside 'negotiating.' I waited half an hour, then started thinking back to when I played high school football. *What if this dude is faking the ol' fullback up the middle play while he's running the ball around end?* If I was going to, metaphorically speaking, stop Egan for no gain, I needed to know where he hid the ball. So, I pulled out my phone and asked it to find your new iPhone. I imagined it as the *ball*. My app told me the *ball* was some thirty miles to the north. Took me right to you. Well, to Egan actually, since by that time he was carrying the *ball* in his own pocket."

The nurse came in and told Becky and Manny they had to leave soon. Time for my nap, she told them. I felt like a five-year-old. "Don't pay any attention to her," I told them through a yawn. "I'm fine. I don't want you to go until you hear me snoring. So, please, go on. Give me a picture of the scene you saw at the house. I'm having a hard time remembering. But what I do remember is a lot different than what you told the doc this morning."

"Well, the signal from the iPhone led me to the farmhouse. I got there in thirty-five minutes. The *ball* told me where Egan was, but not how many teammates might be guarding him. The immediate problem I faced was logistical—how many people were in the house and in what rooms? Couldn't wait for the cavalry, so I had to rely on instinct and good luck. Both served me well, especially the *luck* part. I parked the car half a mile up the road, and hoofed it back.

"Not sure if you remember the topography around there, but the farmhouse was situated in a small copse of trees surrounded by an acre or two of tomato plants. And they were close to harvest time." He laughed. "Real close. Messy close. You should have seen my shoes and pant legs by the time I made it to the front door. SFPD owes me some new duds."

The nurse interrupted again. "Time to go," she said, this time with some irritation in her voice. "Visiting hours are over. Our patient needs his sleep."

"Can we have a few more minutes?" I asked. "We're in the middle of police business here." She arched an eyebrow in a sure-you-are look, and left.

I nodded for Manny to continue. "I opened the front door. It was deathly quiet in there." He emphasized the word *deathly,* which made me shiver. "Because of your phone, I knew Egan was in the house. But not being familiar with the house's layout, I had to force myself to proceed slower than I wanted. It took me ten minutes to work my way back to the kitchen area and another minute or so to find you in that big-ass room behind it."

I smiled. "I can see it in my mind. I'd forgotten how big that room was."

"Absolutely. It was quiet in there, too. I maneuvered to the doorway and peeked in. I saw Egan laying by an overturned chair and you lying about twenty feet behind him near the back wall. All I wanted was to get to you, but training won out. I knelt next to Egan, grabbed his wrist and tried to find a pulse. Nadda.

"Then I hurried to you. You were lying on your left side in a small pool of blood. It was smeared, like you had pulled yourself through it. Your left arm was tucked under you, out of sight. Your right arm was splayed forward, your hand still gripping the Sig. I felt your pulse while I'm calling 9-1-1. Weak, but still functioning. I told the operator I had an officer down and needed immediate assistance. Send a helicopter.

"While waiting for the medics to arrive, I gently pulled your right shoulder up and back so I could see what caused the blood beneath you. What I saw was classic. Your left hand was covering what looked like a blood-soaked hankie that had been packed into the bullet wound in your chest. The hankie staunched the blood flow to a trickle. I talked to the docs after you got out of the first surgery, and they told me had you not packed the wound, you would have bled out." He squeezed my hand. "And I remember you telling me that you slept through those mandatory survival-safety classes."

"Some of it must have slithered unknowingly into my subconscious," I replied through a yawn.

"You were unconscious, so I put my coat under your head to make your breathing easier. Then I went back to Egan. He had taken a round mid-chest. If he didn't die immediately, he didn't last long. A great shot, partner. You had to be fighting your own demons by that time, so congrats on shooting so well. They'll probably give you a marksman medal, among other things."

I shook my head and turned to Becky. "Is this a dream?" I whispered. "Are you really here? Let me feel you squeeze my hand." She did. "Now my face?"

"I'll do even better," she said, bending over and pressing her lips to mine in a long, sensuous kiss. "Does that feel like a dream?" she asked as she softly touched my face.

"Ummm. Okay, you're real." I smiled, hoping it didn't look like a grimace. "Now tell me, is Manny really here, or have I been hallucinating?"

"I can vouch for him being here, if that's what you mean," she said with a laugh.

I turned to Manny and said, "Maybe it's you hallucinating, my man. I remember Egan pointing that gun at me and me taking a half-ass dive to the floor. It was only after being hit that my mind registered the sound of the shot. Odd, huh? You'd think it would be the other way around. Anyway, that's it. That's all I remember."

"*Remember* is the operative word, Deck. Your mind is blanking out on a large part of what happened in that room because of the trauma you endured. Egan did shoot you. You're right about that. But you also shot him. You may not remember that, but I walked into that room and saw both you and Egan laying there. I called the emergency rescue helicopter that got you to the hospital in time to save your life."

"All I remember is diving off the chair as Egan shot. What's forensics got to say?"

"They're saying you shot Egan. You may not remember it, but the evidence tells them that's how it went down."

"I'm telling you that didn't happen."

"Well, somebody shot him. He was dead when I came in. And you had the Sig in your hand just like I described." He stopped speaking for a moment, leaned closer to me and said, "Maybe it's the trauma of almost dying that suppresses your memory. Your mind's way of coping. It happens, you know."

I was too tired to argue, so I changed the subject. "Thanks for buying this damn phone for me," I said to both of them. "Without it, my ass would be in a morgue somewhere."

"Yeah, lucky in a number of ways," Manny said. "If Egan had dumped it somewhere, or left it in Sacramento, you'd have died in the farmhouse. So, I guess we owe him something."

"No," Becky said. "We owe God for creating such a stupid man."

"Not only stupid, but greedy," Manny replied. "We all know

what Egan was thinking when he took Deck's phone with him. He was thinkin' *damn, man, this baby's got to be worth some coin*. He got what he deserved. Sweet justice, if you ask me."

Just then a very perturbed nurse walked into the room, a scowl having taken over her face. Before she could say a word, Becky held up her hand and said, "We're outta here."

I squeezed Becky's hand. "Before you go," I whispered, "how are the Giants doing?"

CHAPTER 39

I don't know how long I slept, but was awakened by a nurse telling me I had a visitor. Not waiting for the nurse's permission, in walked Richard Sherman carrying a colorfully wrapped present which he deposited at the foot of my bed. Looking up at me, he said, "Anybody ever mention you look like do-do?"

The nurse shrugged, gave me an *it's-not-my-fault* look, turned, scowled at Sherm, and left.

"Geez, they just let anybody in these rooms," I said with a big a smile. I motioned him to come closer. "What a great surprise, Sherm. We have to stop meeting like this." We both laughed. "It's really good to see you."

Sherm leaned over the bed's railing and patted my cheek with his left hand. "Was in Minneapolis when I heard you'd been shot. Booked the first flight out." He paused. "How the hell you feelin' man? I was just funnin' when I said you looked like death warmed over. Actually, you look a hell of a lot better than I expected."

"I'm feeling pretty good, tell you the truth. The first couple of days were a bitch. But being a survivor, strangely enough, tends to take away all the pain."

"Yeah, ain't that the truth!" he said with a smile. "So, tell me what happened. I leave you alone for a day or two and you get yourself shot. How'd you end up catching a bullet?"

I spent the next hour telling Sherm about the case. How I'd been working it from the time I last saw him: beginning with the

DENNIS KOLLER

call I got from my nephew; to getting permission to re-open a thirteen-year-old murder case; to waking up in this bed after being shot by an ex-SFPD Homicide Inspector named Barry Egan."

"Son-of-a-bitch, man. Sounds complicated."

"The threads of the case are complicated, and, truth be told, those threads are still hanging out there. But the final verdict, the only one that really counts, is pretty much cut and dried. Barry Egan confessed to robbing and murdering Poppy Garcia by shooting me."

"Did they catch Egan?" he asked.

"Yeah. The best kind of 'catch.' He died at the scene."

"Good going. You got him, too."

"No. That's the big mystery in all this. Hey, I'm glad the son-of-a-bitch is dead. Only thing is I didn't shoot him."

"Who did?"

"I have no idea, Sherm. Everyone tells me I must have since no one else was in the room but the two of us. Forensics says it was my Sig that killed him. But I have zero memory of that." I paused, took a sip of water from the glass on my tray, then said, "I remember him shooting me, but from then on, everything's a blank."

"Well, you can't argue with the forensics. And, as I'm sure you know, there is such a thing as repressed memory. Probably should just let it go, Reg. It'll all come back someday. In the meantime, just be thankful he's dead, and you're alive. Right now, you got more important things to do, like getting your health back." He pulled over a chair and sat down. "I talked to your doctor before I left Minnesota. Turned out he is, like us, retired military, so we bonded quickly. He told me how the bullet, in his words, *miraculously* missed all your vital organs, and came to rest in your ass."

I laughed. "Yep. It's the classic *I've got good news and bad news for you. The good news is you survived. The bad news is you won't be able to sit down on a toilet seat for the rest of your life."*

"Well, it won't be that bad," Sherm said with a laugh. "It'll probably be a little uncomfortable for a while as your butt gets acclimatized to having a foreign object residing there."

"He's talked to me about what to expect. I'm wondering how it's gonna feel when I actually try sit down."

"Well, funny you should ask." He picked up the present and placed it on my lap. "Your good friend, soon to be your best friend, Richard Sherman brought you a present that he carried all the way from Minneapolis. Special delivery."

"You shouldn't have, Sherm," I said, as I started ripping the wrapping away. It took me a second to understand what I was looking at. Then I started to laugh. "Damn, Sherm. You shouldn't have. I'm now a proud owner of a *Luxury Orthopedic Seat Cushion*? Who woulda thunk?"

Sherm laughed. "Not just 'A' *Luxury Orthopedic Seat Cushion*, my friend, but 'THE' *Luxury Orthopedic Seat Cushion*. I wanted to get you something where you'd think of me every time you felt a pain in your ass."

"Well, then, I'll be thinkin' of you often, Sherm. It's one of those gifts I'll never leave home without. At least for the next few months."

He laughed. "And on a nicer note, when you're fully recovered, I still want to talk to you about coming to work for Brigitte Le Pendu. Can you imagine you and me together? We'd kick ass and take names, brother."

CHAPTER 40

Becky and Manny were in my room when the doctor arrived early the next morning. He put out his hand when both started to leave. "No, wait! You don't have to leave. In fact, I'm glad you're here. My staff and I are pleased with the progress Inspector Decker's made this past week, and we're convinced he's no longer in immediate danger of dying."

"Oh, thank god," Becky said, grabbing my hand and pressing it to her cheek.

"Even more good news," the doctor continued, a smile taking over his face. "My staff and I are of the opinion it would be better if the patient were in a hospital closer to home. We cleared this with your department, Inspector. They've authorized us to make arrangements for your transfer to UCSF Med Center."

"Oh, that's such great news, Doctor," Becky said. "When will he be able to leave?" She let a beat go by and then said, "Not that we don't like it here, or anything like that." Everybody, including me, laughed.

The doctor looked at me sternly. "They can laugh. You can't." Then he smiled and said, "You have some paperwork to sign before the ambulance gets here. You'll be in your new digs by four or so."

"How long do you think they'll keep me there, doc?" I asked. "Another week?"

"Sounds about right to me. Course it depends on how good a

patient you are. You're mending well, but it takes a while for the body to heal itself from such a traumatic experience. I'd expect you to be walking with a cane for a while."

~~~~~

Everything he told me was spot on. During the four days I was at UCSF, I was prodded and probed with every instrument known to God or man. Because of my exalted status as one of SF's finest, Becky got to bunk with me, albeit separate beds. Being the last three days in the school year, she was out of class at noon and at my bedside by one. On Saturday of that week, Becky brought her class to UCSF to visit me. Since the school couldn't afford a bus to take the children, Becky enlisted the help of parents to ferry the children from school to hospital and back. There were so many kids and parents at the hospital that Saturday morning, the hospital administration allowed us to use an empty conference room to do our meet and greet. The kids got to stay a full two hours, peppering me with questions from what it felt like to be shot ("it hurts a lot") to being a policeman ("It's a lot of fun. If you study hard and get good grades in school, you can become one") to arresting bad guys ("All bad guys go to jail"). You want to be the good guys so you'll never have to go to jail. Blah! Blah! Blah! After the class left, I slept a full four hours.

The next day, Becky and Manny transported me in a wheel-chair from my room to the hospital check-out station in the main lobby. After a few encouraging words from the hospital staff, I was sent on my way.

Knowing I'd have trouble maneuvering up the basement steps, Becky parked on the street and, with Manny's help, pulled the wheel-chair and me up the front steps. I asked him to stop, that I wanted to walk into my own house. Becky held onto my arm as I stepped into my living room. Felt like heaven being in my own house for the first time in two weeks. Becky asked Morales to go to the pharmacy to pick up the boatload of pills the doctors had prescribed for me. Once he left, Becky closed the door, took me in her arms and planted a warm, wet kiss on my lips. "Wanna play around?" she asked with a sly smile.

"Do we have time?" I asked.

"As soon as we get rid of Manny, you can take all the time you need."

All I could think of was how right Dorothy had been when she exclaimed, "There's no place like home."

When Manny returned, and I was settled on the pillow Sherm bought for me, Becky set about brewing coffee. Manny took the occasion to ask what I thought would happen with the Garcia case.

"I'm guessing we have a day or two," I replied, "before the official report on the shootout in Sacramento will be completed. Once that file is delivered to Bristow's office, I'm sure he'll shut it down."

"That's what I figured, too. Bummer."

"Exactly. I've been thinking that since I'll be on disability leave for at least a week, I'd pursue it on my own time. Unfortunately, that'll leave you out of the equation unless we can come up with something."

Becky returned and set the coffee cups on the table. "Did I hear you say you might pursue this case on your own time? So much for our vacation in Cancun, huh?"

"Cancun? Oh, baby," I replied. "I'm so sorry. You must have overheard me when I was talking to that travel agent. Fact is, though, when I told him I needed a place where I could sit my ass on a donut poolside, he hung up."

"Good one," she laughed.

Manny shook his head. "Just bad luck," he said with a chuckle. "Deck, just so you know, I'm going back to the Hall and have another peek at the notes I made after reading the murder book. Maybe the great policeman in the sky will give me some inspiration."

"And while you're being inspired, I'll call Kincaid to see if he found out anything about Poppy's mother. I'm still not convinced she's an innocent bystander in this sordid affair."

CHAPTER 41

No sooner had Manny closed the front door, than I was on the phone with Kincaid.

"He's baaaack," I said as Kincaid answered his phone.

"I was afraid of that," he replied with a laugh. "You're home finally, huh?"

"Yep. They released me today."

"Bet they couldn't wait to get you out of there. You're just the kind of whiney patient they hate. So, how are you feeling?"

"A lot better than a week or so ago, for sure."

"I can imagine. Since you're at home, maybe I should send you a bouquet of flowers."

I laughed. "Only if you add a bottle of Bombay Sapphire to the order."

"Damn. Did the hospital discharge you knowing you're still hallucinating?"

"Ha-Ha. You're a funny guy, Walt. But enough, already. I've got a bullet up my ass and you're making it hurt. So, before I forget, did you ever get your tracking device back?"

"I did. Thanks. So, what's up with your investigation?"

"I still have some questions about Egan and just about everything else surrounding this damn case. I heard through the grapevine the brass might shut the case down. As far as I'm concerned, that would be a big mistake. Still too many loose ends. I was hoping you took a look at the info I gave you on Mrs. Garcia while I was in the hospital."

"Actually, I did. Turns out your lady friend knew some important people. Probably still does, for all I know."

"Tell me."

"Some background info first. We had to find out where the woman banked. Standard operating procedure in situations like this. If I could get into her account, I'd be able to see her income. Where it came from as well as where it went. Never ceases to amaze me the information you can get from a simple bank account. It's like seeing a person's whole life laid out in front of you." He gave a small chuckle.

"I'd always been told you needed a court order to get a perp's banking info."

"True enough under normal circumstances," he replied. "But in the real world it depends on who you know. In the real world, it goes something like this: SFPD Homicide Inspector Reg Decker knows FBI Special Agent-in-Charge Walt Kincaid. And Special Agent Walt Kincaid happens to know a ton of bankers. So, when Inspector Decker needed some financial data on a suspect, he called his friend Special Agent in Charge, Walt Kincaid, who in turn called his banker friends."

"Well," I said. "That sounds like a good deal for your friend Inspector Decker."

"And, indeed, it was. Turned out Decker's FBI friend knew a banker at JP Morgan Chase in New York. So good friend Kincaid called to see if his banker friend could help him. Guess what? Kincaid's banker friend found that the person of interest to his friend Decker, a woman named Maria Garcia, had an account at Bank of America."

"Great story so far. Can Decker's FBI friend tell him how that helps?"

"Yes, he can. Most of the time, just having a bank account

number doesn't help, but in this particular case, it did." He paused, obviously trying to provide even more drama to his big reveal.

"Come on, Walt. Don't keep me hanging."

"As luck would have it, to say nothing of a number of after-hour cocktails paid for by the good citizens of the United States via your FBI friend's credit card, he's also friends with the VP for Operations at B of A."

My anticipation meter started vibrating. "So, who were her friends?"

"Well, it's more complicated than that. As you can imagine, her moving back to Mexico meant moving her bank account, too. She's no longer a client of B of A so her records were tough to come by."

"Please, Walt. You don't have to keep ratcheting up the suspense. Just tell me."

"Well, when I said your lady knew important people, I didn't mean to imply I could name them. I can't. But I do know that whoever they are, or at least *were*, they were powerful enough to stay hidden."

"Does 'stay hidden' mean what I think it means? These guys are buried?"

"Pretty much. At the very least, they're going to be hard to find. Let me give you an example of what we're up against. For the past three decades or so, your lady friend had money transferred into her banking account on a monthly basis. Care to guess for how much?"

"No. I'm sorry, but my mind is mush right now. Tell me."

"Starting in the early-eighties, someone was transferring a steady three grand a month into her account. In case you're too young to remember, three grand a month in the eighties was a good size chunk of change. By eighty-eighty or so, the amount grew to five-grand. Through the next ten years it never went below that amount. In '98, the monthly amount jumped to seven grand, supplemented every now and then by another grand or two. It was like whoever was funding her decided she needed more money this particular month but not the next month. Or could be Garcia had more expenses so demanded more."

"So, if her daughter needed something like braces, or clothes for school. Books. Stuff like that," I said. "She'd ask for extra?"

"Exactly. But there's more. When the new century rolled around, the monthly amount increased to a steady eight grand. A month, for god's sake. That amount held steady for the duration."

"And the 'duration' means what?"

"Until she moved back to Mexico after her daughter was murdered. And what's more, for the time Maria Garcia lived in this country, we have no record of her ever paying a penny for rent. I've seen a list of all the checks she wrote during the time she lived here. At least the ones she wrote through her B of A account. Not one for rent."

"You sure she didn't own those flats?"

"She didn't. Those flats were purchased in 1982 by a company named PC Resources out of Bermuda.

"Bermuda? Damn, Walt, this case is getting weirder and weirder."

"You ain't heard the half of it, Decker my man. Mrs. Garcia's monthly income checks, those six, seven and eight thousand-dollar ones? They were written on PC Resources' Bermuda account."

"Have you gotten in touch with them?"

"Tried to. Again, funny stuff. PC Resources was first incorporated in Delaware in 1981. The year before the condo was purchased. The contact person listed in the papers is a DC law firm. I called even though I knew the answer I would get."

"Which was?"

"Sorry. We can't give out that information unless you have a court order."

I laughed. "Sure! And I'm guessing you can't get a court order, huh?"

"Not without the Bureau getting involved. And that ain't gonna happen. At least, not in the short run."

"You said the condo was purchased by PC Resources? Both the upper and lower unit?"

"Yep."

"Do you know who the person was who lived in the lower unit when Poppy was little?"

"We do. The bottom unit was rented to a couple named Bob and Judy Gold. According to Mrs. Garcia, they only lived there for a year or two. I'm running a search for them now in the off-chance we can find them and they know something."

"Damn, Walt." I shook my head in disgust. "What's your gut take-away from all this?"

"My gut take-away? Simple! Whoever these guys are, or were, they wanted to make sure they were never found."

~~~~~~

"That didn't sound too helpful," Becky said as I hung up.

"Complicated is all. Hard to figure what to do next."

"Well, what *we're* doing next is get your cute little butt into the living room. You'll at least be more comfortable sitting on the sofa." Once there, she helped lower me onto Sherm's cushion.

"This cushion really works," I told her. "remind me to thank Sherm. I think I'll be carrying this cushion around for the foreseeable future."

"Remind me to walk behind you when we're out together." She laughed. "But you like, huh?" she said snuggling up. I flinched a little as her hip bumped close to where the bullet rested. "If you weren't such a wuss, we could have some serious fun on your cushion."

I laughed. "You sure pick a bad time to get horny knowing I'm going to be outta business for a while. Last week when I was here and available, you rebuffed every time I wanted to jump your bones."

She kissed me on the cheek. "Not every time, darling. I remember you flashing a big smile when you woke up the last Friday morning you were here. The Friday you were shot."

"Oh, yeah. Hmmm. Forgot that one." I smiled and put my good arm around her. "Okay, disregard everything I just said."

"I will." She burrowed in even tighter.

"Hey, you heard anything lately about how the little guy's doing up in Mendocino?"

"No. Haven't had a chance to check on him."

"Maybe we should go see for ourselves. You game?"

"Oh, Reg, that would be so much fun. Could we?"

"Well, hell yeah. How 'bout Sunday?"

"You know I'd love to, but will you be well enough to sit for all that time? I mean it's like a three-hour drive up there."

"I know how far it is. Piece of cake, Babe. Just stretch me out on the back seat with my *Luxury Orthopedic Seat Cushion* and forget about me."

"I'd rather have you and your donut up front with me."

"Come on. It's not just a *donut*."

"Oops, almost forgot." She smiled and squeezed my arm. "I'll call them tomorrow, and make an appointment to visit. You know we're footing the bill for him being there, don't you?"

"I heard the rumor." I smiled and put my arm around her. "I'm sure we can afford it."

She leaned back into me and said, "You're the best."

CHAPTER 42

I awakened the next morning in my own bed for the first time in almost two weeks. Even better, I woke up in my own bed with Becky beside me. But the icing on the cake was when she walked me out to the kitchen for breakfast, there wasn't a sullen eight-year old slopping milk from his cereal bowl on the table.

I was thinking we could spend the day together. Maybe take a ride somewhere. Just the two of us. But when you're married to an elementary school teacher, you find there's no escaping schoolwork. "You won't mind me going to school today, would you? I have to finish packing."

Hell yes, I'd mind, I thought, but instead said, "No problem, babe. I'll take a nap." Just then the phone rang.

"That's no doubt for you, Reg. I'll go now. Be back by noon at the latest." She picked up the receiver and handed it to me. "Tell whoever it is I said 'hi'." With that, she gave me a peck on the cheek and left.

It was Bristow. "How you feelin' Decker?" he asked.

"Are you really concerned or just checking up on me?" I replied with a laugh.

"Oh, concerned, Deck. CONCERNED, I tell you," he replied, finishing with a laugh of his own. "Bet you're glad to be home, huh?"

"Amen to that, Matt. Much better than laying in those damn hospital beds in Sacramento and SF, I'll tell ya. But, to be clear, both those hospitals were infinitely better than laying in the morgue."

"Amen to that," Bristow replied.

"How're the guys getting along without me?"

"It's hard for me to believe, Decker, but they say they really miss you. Everybody's been asking when you'll be gracing us with your presence?"

"I'd be in today if the docs would let me, but they're telling me I'm still looking at maybe a week or two. I'm still a little tender and walkin' slow."

"Just let me know, okay? We're planning on having a party for you. It's not that you're liked or anything, just the guys are hoping they'd be given the afternoon off." He laughed again and said, "Wanted to tell you Egan's autopsy and the Sacramento PD's summation of what happened in that farmhouse is complete. Everything is buttoned up. Since there are no outstanding issues or lingering doubts, I'm officially closing the Garcia case. Wanted you to know."

"Thanks, Matt. I expected it."

"You know where Manny is? I called his house, and he didn't answer. I hoped he was with you."

"Nope. Not here, Matt."

"Too bad. Just wanted to tell him in person the Garcia case has officially closed. If you talk to him, can you relay the message? And tell him his supervisor wants him back in the building."

"Of course. I'm sure he'll be at the Hall tomorrow."

Hanging up, I placed a call to Manny. When he didn't answer, I left him a voice mail, shuffled back to the bedroom and promptly fell asleep.

~~~~~~

I was awakened at twelve-thirty by a call from Becky, telling me she was on her way home. When she arrived, she fixed lunch for both of us and we went into the living room to watch the news. Just as we settled in, Manny called.

"Glad you're up, Deck. You doing well enough to have me stop by for a few minutes? I've got some news that's kick ass."

"Of course, you can come over. Becky just got back from school, and we're watching TV and eating lunch. You hungry?"

"Nah, I've eaten. See you in about twenty minutes."

When she heard Manny was on his way, Becky decided she should go food shopping. I walked her to the door and gave her a hug. "Buy something sexy to wear later tonight," I said.

"While you lay flat on your back with a donut under your butt? Forgive the pun, Inspector Decker, but I'm not sure you're *up* for that just yet." She squeezed the back of my neck and gave me a kiss. "But we'll give it a shot, my love."

Fifteen minutes later, I was seated on my donut in the living room with a visibly excited Manny Morales. He pulled a file folder from his briefcase and laid it on the coffee table in front of him.

"Before this case is taken away from us and we're told we have to head back to our dreary jobs . . ."

"Stop right there," I said. "Bristow just called. The case has been taken away from us."

"Son-of-a-bitch, Deck. Too damn soon." He paused. "Oh well, you can take it from here since you are technically on disability leave."

"You can count on it."

"Good. Okay . . . I decided find the damn person who started all this. The so-called *Twitter Dude*."

"If only you could," I said.

"Deck, you told me from the get-go that whoever the Twitter

DENNIS KOLLER

person was, he had to be a friend of Poppy Garcia's. I went back to the office last night and reviewed all my notes from the beginning of this damn case. I picked out the two people that Egan identified as Poppy's closet friends." He paused for effect. "Just finished talking with both of them. They're both women."

"Women? Geez, that sure changes the equation, doesn't it? Good for you. Who would've thought, huh?"

"The first woman wasn't all that helpful. But . . ." he handed me a file, "this woman was a freaking gold mine."

I gingerly leaned back and opened the file. Staring at me from a five-by-seven professionally produced picture was an attractive, forty-something woman with short blonde hair and brown eyes.

"Meet Connie Fiorentino," he said. "Your *Twitter Dude*."

"Son-of-a-bitch. You sure about that?"

"Absolutely. She showed me her Twitter account. It's all there."

I leaned back further into the sofa, maneuvering my donut in an effort to become more comfortable. "I'm impressed, Manny. You've got to tell me how you went from a simple interview to seeing her Twitter account?"

"Learned the art of persuasion from you, Deck," he said, clapping me on the shoulder. "As we were talking about what happened to Poppy all those years ago, Connie alternated between weepy and being angry. Turned out the anger came from my being only the second police officer in thirteen years to talk to her about Poppy Garcia's murder. And the first officer, she told me, didn't seem all that interested in finding out who killed her. The only thing he was curious about was did she, Connie, have copies of the pictures Poppy took."

"Let me guess. The first officer couldn't have been our now deceased pal Barry Egan, could it?"

He laughed. "Hey, not only the first officer she met, but the

234

only officer she met until I showed up on her doorstep." Morales smiled and folded himself back into the sofa. "Probably be easier to understand if I started from the beginning." He paused for a minute, then continued. "As I said, I interviewed both Connie and Joyce Wilson. No need for me to go through Poppy's history with them. Just know it was extensive."

"Were either of them cab drivers?"

"No. Merely good friends from high school days. I interviewed Joyce Wilson first. Lasted a little under an hour. Then I went to Fiorentino's house. Was there two hours. The amazing thing about both interviews was their similarity."

"Had they rehearsed beforehand?"

"Nope. Completely off the cuff. They both concluded, separately I might add, that Egan wasn't at all interested in who killed their friend. That observation was the genesis of Fiorentino's tweets about a police cover-up."

"I don't blame her," I said. "Incompetence on our part is the number one reason why citizens come up with this 'cover-up' crap. In this case, though, it wasn't incompetence, it was corruption. And now, dammit, except for knowing Egan was dirty, we aren't any closer to finding out who killed Poppy. Damn discouraging."

"Hold on, Deck, I ain't finished yet."

I wiggled around in my seat, trying to maneuver into a better position on my "magic" cushion. Didn't work. My butt was hurting something fierce. *Nothin' you can do about it, Decker, so suck it up*, I thought. "So, what else you got?"

"You okay, man?" Manny put his hand on my shoulder. So much for sucking it up.

"I'll be okay. Go on."

"I asked both women whether Poppy had any boyfriends, someone she may have jilted or made jealous. A motive sufficient to get her killed. Both women answered the same way. *Not from a guy*. Poppy Garcia, as we found out earlier, was gay. That's why Connie's tweet accused our department of being 'homophobic'. She told me Poppy had been gay since high school. She also told me the three of them were pretty promiscuous all through their high school years. They belonged to a club of teenage girls who were, as she put it, 'going through a phase of being sexually active.' Within that sexually active phase, the three of them had sex together dozens of times. Connie refused to classify any of it as a *relationship*. More an *experiment*, she said. For Joyce, the experiment lasted all through high school. For Connie, just her junior and senior years. Whatever, it was a long time ago."

"And this Connie woman actually admitted all this?"

"Both women told me they weren't really gay, just inquisitive and adventurous. It went with the times. Both are now married. Connie's got three kids, two from her husband and one from a previous boyfriend. Joyce has two. Doesn't change things for us, though. Jealousy could still be a motive for her murder. Maybe we've been too focused on the wrong sex."

"Maybe, but Bristow isn't going to let me go digging up all that thirteen-year old sex stuff on the remote chance it would lead to her killer."

"Well, if you see it that way," Morales replied, "maybe we should just go with that and call it a day. We don't have too many other options as far as I can tell."

"I hear you, Manny. And I already told you Bristow's officially closed the case." Morales nodded. "Honestly, the thing eating at me the most is not finding her killer. We're thirteen years removed from finding that out. My problem is whether Poppy's mother, and now these two friends of Poppy's, would ever forgive us if we just walked away."

"Being forgiven isn't in our job description," Morales

countered. "I feel sorry for Poppy, Deck, I really do. And I feel for her friends. But you know the stats. In the best of years, the department only closes eighty-five to ninety percent of the homicides in this city. Poppy happened, unfortunately, to fall into the ten to fifteen percent unsolved."

I shook my head side-to-side. Tell you what! Before we call it a day, Manny, let me take a few days to look at it in its fullness. You said we know zip about the murder. That's not quite true. We know a full investigation into Poppy Garcia's murder was thwarted by one of our own. Egan wanted to make sure that no one would dig too deep into this case. All he was after was making a few bucks fencing junk he took from the house, then shutting down the case as fast as he could. Period!"

"Believe me, Deck, I get it. I was his partner, for goodness sake. For Egan, Poppy Garcia was nothing more than an inconsequential Hispanic bitch who was in the wrong place at the wrong time and happened to get herself whacked. So why not, he thought to himself, make a few bucks pocketing the money that was on the table along with anything else of value in the house, plant a little cocaine to make the hit look justified and call it a day?"

"Exactly. Come on, Manny. Looking back on it, you can't be satisfied with that, can you? Especially since your name is on the murder book. We're talking about a young woman who was murdered. Just because Egan took the easy way out, we can't."

CHAPTER 43

Y ou want something to drink?" I asked during a lull in the conversation. I tried to push myself erect.

"Sure. You stay put," Manny said, his hand on my shoulder to keep me from rising. "You and your donut were made for each other," he teased. "I'll get whatever you want. Coffee?"

"Perfect. There's still some in the pot from this morning if you ain't persnickety about it not being fresh. I think it's still hot, though."

He came back a few minutes later and handed me a cup. "One more thing I have to mention, partner. I don't think it has anything to do with the case, but if you end up questioning the two women, you're gonna hear it."

"So, tell me."

"Remember we talked about her missing camera? When I mentioned it to the two women, they were surprised to hear it was gone. They told me how Poppy had become consumed by photography. Took classes and everything. After a lot of experimenting, she decided to become a chronicler of the San Francisco street scene. She did just that, and even won a few awards."

"And why do they think this is important?"

"Important because, in our conversation, they mentioned Poppy had posted pictures of the Pride Parade on her Facebook page."

"Let me ask again. That's important why?"

"Important because Facebook took them down."

"Come on, Manny," I said, hearing the peevishness in my voice. "What's that got to do with anything? It's their damn site. They can do what the hell they want with it. What's the big deal?"

"It's just weird, Deck, that's all. I called a number of friends who are Facebook followers and they never heard of Facebook doing anything like that unless the post was pornographic. Whatever they considered pornographic came down. It may have been different back in '07, but I seriously doubt it."

"I heard about the porno thing. I give 'em kudos for it."

"But according to both Joyce and Connie, the pictures they took down were nothing more than street scenes of the Pride Parade."

"So, what are you driving at? What's any of this have to do with her getting whacked?"

"That's the question Connie and Joyce said they asked back in '07 and are asking now. Both were, and still are, convinced that those pictures had something to do with her murder."

"Oh my god. Not another crazy conspiracy theory. We don't want to go down that rabbit-hole, do we?"

"Normally, I'd run away from something like this faster than a dog could trot, Deck. But, I gotta tell you, this has a different feel to it."

"Sure!" I scoffed.

"No, it does. Listen! Poppy was furious and contacted Facebook. They told her they took them down because her photos were deemed homophobic. Joyce and Connie told me that Facebook made all that up. They said Poppy was so angry she threatened to go to the press. They . . ."

"Hey, do me a favor," I interrupted none-too-politely. "The next time you see her girlfriends, tell them we all feel sorry about Poppy's pictures, but those photos have absolutely zip to do with finding her killer, or killers, and bringing them to justice. Tell 'em we have so many other things to worry about, we can't afford to be distracted with trivial issues like this."

"I'm gonna push back again, Deck. I think those pictures might have something, maybe everything, to do with her getting whacked."

I shook my head. "Tell me what I'm missing, Manny."

"Coincidences."

"Coincidences?" I said in a loud voice. "I can't believe we're having this conversation. My partner of five years is gonna lecture *me* about coincidences?"

"Ironic, isn't it?" he said with a smile. "Weren't you the one who impressed upon me there were no coincidences in the murder business?"

"Guilty," I responded, looking at my watch, hoping this conversation would be over soon.

"Well, try this on for *coincidence*," Manny replied testily. "Two days after her photos were posted, and one day after she complained about them being taken down, she was laying on her kitchen floor with pieces of her skull missing."

I looked at him skeptically but couldn't argue with my own logic. "Okay. You win round one," I told him resignedly. "Show me the pictures Poppy sent to Facebook."

"That's another issue that falls into the 'coincidence' category." He looked at me and shrugged. "I can't."

"Can't what?"

"I can't show the pictures to you."

"You're telling me those women refused to give you the photographs?"

"It wasn't that they refused, Deck. They don't have them. And you know why? Barry Egan confiscated their photographs of the Parade two days into the murder case, that's why." I thought

241

back to the murder book. As far as I remembered, there was no mention of flash drives being confiscated as evidence.

"In fact, the day the photos were taken down, which as I said was just a day before she was murdered, Connie and Joyce went to lunch with Poppy. They both independently told me the same story. Poppy was furious that Facebook would dare suggest her photos were homophobic." He paused.

"And?"

"And after both her friends reviewed the drive, they, too, came to the same conclusion. That Facebook willfully misinterpreted a few of her pictures. Two, to be exact. Both were of people marching down Market Street with rainbow flags. On the bottom of those two pictures, Poppy captioned, 'What's wrong with this picture?'"

"Well, come on then," I said, shrugging my shoulders as if those words wrapped it all up.

"I know what you're thinking, but wait a minute. According to the two women, Poppy was merely highlighting the fact there were no American flags along the Parade's route. At least in the picture she took. For her, it was a patriotic comment, not a homophobic one. She contacted Facebook to explain, but no one responded." Morales paused to take a sip of his coffee, then continued. "That was the last time the two women saw Poppy. She went to work that night, and sometime the next morning she got popped."

"When did Egan call on them?" I asked.

"Two days after the murder."

"So, essentially it was his first full day on the case. Must have gotten their names from the mother."

"Looks that way. Anyway, he called both women. Told them he'd heard they were Poppy's best friends and wanted to interview them. They agreed, so he set up a meeting for the following day."

"He was quick, I'll give him that. So, how'd the picture thing come up?"

"After the obligatory questions about motive and such, Egan brought up the Facebook issue, wondering if they had seen the pictures on the site. When they said yes, he asked if Poppy had given them copies of the photographs."

"And they both said yes?"

"Exactly. What would you expect from two law abiding citizens?" he said with a smile.

"And, what? You're thinking he was just trolling?"

"No doubt in my mind. He asked both if they knew of any other friends she may have given a copy of the pictures to."

"Did they give him names?"

"No, but get this. Egan told them if they came across anyone who had a copy of those pictures, he'd buy that person a flash drive to replace the one the pictures were on."

"Okay. I'll agree with you that what he did was weird, but the two women agreed to take the money and run?"

"Hell, yeah. Fifteen bucks plus a new flash drive? Wouldn't you?" Manny looked at his watch. "Speaking of running, I've got to go, Deck. Don't know about you, but I'm bushed."

"Wimp!"

"You got that right. Thanks for listening. I'm glad you're still interested in seeing the case to its proper conclusion. By the way, Connie said she'd stop the tweets. She made a point of telling me, however, if it looked like we weren't serious about finding Poppy's killer, she'd start them up again."

I shook his hand and gave him a hug from my sitting position. "Does Connie work?"

"Yeah. The second shift at the post office over on 24th Street. She does her Twitter work in the morning."

"You have her phone number?"

"Why? You thinking of calling her?"

I nodded. "Just to say thanks for her help. I think I'll give her a call this afternoon."

"Go for it. She'll be flattered." He wrote down her number and handed it to me.

CHAPTER 44

Manny's visit re-energized me. I stood and shuffled warily from the living room to the kitchen to get some more coffee. On the way, I stopped and pulled out my cell to check the time. A little before three. Manny said Connie Fiorentino worked the second shift at the post office. On the off chance she hadn't yet left for work, I called her. She answered on the second ring. Introducing myself, I thanked her for helping our efforts to find Poppy's killer. I told her we were doing the best we could and would follow-up with Facebook as to why they rushed to take her photos down. We chatted another five minutes before I hung up. A few minutes later, Becky called telling me she would be home within twenty minutes.

I padded back to the living room and gingerly sank on my donut. I'd heard somewhere that CK was a Facebook fanatic. I decided to call to see if she knew anyone at the company I could talk to.

First thing she said was how weird to even think there might be a connection between Poppy Garcia's murder and Facebook. "Maybe they had some strange algorithms back in the day," she said to me, "but I can't imagine them pulling pictures in today's world for something so innocuous."

She laughed and spent the next ten minutes telling me what a wonderful company Facebook was and how much she'd made on their stock over the years. "Pretty sure Facebook has never heard of me, but I can give you the name of someone who has contacts there. Guy's name is Ralph Jackson. He used to work at Facebook, so he knows everyone. Ralph actually works for us now. In PR. I'll give you his extension." I scribbled down the number and gave Ralph a call.

"Sounds complicated," Jackson said after hearing my story. "Complicated like *senior level management* complicated. The problem dealing with Facebook is it's tough getting anyone's attention, let alone someone in senior level management. Couple that with an incident that happened thirteen years ago, and you got to hope your being from SFPD Homicide catches someone's attention."

"I can only hope, my friend."

I must have sounded dejected because Ralph immediately brightened his tone. "But I do know some people in their PR division who might be able to hook you up with someone who might be able to give you some answers. I'll call over there and see what pops up. Sorry, but that's about the best I can do." I thanked him, gave him my cell number and hung up.

Eight minutes later, my phone chirped. It was Jackson. "I connected with a guy from Facebook's PR department," he said. "He's an associate manager named Benjamin Gribner. Best I could do. He's cleared to talk to you for five minutes. I gave him your number. He should be calling any minute."

"Boy, five whole minutes, huh? I must be important."

Ralph laughed. "Don't feel bad, Inspector. Five minutes for a guy like this is an eternity. Good luck." I thanked him and disconnected. Twenty seconds later, my cell rang.

"My name is Ben Gribner from Facebook. I heard you had a question for me."

"I do. Thanks for calling back." I introduced myself and started my spiel when he cut me off. "Excuse me for interrupting,

Inspector. I presume you are as busy as I am, so let's forego the 'get to know you' phase. I was told you're investigating a murder that occurred in two thousand and seven."

"That is cor . . ." is as far as I got before he blew right past me. "And your murder victim had her Facebook photos removed from our site a day or two before she was killed, and you're calling Facebook to see if there might have been a connection between the two events. Do I have that right?"

Just then Becky walked in the door, hands full of bags.

"You do," I answered, nodding to Becky as she walked past. "I won't go into the details, but . . ."

"This is a different world we live in today, Inspector," he said, cutting me off for the third time. I felt like reaching through the wires and slapping him upside the head. "Back then, photos could be removed if our internal monitoring system flagged a post, or we received notice from a respected outside source that a particular post bordered on social impropriety, neither of which happened very often."

Must have caught him between breaths because I got to say, "All I want to know is why you took Ms. Garcia's pictures down. Was it a purely administrative decision or prompted by outside interference?"

"Did you know, Inspector, that last quarter Facebook had a net worth of six hundred billion dollars?" He emphasized the word *billion*.

I gave an exaggerated sigh. He took that as my reply and quickly continued, "Don't be impatient, Inspector. That information is relevant to the question you asked. Like I said, we are a much different company now than we were in '07. Back then we were frightened that negative publicity would offend not only our constituency base, but our corporate partners as well."

"Was it outside interference, Mr. Gribner?" I asked again, an impatient edge to my voice. "Or administrative decision? Easy question."

Becky was now back in the room. She kissed the top of my head as she walked by on her way to the kitchen.

By now, Gribner had gone silent. I could almost hear his brain clicking through the possibilities as to whether the information I wanted was proprietary. His brain, thank god, told him it wasn't.

"Outside interference or administrative decision?" he asked. "Seems it might have been a little of both," He paused. I heard his keyboard clicking, then he said, "When I went through our files, it looked like her photographs received some corporate blowback. In cases like that, our internal monitoring system flags the post and removes it from the system. In the incident you are referring to, it was no more than two hours before our internal system cleared the photos. They were back on her page late the next afternoon."

Too late, I thought. *By then Poppy was already dead.*

"I'm reading here," said Gribner, "that two days after the photos were reinstated, Facebook was notified that the account owner had passed away and to please delete the entire account immediately." That bit of information surprised me, so I asked who contacted Facebook to make such a request. "It says here it was a Mrs. Maria Garcia. Claimed she was the account holder's mother," Gribner replied.

"Is it possible you could you tell me the name of the corporate entity who complained that the photographs were homophobic?"

"This is above my paygrade, Inspector," Gribner said, "but it says here the corporate entity was a woman by the name of Brigitte Le Pendu who, at the time, was one of Facebook's advisory board members."

"Brigitte Le Pendu?" *Son-of-a-bitch*, I thought. *Talk about being blindsided.*

"Do you know her?" he asked.

"Yeah, I do. Do you?"

"No. She was before my time and above my paygrade."

"Well, just so you know—in the years we're talking about, she was the girlfriend of your then Board member, Derek Cora. He's the guy who is now being investigated by your child porn operation?"

"Again, above my paygrade, Inspector. I'm just telling you what it says here on my screen."

CHAPTER 45

I disengaged with Gribner, sat back in my chair and reviewed my notes. Poppy's pictures were taken off the site at the request of the Le Pendu woman. I put an asterisk next to that line. The next day the photos were back on Facebook, though Poppy was already dead by then. The day after Poppy's death, her mother called Facebook and requested that both her daughter's account be closed and all her pictures taken down.

"This whole scenario doesn't add up," I murmured to myself. *There are no coincidences in the murder business.* I looked at my watch. Four forty-five. I picked up the phone and called Mexico.

Maria Garcia answered on the second ring. "Hola, Inspector," she said, obviously having caller ID. "Tell me you found my daughter's killer."

"I'm working on it, Mrs. Garcia. I'm working on it."

"I know you are working on it, Inspector. The question I want answered is, are you getting anywhere? And please, call me Maria."

"Thank you . . . Maria." Somehow calling her by her first name didn't seem professional, but since she asked, what the hell. "To answer your question? Yes, I'm getting somewhere."

"Santa Madre de Dios," she whispered. "Please tell me."

"You're aware Poppy experienced some issues with Facebook a few days before her death."

There was silence for a few moments, then a slew of Spanish

assaulted me all the way from Durango. While I don't speak the language, I felt the fury behind the words, and knew if those phrases had escaped from my mouth in Becky's presence, it would've cost me a bundle.

I waited for her to calm herself, then said, "I understand how hard this is for you, Maria. I recently spoke with a representative of the company, and he apologized for their actions in removing your daughter's photos."

"They killed her," was all she said.

I let the thought linger for a few moments so she wouldn't think I doubted her feelings, then remarked, "They told me about her photos. How they took them down but reinstated them a day later."

"Poppy never knew," she replied, a catch in her throat. "She was with God by then."

"I'm interested in her work, Maria. It's one of the reasons I'm calling. I asked a few of her friends if they still had those photos, but, sadly, they didn't."

"That's because they gave them to that horrid policeman."

"You're talking about Inspector Egan?"

"Yes. He tried to take them from me, too. I refused, so he offered to buy them from me. My own daughter's pictures. I told him I didn't have any copies of those photos. Besides, I knew he had taken them from Poppy's friends. He didn't need mine, so I told him Poppy never shared those pictures with me."

"Good for you. I'm glad you told him that." I wondered if I should tell her about the demise of Barry Egan. She'd probably be ecstatic. But then I thought the hell with it. It was of no consequence to what I was after. "Would you mind if I saw those pictures?" I continued. "Poppy's friends told me they've never seen her do better work."

"I will not send you the originals."

"No, of course not. I'm only asking you to email them to me."

"Of course, I will do that, Inspector. Are you at your computer now?"

"I am."

She hung up. Six minutes later Poppy's photos were on my computer, and two minutes after that they had safely been copied to my flash drive. I took a quick peek at them, then called Mrs. Garcia back.

"Thank you for sending the photos. Your daughter had a great deal of talent."

"Thank you, Inspector. Please find the people who did this to her. And to me."

"I promise you I will. One question, if you don't mind." She remained silent, so I continued. "Do you know a woman named Brigitte Le Pendu?"

This time there was such a long silence I was afraid we'd been disconnected. "Why do you ask?" she finally said.

"Just curious. She was on Facebook's Board of Advisors the year your daughter was murdered. I was told by a Facebook executive that Brigitte Le Pendu was the person who requested Poppy's photos be taken down, claiming they were homophobic."

After a long silence she said, "I do not know the woman."

"No problem," I said, wanting to believe her. "I've lived in the city my whole life and this is probably only the third or fourth time I'd ever heard the name Brigitte Le Pendu. At one time, long ago, she was known as a close friend, even the girlfriend, of a man named Derek Cora. Have you heard of him?"

"Never!" was the cryptic answer.

The quickness and force with which she denied knowing Cora surprised me. *Strange answer,* I thought. *Probably wise to sometime take another look at this woman.* But to her I merely said, "I want to thank you for the pictures, and please know I will find the

253

person or persons responsible for murdering your daughter." I heard her quietly sobbing as I hung up.

~~~~~

I immediately called Manny telling him I had a copy of Poppy's *Pride Parade* photos. "You got time to look at them now?"

"Hell, yes, I do. I've got a big screen TV. We'll be able to see a lot more on my set than that two-inch screen you have"

I laughed. "I hear you. Let me see if Becky can drive me to your house."

"Don't be silly, Deck. Becky's not gonna want to stay here through our slide show. I'll come get you."

"Tell you what, Manny. If you can come to get me, I'll have her pick me up after we're finished. I'll bribe her with dinner out with a handsome man and his *luxury* seat cushion." He laughed. "So, if you can come get me, that would work."

"Be there in ten minutes."

When Becky heard my plan to take her out to dinner after my meeting with Manny, she said, "That's a schedule I could get used to."

CHAPTER 46

Manny lived alone in a modest three-bedroom house in the outer Sunset. His wife had passed six years ago, a year before he and I came together as partners. He had two grown sons with families who lived on the East Coast. He was looking forward to retirement so he could move east to be close to them

He ushered me into his living room where he had a computer hooked up to his seventy-five-inch flat screen television.

"I added some extra cushions on the couch in case you forgot yours," he said with a smile. "Glad you didn't."

"I never leave home without Sherm's cushion," I said, placing it on his couch.

He laughed. "So, make yourself comfortable while I open a couple of beers." A few minutes later Manny placed two schooners on the table in front of us. "Hope you don't mind IPA?" he asked, knowing there wasn't a chance in hell I was going to turn it down.

"If that's all you got, I guess I'm stuck with it," I joked.

"Figured as much," he replied as he sat next to me on the couch. "Before we settle in, mind telling me again what we're looking for? Anything in particular, or is it just morbid curiosity?"

"Good question," I replied. "After my conversation with Mrs. Garcia today, I asked myself the very same question. I ended up taking a few minutes to give the photos a look-see. I've got to tell you my first reaction to them was why the hell did Facebook ever get involved. Nothing there I could see that warranted such an action. Forced me to start thinking in a different direction." I took another swallow, burped and then continued. "But before I tell you what I thought, I want to hear your take on these pictures. If you see anything that merits the fuss they caused, please tell me."

"Then let's get to it." Manny said. He pushed a few keys on the computer, and the giant Sony screen came to life. "With your Pride Parade history, Deck, you'll probably recognize almost everyone in the pictures."

I laughed. "I wouldn't be surprised. When you're as cool as I am, you get invited to a lot of decadent parties."

I'd been part of the SFPD's presence at every Pride Parade since '09. I had to admit they were fun, rivaled only, in my view, by the Giant's parade down Market Street celebrating their 2014 World Series victory over the Kansas City Royals.

While not everyone in San Francisco appreciated the Pride Parade's good-natured bawdiness, I always looked forward to its sophisticated earthiness. And to think I got paid double time for the privilege of hanging out with all these fun people was just icing on the cake.

Right before Manny picked me up, I called the help desk at City Hall to get the official estimate for how many people attended the '07 Pride Parade. Back then, they'd come up with an estimate of three quarters of a million people. When I told Manny that number, he was surprised. "I was there, Deck. Didn't look like that many people to me. Not even close."

"Well, they could be as mistaken as the rest of us who lived through those years."

Poppy's pictures were mostly a mish-mash of various street scenes cataloguing outrageously dressed people having a hell of a time. From the background in each photograph, I could identify exactly where she had been standing when she snapped the shot.

After Manny and I had carefully viewed each photo, he went back to the beginning and slowly clicked through each frame again.

"Be sure to give a shout if anything jumps out at you," I said. "Except for the Parade's performers and wannabe performers, tell me if you see anything out of the ordinary. Anything that would make you say 'Whoa, who or what was that?'"

After we finished our slow walk through the slides, Manny took a sip of beer, wiped the foam from his mouth and said, "Except for some of the participants and their crazy antics, there's nothing here that would have gotten anyone's pants, or in this case panties, in a twist."

"I'm thinkin' the same thing," I replied. "So, what are we missing, if anything?"

"That woman on the Facebook Advisory Board certainly thought she saw something objectionable on these photos. So, what's her story? Who the hell was she, or is she, anyway?"

"Her name was, and is, Brigitte Le Pendu. If you'd hung around the right circles back then, you'd know who she was."

"I never made a habit of hanging' around people like that," he replied with a snort. "Bad for your reputation. At least with the guys I hung with."

I smiled and then said, "Just found out a week or so back that an old friend not only works for her but is also dating her."

"Don't tell me your friend Sherman?"

"Yeah. She's not only his girlfriend, but his boss."

"Ouch."

"Yeah! Tell me about it." I paused, then said, "In any case, I did a quick Google search of her this morning. There was lots of stuff on her. She was born and raised in France. Her father, before his death the early part of this century, was owner/operator of a one of the wealthiest European hedge funds in existence. It looks like our girl Brigitte wanted for nothing. They sent her to the finest European boarding schools. She's hung around with the rich and famous most of her life.

"By the time she was twenty-two, her father had taught her all the ins-and-outs of the hedge fund business. In the late '80's, he sent her to the States to manage his office in New York. Because of who she was, or more precisely, who her father was, she was immediately accepted into the upper echelons of American wealth. She'd been here only four months when she became the live-in girlfriend of guess who?" I paused for maximum effect.

"Sorry, not familiar with the rich and famous in this country," Morales said.

"The live-in girlfriend of our friend, Derek Cora. Though she's been the ex-girlfriend of Cora for over a decade now."

Morales looked over at me and then back at the darkened television screen. "Come on, Deck. You don't think Cora's involved in this, do you? That poor dude is in enough trouble with the photographs he took of those underage girls at his parties."

"You're right, and I'm not for certain he's involved in the 2007 Facebook thing, either. His then-squeeze Brigitte sure was, so why not him?" I took a last big swig of beer and said, "So, let's speculate that one of Poppy's photographs captured the famous Ms. Brigitte Le Pendu in a compromising position." Morales laughed. "And let's say her people in France would not be at all proud of her, the daughter of the founder of the company, being seen on Facebook cavorting around in a Gay Rights Parade."

"Want another one?" Manny asked, pointing to my empty schooner. I nodded. "I can see where you are going with this, Deck," he said, walking into the kitchen with both glasses, "but that looks to me like a dead end. I mean, we didn't see her in any of the photographs, did we?"

I waited until he came back from the kitchen and handed me a beer before I said, "No, you're right, Manny. But somebody went to a lot of trouble to make sure none of those photos saw the light of day. Remember, Egan went around and personally collected all the flash drives containing Garcia's photos."

"Yeah, I know." He sounded pouty, like "you've got me again."

"And it's even a possibility," I continued, "that it's not Brigitte that's at issue here, but Derek Cora."

"I'm thinking you're right, Deck. It's becoming clear to me that I may have missed something. Let's run through all the photos again. See if anything jumps out at us."

I agreed, so Manny went back to the slides. The first photo up showed a guy walking down Market Street wearing angel wings and a Speedo. Behind Mr. Angel Wings & Speedo was the Palace Hotel, one of the most iconic luxury hotels in the world. In my mind's eye, I could see Poppy standing on the corner of Montgomery and Market Streets looking south when this photo was snapped.

"You see anything here, or should we go to the next shot?" Manny asked.

"Wait," I said, leaning closer to his television screen.

"Camera's pretty tightly focused on Mr. Speedo, Deck. Only parts of other people can be seen. No faces."

"I'm aware of that, but we've got to look at everything." I pointed to the background. "Like the Palace Hotel behind Mr. Speedo, for example. Can you zoom in on just the hotel? Lots of windows. Hell, could be someone in one of those rooms that didn't want anyone to know he, or she, was there."

"Long shot," he snorted, "but here goes." Manny clicked the mouse, dragged the hotel to mid-screen and enlarged the photo. There was too much glare from the street and sky on the windows to determine one way or another if there were people in any of the rooms.

"Okay," I said. "Nothing clear enough to see, so let's push on."

He clicked to the next picture. This one showed two women standing on the base of the Mechanics Monument kissing. Since you could see the One Bush Street building behind the two women, Poppy had to have been standing on the north side of Market at the intersection of Market, Bush and Battery streets.

"Zoom in on the Bush building, okay?" I asked.

"Got it!" He twisted the projectors lens. "This one is definitely at a better angle for us voyeurs, that's for sure." he said with a laugh. "And this is an office building probably constructed what, maybe seventy-five years after the Palace Hotel? The windows are huge in comparison. They're like big mirrors."

He was right. Mostly what you saw in their "big mirrors" was the reflection of the buildings on the opposite side of Market Street. Manny slowly dragged the photo up and down, side-to-side. In two or three of the windows, we could see standing lamps, but nothing else. If there were people in those rooms, they were invisible.

The next photo showed a large of group of people carrying rainbow flags marching down Market Street towards Poppy's camera.

"This, by the way, was the picture that got Poppy in all the trouble," Manny said, "The one that caused Facebook to pull her content,"

"Interesting. Can you zoom in on the people in the photo?" He did a slow scan of all the faces in the crowd. "You recognize anyone? I sure don't."

"Me neither," replied Manny.

"Then, what the . . ." I stopped in time, thinking of Becky.

"You can say anything you want around me," Manny said with a chuckle. "I won't fine you."

I shook my head and smiled. "Amazing. Who would've thought she could affect my word choices like this? Hope you don't mind me saying something like "it surprises the poo-poo out of me." We both laughed.

"I think it's cool you even care. Shows how much you respect her. If Maureen had tried this on me, I would have divorced her long before she died."

"Nah. You would've never divorced her. I can tell just the way you talk about her." I quaffed down another slug of beer, then said, "Anyway, back to the rainbow flag photo. Can you tell me what the hell's wrong with the picture? As far as I can see, it's nothing more than a group of people marching down Market Street with those damn flags. You'd have thought if someone went to the trouble of suppressing this photo, it would have at least contained a picture of someone recognizable."

"Agreed, but apparently the push-back wasn't the picture itself, but the caption *What's Wrong with This Picture?* And the push-back was strong enough to get all of her photos taken down. Connie told me Poppy captioned each picture she sent to Facebook. Most bordered on cutesy, you know, like 'Sisters Having Fun', which was her caption under the shot of the two women kissing or 'Nice Butt' which was under Mr. Speedo's."

"And they took down all of her pictures," I said, "because she had captioned one with *What's Wrong with This Picture?*"

"At least they admitted their error. Thirteen years and a murder too late, but at least it was something." He pushed the arrow for the next photo. "Only six pictures left."

CHAPTER 47

The Flatiron Building was a three-sided, ten stories structure, built sometime before the end of the first World War. Poppy had taken three different photos of the Pride Parade which featured the Flatiron Building as a backdrop. One photo had two guys in tuxedos riding in the back of a pickup, holding hands and carrying a sign saying, "Just Married." Because Poppy had taken the photo standing directly across Market from the Flatiron Building, virtually all the windows looking out on the Parade route were visible, and none cast a glare.

When Manny zoomed in on the windows and went slowly one to another, we could see people in some of the rooms. In the first of her photos, there was a room on the second floor where we could make out three distinct people. In the second photo, there was of a room on the fifth floor that had four people in the room. Unfortunately, because of Manny's off-the-shelf software, we couldn't clearly see, nor define, any of the facial features.

In that four-person room, a small banner strung across the window proudly stated McGinnis Realty would be happy to rent this room and listed an 800 number to call. *Calling is exactly what I have in mind, Mr. McGinnis,* I thought, as I jotted down his number. *You'll be hearing from me as soon as I get back home.*

The third photo was from the Sutter Street side of the Flatiron Building. It showed five guys in feather boas, leather pants and high heels vamping in front of what looked like a vintage

Seventies muscle car. One guy even stood on the car's hood. Poppy's photo caught all of the Flatiron's upper windows, minus the ones that were obliterated by the guy standing on the hood.

In one of the windows on the sixth floor, you could make out two people facing one another, one person's arm outstretched, looking as if it was poking the other image in the chest. Strung across the window, obscuring the two guys from the waist down, was another "McGinnis Realty—For Rent" sign.

"Tell you what, Manny," I said. "Old man McGinnis must have made some good coin renting out his excess inventory for the Parade. Come tomorrow morning I'm gonna have to talk to that guy about his renters. Get some names."

Manny and I went through the remaining photos and didn't find any more faces. "Okay," I said. "Getting late. Got to call Becky."

"It was a worthwhile night," Manny said, more a question than a statement.

"Absolutely," I said. "At least we've got something for Kincaid to analyze." I looked at my watch. "In fact, I think I'll give him a quick call"

"So late?" Manny said, already starting to disconnect his equipment. "You think he's still at the office?"

"The guy never sleeps," I replied, punching his number into my cell. He answered on the third ring. I gave Manny the thumbs-up. "Hey, Walt. It's me."

"I was afraid of that."

"Ha-ha! You're a funny guy. Hey, I need another favor. The case I'm working has a new wrinkle." I paused. "You know Derek Cora, right?"

"What, you think I've been living under a rock for the past two or three decades? Of course, I know who he is."

"His girlfriend, well, actually a former girlfriend, a woman named Brigitte Le Pendu, was on Facebook's Advisory Board in 2007. That was the year Poppy Garcia was murdered. The Le Pendu woman was the one who put the pressure on Facebook's Board to take those photos down."

"Okay, so they were taken down. In one of our conversations recently, you told me Facebook restored the pictures next day. So, problem solved. What's the big deal?"

"She posted sixteen pictures, Walt. Only one photo was deemed offensive, but they still removed all sixteen. For the sake of argument, let's agree Ms. Le Pendu was offended by one of the photographs. That's what she told Facebook, anyway. I'd like to know why all of them were removed, not just the offending one?" I paused. "It just doesn't feel right, Walt. Both Manny and I are thinking the same way. Could be it's not this particular photo she was worried about, but another photo in Poppy's set of sixteen. One that could be incriminating. Maybe showing something the complainant didn't want anybody to see."

"By complainant you mean Ms. Le Pendu?" Kincaid asked. "Talk about a stretch."

"I'm not at all saying she was the sole complainant. In fact, this could have been all Cora's schtick. He could have just used her name, for all I know. Remember, this is part of a murder investigation, Walt. I've got a young woman murdered two days after her photos sparked the girlfriend of one of the wealthiest men in the country to force Facebook to take down her photos. By the time Facebook reposted them, that young woman was lying dead in her own house, the front of her head blown off. And you want to hear something else?"

"Not particularly, but I know that won't stop you."

"The day after Facebook reposted her pictures, the girl's mother called all the way from Mexico to ask Facebook to take down her daughter's site. Too coincidental, Walt, if you ask me.

You know as well as I do there are no coincidences in the murder business."

"Okay," he said resignedly. "Send me the pictures. Can't promise anything, but I'll take a look."

CHAPTER 48

The next morning, I retrieved the notes I'd made at Manny's, found the McGinnis Realty phone number and dialed.

"Deacon Financial," a pleasant female voice said.

I hesitated, looked at the number I'd written down, and apologized. "Sorry, I must have copied this number down wrong. I'm looking for a McGinnis Realty."

"Oh, my," she said. "Where'd you get their number?"

"From a banner on Market Street."

"That must've been a really old banner," she said. "The Realty hasn't been in operation since Mr. McGinnis passed. Close to thirteen years ago."

My antenna went up "Thirteen years ago?" I repeated.

"Yes. It was such a tragedy. My boss knew Mr. McGinnis well. Told me he had this Realty business for over thirty years, and it had proved to be very successful. Then he died in a traffic accident. A hit and run."

"Killed in a hit and run?" My antenna was waving in the atmosphere. "When did this happen Miss . . . I'm sorry, what's your name?"

"Shirley Monson," she replied. "And it's Mrs. And you are?"

"My name is Reggie Decker. I'm a homicide inspector at San Francisco PD. Can you tell me when this hit and run occurred?"

"Let me see. I might have it here on my computer. Hold on, let me search. It won't take but a minute." While waiting for

Monson, I flipped on my computer. If she could give me a date, I'd be able to pull up the case-file. She came back a few moments later. "July 2, 2007," she said. I punched the date into the computer. "It's right here on my calendar. Mr. McGinnis was crossing . . ."

"Can you hold for a moment, Mrs. Monson? I'm looking at the official police report as we speak. I'll just be a minute."

"Of course," she replied.

I went to the summary page. It said Ian McGinnis, age 67, crossed the intersection at Golden Gate and Jones Streets at 11:15 p.m. on Sunday, July 2, 2007, and was struck by a vehicle traveling southbound on Jones. From the distance the body traveled after impact, they calculated the vehicle to be traveling in excess of eighty miles per hour. The medical examiner's report said the victim was killed on impact. Two witnesses came forward. Both agreed the driver to be a male Caucasian in the forty to fifty-five age range. They described the vehicle as a Ford sedan, but neither knew the model. It turned out to be a stolen 2005 Ford Crown Victoria found the next day abandoned in the 100 block of McAllister Street. Police found no usable prints.

I keyed to the end of the case file. No arrests were made and the case officially closed on February 20, 2010.

"Okay, Mrs. Monson. I'm done reading. I appreciate your telling me about it. I'll let you go so you can get back to work."

"Wait. Did they ever catch the person who hit him?"

"No, I'm afraid not, and the case was shut down long ago."

"What about the fire? They arrest anyone for that?"

"The fire?" Another grenade lobbed into my lap. I sat back in my chair. "What fire?"

"The one that burned his office building almost to the ground. Happened only a few days after Mr. McGinnis was killed. Arson. At least, that's what the fire department told us."

"How and why were you folks involved in any of this?"

"As I told you, the man who owns Deacon Financial, my boss, was a friend of Mr. McGinnis. He'd already had a deal in place to buy this building at the time of Mr. McGinnis' demise. The arson investigators, of course, saw him as a prime suspect. Burn the building down and graciously offer to buy the ruins for a pittance of the agreed upon price. But my boss isn't like that. He paid Mr. McGinnis' widow full price for the building and then spent another million or so to make it habitable. He bought the property in January of two thousand and nine. We didn't open until November of that year. Gives you an idea about how much work needed to be done. The good news is our eleventh anniversary is coming up in a few months."

The mention of time passing caused me to reflexively check my watch. Dammit. Time was spinning by. "Mrs. Monson," I said, "I'm sorry, but I have to get going. I want to thank you for helping me get my head around the case I'm currently working on. If I find anything new, I'll contact you. I hope we'll at least find the arsonist."

"I hope so, Inspector. Good luck to you."

I called Ed Troop, a cop I knew in the Special Investigative Division. The SID was the brainchild of the chief who took over for Nowak. Even though we didn't completely see eye-to-eye on how the Department should be structured, or restructured, in this case, I gave him credit for forming the SID Unit. He set it up so the Division had jurisdiction on crimes that overlapped. Like this crime, for example. A hit and run victim whose property got torched. As the Chief set it up, the SID featured a police officer assigned to the Fire Department's arson unit. As it happened, Troop was the officer assigned so remembered the case well.

"We combed through the ruins for a week," he told me. "Not much of the interior of the structure was salvageable. If the

269

arsonist's objective was to destroy any paper trail that showed he, or they, might have been involved in that felony hit and run, he, or they, were successful." *Or*, I thought, *any paper trail that he, or they, rented office space from McGinnis during the Pride Parade that year.*

"An accelerant was used. Propane to be exact. No need to go into the chemistry of it all. Suffice it to say it was a hot-ass fire. Melted most of the metal file drawers, even the supposedly fireproof ones." He paused, then said, "You may want to talk to another of our SID people—Sarah Howard. She handled McGinnis' hit and run case. If there was a connection between the two cases, and both Howard and I were on the same page, the perp, or perps, hid it well. They knew what they were doing."

CHAPTER 49

The adrenaline squirt coursing through my veins from talking to Troop prompted me to make another call.

"Well, I'll be damned," Bristow shouted in my ear. "The Phoenix has risen from the ashes. How the hell you feelin'?"

"Doing okay, Matt." I said. "Well, to be truthful, sitting at home doing' nothing is freaking me out. I was thinking I'd come by the Hall this afternoon. Say hi to everyone. That be okay with you?"

"Well, hell yeah, Deck. Everybody would be delighted to see you. What time you thinkin'?"

"Around two. That work?"

"Absolutely. I'll put out the word right away so the guys won't scatter after going to lunch. Does Manny know you're coming in?"

"Nah. Just thought about this a few minutes ago."

"I'll tell him. You want him to come get you?"

"Too much of a hassle. I'll cab it in."

"Okay, but I'll let him know."

Manny was waiting by the door as my cane and I limped into the Hall's foyer a little before two. We took the elevator up to the fifth floor. The room was packed with officers and staff from every department. One of the perks of having been around awhile is more people come to your funeral or, better yet, to a "glad it was you, not me, who caught the bullet" party. There was a good amount of applause, and then Bristow handed me a Diet Pepsi and escorted me to a chair placed in the center of the room. Somebody had already put a rubber donut on the seat. It wasn't as good as Sherm's, but, hey, any port in a storm. As I sat there on my *throne*, each person came over, shook my hand and gave me a congratulatory pat on the back. The last person in line was Manny Morales.

He shook my hand, leaned forward and whispered, "You and Becky get to dinner last night?"

"You bet. A nice one as it turned out. Why are you whispering?"

"Just don't want the guys to know we're still working the Garcia case."

"Good thinking. Can you get some time this afternoon to come over the house?"

"Sure. Why don't I drive you home?"

"Perfect."

At that moment, Bristow came up and stood beside me. "Hey, everyone, listen up," he shouted. "I've got an announcement." He made a big deal of unrolling a scroll he held in his hand. I peeked. It was blank. "The Mayor's office called and told me the Police Commission voted to award homicide inspector Reginald Decker, here seated on his donut throne before you . . ." the room exploded in cheers "the SFPD's Bronze Medal for Valor in the Line of Duty."

My colleagues whooped it up and applauded. "Damn," I shouted. "There goes my reputation."

"This is a huge honor, Deck," declared Bristow, making an even bigger issue of it by turning and clapping me on the back. "They're scheduling the ceremony for this Friday at two-thirty in the City Hall rotunda."

"You sure they're not awarding me the medal as a gentle reminder that in my shape I should start thinking about doing

THE RHYTHM OF EVIL

something else for a living?" Everybody laughed. "See?" I said loudly, pointing to Bristow. "He didn't say no. You're all witnesses. I'm leaving a complaint in HR on my way out." I took a quick glance at Morales. He smiled and gave me a thumbs up.

"Come on, Reg," Bristow broke in. "You're a rock star now. Better get used to being the center of attention at a big-time media event."

"God in heaven, save me," I groaned. More laughter.

"Just show up Decker, smile like you were the happiest dude in the world, and receive your Bronze Medal. They'll want you to give a short *thank you*, of course, and take questions. That sort of thing."

"Do we have to come?" I heard someone cry out from the back of the room. "Please say 'no.'"

"Yes, you have to come," Bristow replied. "Not only that, but no taking the rest of the day off, either. Now, let's get back to work."

Just then, someone yelled, "Speech! Speech!" Soon everyone was chanting it. Bristow called for quiet, then turned to me and said, "If you're feeling up to it, you're on."

Good thing there was a round of applause as it gave me a few seconds to figure out what the hell I was going to say. Not much, as it turned out.

"As I stand here looking out on all my friends," I began, "I can't help but feeling you're all nothing more than a big pain in the ass." I let that sink in for a millisecond and then said, "Oh, wait! It's not you. It's this damn bullet that's still lodged in here." I stood, turned around, stuck my butt out and pointed to the spot. That drew laughter and applause. *Good schtick to give me cover for not continuing*, I thought. "Sorry, I have to sit down now if you don't mind. Know, however, I appreciate you all for being here today."

Bristow came over and helped Manny walk me back to my desk. "How you feeling, Deck? For real." he asked, as I put the rubber donut on my chair and gingerly sat down. "Well, if you must know," I leaned over conspiratorially and said, "being shot has been a real pain in the ass."

He smiled. "I can only imagine. Hey, I'm really happy you and Manny have made a *go* as partners."

"Me, too. He's been a real help. In every way. He's still here, right?"

He peeked behind me, gave a wry smile, and, in a conspiratorial whisper, said, "No. I think he left. Probably out in the hall calling Nowak trying to get Egan's old job."

"Good one," I said. "Though if I were him, I'd be trying to get away from me, too." We both had a good chuckle at that.

Bristow left shortly afterward. Manny walked over and said, "Walt Kincaid called about ten minutes ago while you were yucking it up with Matt. Said to tell you he was sorry he couldn't make your party this afternoon and wanted you to know he received the results from HQ on your facial recognition request. Asked if you could come by his office tomorrow morning at nine and look at them."

"Well, hell yeah," I said, pulling out my cell and punching in Kincaid's number. "Get yourself free so you can come, too."

CHAPTER 50

Morales told me he couldn't get the day off, so at seven-thirty the next morning, a cab dropped me off in the underground garage of San Francisco's Federal Building.

Cane in hand, I rode the elevator to the thirteenth floor. Walt was waiting for me when the door opened.

"You look like something the cat dragged in," he said as he shook my hand.

"You're such a smooth talker, Walt. No wonder they made you the Special Agent in Charge."

He smiled. "Read about you in the paper. Being such a big celebrity and all, guess I'm gonna have to start asking for your autograph. How're you feeling, by the way?"

"I'm okay. I'll be off the cane in a week or two. I'm really looking forward to that day. Having to walk with this damn thing makes me feel I'm about eighty. And having this bullet in my ass is no fun either."

"I feel for you, man. But you've always been a healthy bastard, so you'll be like new soon enough." He turned a corner, leading me into a medium sized conference room and introduced Agent Andy Metzer. "He's our tech wizard. Going to show you what we got from the pictures you sent."

I shook Metzer's hand and delicately eased myself into the chair beside him. "At the request of Special Agent Kincaid, I transmitted two of the seven photos you gave him to our Facial

Recognition Photo Group in DC. We sent those particular photographs because they captured images of people in the buildings behind where Poppy Garcia was focusing her lens." He put both photos side-by-side on the computer screen.

"Only two, huh? Damn," I said.

"That's a matter of perspective, Inspector. Like I told you, the two photos I sent to DC were the only ones that showed people in a particular office in a particular building. In this case, the Flatiron Building. The first image here," he tapped the screen gently, "is one we, in a fit of genius, named *Photo One*." He was the only person in the room who laughed. He shrugged, and then continued. "You'll notice it shows three people in the frame while Photo Two here," he again tapped the screen, "shows four people."

He let me quickly study both images before he enlarged Photo One. "The Lab was fortunate here," he said. "It doesn't happen often where a photo is of such quality the Lab actually achieved 'recognition certainty' on all three of the people featured in the photograph. They weren't so fortunate, however, with Photo Two.*"* He paused, made a few changes in the screen orientation and then continued. "Of the four people in that photograph," he minimized Photo One so I could see Photo Two again, "three were the same people identified in Photo One." He pointed them out. "The fourth person in the room was in dark shadows, the worst possible config for our software. We can tell from various body characteristics the shadow was a man. HQ promised they'd get their best guys on it. Maybe they'll get lucky by the end of the day. It could take them as long as Monday. It's possible, however, that we'll never get a match. Just have to keep your fingers crossed."

"Let's be clear about our procedure," Kincaid interrupted. "The Bureau measures facial characteristics like the size and shape of eyes, cheekbones, lips . . . things like that, and compares those measurements to the millions of faces we have in the data-base. For our purposes, a 65 percent match counts as measurable equality."

"The pictures came back yesterday morning," Metzer continued, clicking an icon on his computer. It caused the large screen on the back wall to come to life.

"Was this one of hers that got taken off Facebook?"

"Correct. Care to guess who this might be?" He tapped his computer, and the wall screen turned into a dark blob with a few specks of light scattered here and there.

After a looking at the blob for a few moments, I smiled and said, "Nope, I give up."

Metzer, with a sly grin, said, "Watch the magic." He moved his cursor to the blob's lighter specs and clicked. The screen went black, then came back to life with the blob now featuring a pair of gray-hazel eyes covered with medium bushy eyebrows. Something was vaguely familiar with the face, but I couldn't place it. Then Metzer did the same thing with another of the lighter specs. The screen went black again, and when the photo returned, the dark blob with gray-hazel eyes and bushy eyebrows now had a definitive mouth. Metzer worked his magic once more, bringing this time a cheekbone structure to the face. Before his cursor could hit one of the few remaining light specs, the screen flashed "You Have a Match", and the "blob" was replaced by a facial photo of Barry Egan. Under his picture read: "There is a 69.4 percent likelihood that the man in your original photograph is Barry Egan."

Kincaid slapped me on the back. "I know you're thinking 69.4 percent leaves a lot of wiggle-room as to who the faceless man in the photograph might be. Let me tell you my friend, in our world, 69.4 percent is the same as 100 percent. I'll flat out guarantee Egan is your guy." He paused and then said, "But I'll also guarantee the next picture won't be so easy."

Metzer turned to me and said, "Remember I showed you that first photo with three men?" I nodded. "You've seen the first perp. What I'm going to show you now is the second man in that photograph. Then I'll show you who the computer says that man is."

"All the photographic images came back to us yesterday morning," interjected Kincaid. "The one you just saw was pretty straightforward."

"Yeah, right," I said.

"No, seriously. It didn't need any special handling from our office. However, the other two images that came back weren't of good enough quality for our computers to recognize. I sent both back to DC yesterday afternoon requesting they be run again, but this time on their highest intensity setting. Got them back today at 4:40 a.m."

"Both Special Agent Kincaid and myself had a chance to view them about an hour ago. The photo I'll put on the screen now is the second person in Ms. Garcia's photograph."

"Wait until you see these two dudes," Kincaid said. "You'll be utterly blown away."

Metzer went through his "magic" show once more. In the same way I couldn't make out Egan in the original photo, I couldn't figure out who the second man was until his photograph flashed on the screen with the tag that said there was a 72.1 percent likelihood that the man was Derek Cora.

"Unbelievable," I said. "You're sure that's Cora?"

"If our program says it's him, it's him."

"That's music to my ears, Walt. We got his butt."

"Think you might be jumping the gun a wee bit too quickly, Deck. What exactly do we *got his butt* for? Showing up in a photo taken at the Pride Parade? No crime in that. But," he chuckled, "we do have something here that's gonna warm the cockles of your heart." He turned to Metzer and nodded.

A red square box controlled by Metzer's computer software appeared on the screen framing what the FBI's computer in DC identified as a possible face. Again, hard as hell for me to make out anything definitive as the area was virtually shrouded in darkness. Without the Agency's enhanced recognition software, there would be no way to ID the third person in that room.

"This won't take too long," said Metzer. "The computer is intensifying the facial areas and going through hundreds of thousands of contrast levels to optimally lighten the photograph. Once it internally gets all those levels adjusted to the expectations of the software, then the program will start working on the person's most conspicuous facial features." He leaned back in his chair.

"When we first asked the computer to come up with a match," Kincaid said, "it took thirty-two minutes to chew through its own algorithms. Lucky for you, the computer has a memory bank."

No sooner had he said that than a photograph of a chubby faced fellow with a heavy mustache flashed on the screen with the tag that said there was an 84.1 percent likelihood that the person in the photograph was Ismael "El Mayito Gordo" Zambada. I looked over at Kincaid and shrugged my shoulders in a who-the-hell-is-he gesture.

"That, my friend," he said, "is the second-in-command of the Sinaloa Drug Cartel. A very bad hombre."

CHAPTER 51

There haven't been very many times in my life when I've been speechless, but this was one of them. I leaned back in the chair as far as that damn bullet in my butt allowed and cupped my hands behind my head.

"Yeah, I know exactly how you feel," Kincaid said, replying to my body language.

"So, what do we have here?" I asked haltingly, trying to piece it all together as I spoke. "Let's see, we have a now deceased San Francisco homicide inspector along with arguably the wealthiest and most politically connected man in the State of California, maybe in the nation for all we know, taking a private meeting with the second in command of one of the most notorious drug cartels on the planet." I paused and looked at Kincaid. "What the hell, Walt!"

"You know what first crossed my mind when I saw Cora in that picture?" Kincaid asked. He didn't wait for my reply. "I thought here is one connected son-of-a-bitch, and if we're going to tangle with him, we better have all our ducks in a row."

"If he had something to do with Poppy's murder, I'd gladly tangle with him, row of ducks or not." Pointing to Metzer's screen, I asked, "What the hell are we going to do with this?"

"Not sure *we're* going to do anything with it," Kincaid replied. "Right now, this is a thirteen-year-old murder case, a cold-case at that, committed in the City and County of San Francisco.

The FBI is involved only because I'm a friend of yours and you asked me for help. There is nothing here that directly involves the Agency."

"Come on, Walt. These photographs got a young woman murdered. Why? Well, one plausible explanation could be she captured the facial image of a wealthy, well-known San Francisco businessman in a meeting with the second ranking member of the Sinaloa drug cartel. If that's not FBI territory, I don't know what is."

Before Kincaid could reply, Metzer interrupted. "Don't mean to hurry you guys up, Boss, but we've got a group of agents waiting to use the room."

I turned to Walt. "Before we get kicked out," I said, "can I show you something else in those photos that you need to see and understand?"

"Go for it," he replied.

I politely asked Metzer to pull up Photo Two again, the one where we couldn't identify the fourth person in the room. Metzer looked to Kincaid, who nodded and said, "Give us another five minutes, Andy, and I promise we'll be out of your hair."

When Metzer brought up the photo, I pointed to the McGinnis Realty banner strung across the bottom of the window and painted what I considered to be a graphic link connecting Poppy's pictures to her murder *and* the hit and run murder of Mr. McGinnis *and* the subsequent torching of his office complex.

"There are no coincidences in the murder business, right?" I said to Walt, as he helped me hobble back to his office twenty-five minutes later.

"Okay, okay, already," he said with a laugh. Opening the door to his office, he settled me in a chair. "I've been wondering what would've prompted Cora to hire a guy like Egan in the first place. The Derek Cora's of this world don't need lightweights like

Egan."

"I had the same thought, Walt. Made me remember something Egan told me in that farmhouse right before he pulled the trigger. He started bragging how he'd been recruited by some big shots in Mexico. They needed his expertise and connections to help improve their 'business interests' in California."

Kincaid laughed. "Gee, wonder what those 'business interests' could have been. You thinking maybe the Sinaloa Cartel convinced Cora the pictures Poppy Garcia posted on Facebook presented a clear and present danger to those business interests?"

"That's exactly what I'm thinking, Walt. It's why I'm asking you to help me put Cora's ass in jail forever. Could you guys bring charges against him for having ties to the cartels? Then see what your investigation shakes out?"

"Well, Deck, it wouldn't be easy. But hell, we are the FBI after all, and we can manufacture a lot of ways to become involved." He laughed. "But for you, it's nothing more than an out-and-out murder case. That's your baby."

"Yeah, I know, but unfortunately Bristow has already shut our case down. To him, it was a cold-case murder that has been solved. Egan was the perp! Perp now dead! Case closed!"

"Yeah, that's a pisser," Kincaid said. "But you and I both know that in our world, lots of bad guys walk free. At least they got Cora. He didn't walk free. Serving time right this very minute on an underage sex crime charge."

"Come on, Walt. What, thirteen months? He was convicted for molesting a fourteen-year-old girl, for god's sake. And somehow the SOB gets the case reduced to a state-level offense where he pleads guilty and ends up with only a thirteen-month sentence. And does he do hard time? Hell, no. He's serving his time right this very minute under 'house arrest' in his eight million-dollar Pacific Heights mansion. It's what happens when you've got friends in high places."

"I'm not condoning any of that," Kincaid said. "But it happens, and there just ain't nothing you or I can do about it."

"I know," I replied. "I'm just pissed off is all." I readjusted the donut under me, and said, "But there is a 'good news-bad news' scenario in all this. The bad news is Bristow closed our murder case. The good news is I'm on paid disability for another week. I'm going to spend that week finding out who the fourth son-of-a-bitch in that room was." I looked Kincaid in the eye and said, "And for that, I'm gonna need your help."

"Can't guarantee I could be a big help, but I'll do what I can. What about your friend who worked for Cora? He was around that operation in those years, wasn't he? Why not ask him?"

"Well, he's a friend, yeah, but not what you'd call a good friend. At least not yet. Just a guy I was in the service with years ago. But I was thinking the same thing, Walt. I'm going to give him a call as soon as I get home."

CHAPTER 52

W alt excused himself, saying he had a meeting to attend. He told me, however, to use his office for as long as I wanted. First thing I did was call Morales and asked if he'd be free this afternoon. He told me Bristow called his own meeting and the entire office staff was ordered to be present. I asked if he had the time to make a call and set up a meeting on my behalf.

Thanks to him, twenty minutes later I was in a cab on my way to see Connie Fiorentino, Poppy's friend whom Morales interviewed a few days before.

When I arrived at her office, she asked if I minded going somewhere that was far enough away so snoopy people wouldn't be within earshot. We ended up at a little hole-in-the-wall eatery six blocks from her office. When we got there, I made a big deal about where to put my cane, finally asking the waitress to take it somewhere for safe keeping. Connie noticed.

"Sorry I had to make you walk so far, Inspector."

I smiled inwardly. Sympathy was a great analgesic. "No problem," I lied. "Glad you had the time to speak with me. I know you had a good conversation with Inspector Morales a few days ago. He told me you've been instrumental in keeping Poppy's memory alive through all these years. We are this close," I held my thumb and index finger an eighth of an inch apart, "to wrapping up this investigation. I'm aware Inspector Morales informed you we know who murdered Ms. Garcia. We're not yet clear on whether there were other persons involved in her death."

"Do you think there might have been, Inspector? Like a gang or something?"

"There's always that possibility, of course," I replied. "My interest as of this moment is that while you girls were still in high school, you attended some, shall I say, rather promiscuous adult parties. Is that a fair way to describe what you told Inspector Morales?"

"That was a long time ago, Inspector."

"I understand that, Connie. Please don't think I'm judging you. We all did things in our youth that we're not real proud of." I smiled and shrugged my shoulders. "I was no saint growing up, Connie. It's why, as an adult looking back, I dismiss those missteps as 'youthful indiscretions.' You know what I mean."

"Believe me, I do," Connie said, shaking her head, "I'm surprised we're all still alive to talk about it."

"Unfortunately, not all of us are still alive," I said. "For example, Poppy."

"Oh my god! You're not telling me that those parties we went to had something to do with Poppy's death, are you? How could that be? We're talking about the mid-nineties here. Ten years or so before Poppy was murdered."

"Let me be clear. I don't know one way or the other whether those 'promiscuous' parties you went to had anything to do with her death. However, they'll be one of the things I'll be looking at very carefully." I paused and glanced at my watch. "What say we order lunch?"

While we waited, I asked Connie to tell me about the parties.

"Well, first of all, we didn't go to many. I think Poppy and I attended maybe five or six, max, before our parents found out and put a quick end to them. Secondly, from our perspective, the parties were just a bunch of old people. I mean, we were barely fifteen. The majority of the people at those parties were in their late thirties or early forties. Our parents' ages, for god's sake."

I smiled. "Were the people at the parties mostly couples or singles? And give me a sense of the wider age range, especially the ones older than your parents."

"The wider age range would have been from maybe the late thirties to people in their sixties. Maybe even seventies. When you were as young as we were, it's hard to tell how old people are. To us, they all just looked old."

I smiled and nodded my head. "I know what you mean. Been there, done that." I waited a beat and then said, "So, go through a typical evening for me. You arrived around what time?"

"They told us to arrive no later than five. We were going to be the cocktail waitresses and had to be on premises and good-to-go before the guests arrived. We were ushered into one of the fancy bedrooms on the second floor where we changed into our costume for the evening. Pretty sexy stuff. Almost always a variation of a 'mini' mini-skirt, and some type of crop top that just barely covered our boobs."

"So, your job was to take liquor orders from the guests, and then bring the drinks back to them from the bar?"

"Yes, they had a huge bar in one of the large rooms on the first floor." She stopped to take a sip of water, the said, "They all tipped very well. We made a lot of money."

"Were you expected to have sex with anyone?"

"No. In general that was left to the girls who showed up at nine. The ones supposedly over eighteen. They made really big money. But we did get good tips if one of the men, or even one of the women, wanted to kiss us or maybe wanted to feel us up."

"And you did this how many times a month?"

"Maybe twice. Poppy and I lasted just three months. Joyce did it for a whole year."

"So, you were always in a house, right? I mean, they didn't hold these parties at the Irish Cultural Center."

She laughed. "No, never there. Poppy and I were only at private homes."

"Did they rotate the homes where the parties were held?"

"Not the summer Poppy and I were part of it. The three parties we worked were at the same house. A mansion in Pacific Heights. They never told us who owned the house, and we never asked."

"Do you remember anything about the house? What it looked like? Any distinguishing features? It would really make my day if we could find that house and identify the owner."

"You know? I thought you may ask that question when we met today. After your partner called this morning to set up our appointment, Inspector, I called Joyce to see if she had any recollection about that house and its address. She had more than a recollection, she actually had the address in her file drawer." Connie reached into her purse, pulled out an index card and slid it across the table.

I wasn't completely surprised, but jarred nonetheless. I was staring at Derek Cora's address.

CHAPTER 53

I took a cab back to the Hall. On the way, I placed a call to Morales. No answer. 'Thank you, Lord," I whispered. I called CK asking if she could give me a minute or two when I arrived. She told me to come to her desk and she'd have the pillow waiting.

"Hey, Wyatt Earp," she said as I hobbled toward her. "You don't look half bad for a guy who was in a gun fight two weeks ago."

"And you have my pillow waiting," I said, gingerly taking a seat. "If nothing else, you run a first-class operation here."

"Nothing but the best for our wounded warriors. To tell you the truth, though, I figured you'd bring your own donut. Maybe even one autographed by all the people you've shown it to." She laughed and then paused, making sure I was seated comfortably before continuing. 'I'm guessing you're not here to brag about your two-fer."

"Two-fer?" I asked. "No comprendo. Tell me what you're talking about."

"That's Manny's line. You got two bullets in him before he got that one in you. Hence, a two-fer."

"Cute," I said. "Actually, the only thing I remember is Egan getting that *one* in me. Have no clue how I got one, or even two, in him. And you're right. I'm not here to talk about any of that." I paused, leaned in closer to her and half-whispered, "I need a favor, CK, and I need it kept quiet. And I mean—quiet. No one,

including your boss, can know. At least until I have some answers. Can you do that for me?"

"Tell me what you need, Deck. Until I hear, I can't promise
anything."

I told her what I wanted. She raised an eyebrow and looked
at me skeptically. "I see where you're going with this, Deck.
Question is . . . are you sure you want to go there?"

"Have to, CK. I may be wrong. Actually, I hope I'm wrong,
but I won't know until I get some answers."

"It's noon on Friday. Gonna be hard to get that info to you
today. I'll try. It's all I can promise."

"You're a sweetheart, CK. I appreciate it. If you can't get it
today, Monday will be okay, too. Not perfect, but okay."

"I sure hope you know what the hell you're doing."

"So do I."

I looked at my watch as I made my way back to my desk.
Twelve-thirty. I picked up the phone and dialed Maria Garcia's
number. I had come to the conclusion the key to solving her
daughter's murder rested squarely on her shoulders. This time I
wasn't going to let her go.

"Hello Mrs. Garcia. This is Inspector Decker calling."

"I knew it was you. I recognized the area code," she replied.
"I'm glad you called. I heard you were shot by the man who murdered my Poppy. I wanted to call you but didn't know if you were
still in the hospital. Are you home now?"

"I am, Mrs. Garcia," I said, switching from my Mr. Nice-Guy
voice to my formal interrogation persona. "I got out of the hospital a few days ago. Thank you for asking."

"No, Inspector. It's me who must thank you. After all this
time, you answered a mother's prayer." Her voice cracked. "You
found the person who killed my daughter, and you exacted justice
on him. I can't thank you enough."

"I'm surprised you heard about what happened to me." I was now in full interrogation mode. "Did someone call you?"

She hesitated for a moment, then said, "I still have a few friends in your city, Inspector. I received a call from one of them when the news of your shootout with that awful Egan was made public. I knew in my heart it was he who murdered my daughter. A mother knows."

"That's one of the reasons I'm calling, Mrs. Garcia."

"Please, I told you to call me Maria."

"Mrs. Garcia," I said, ignoring her request. "This is not just a friendly call. I need some answers from you," I paused, squirming in my chair. "I am not at all convinced that Mr. Egan was acting alone when he killed your daughter."

I heard an audible gasp. "But he said . . ."

She stopped, obviously realizing her faux pas. I knew I had to be careful here, not wanting to spook her into hanging up before I got her to reveal who the *he* was.

"Mrs. Garcia, I've come to believe that your daughter was murdered over the pictures she posted to Facebook. The same pictures you sent me. There were people in those photographs who couldn't afford to be seen together. Unfortunately, that's exactly what Poppy's pictures did, put those people together in a room above the Parade. The people photographed together in that room had enough power to command a social giant like Facebook to remove those pictures from their site. As you know, your daughter was a headstrong young woman and was prepared to tangle with Facebook over their removal of her pictures. The people in those pictures couldn't take a chance she would post them on other popular social media platforms. She had to be stopped, so they stopped her."

I let that sink in, and then changed gears. It was time to play Mr. Nice-Guy, the one sympathetic to her pain. Get back her trust before I hit her with the hammer.

"I know you're a religious woman, Mrs. Garcia. I'm a religious man. We both know that God is good. He is so good, he blessed you with a wonderful daughter." *Probably too preachy*, I thought, *but what the hell*. "We also know from our own experience that our God can be a cruel god. Or, at least, sometimes it looks like he's a cruel god. In any case, we know that God allows cruel and evil people to exist. And to make matters worse, we sometimes mistake those cruel and evil people for good people. Evil people can fool people like you and me, Mrs. Garcia. They make us think they are just like us, when they're not." I took a deep breath.

"There were two photographs that your daughter took that showed four people in a room above the Parade. So far, we could only identify three. One was the second-in-command of one of the largest, and most dangerous, drug cartels in all of Mexico. He took a great risk to sneak into this country in order to meet an American he thought could be a major US drug distributor for them. Another person in that room was Barry Egan. You remember him, don't you?" She cursed in Spanish. I could feel her hatred of the man. "He was the man we think killed your daughter."

"Think, not know?" she replied immediately.

"Sorry, that came out badly. There's no doubt in anyone's mind he was the one who shot your daughter. But we're at a point now where we think he was ordered to kill her. By the man he worked for."

"Ordered? I don't understand."

"Right before Egan shot me, Mrs. Garcia, he told me he was nothing more than a paid employee. That he did exactly what the boss told him to do." I paused, letting the import of his words convict him. "Do you understand what I'm telling you." She didn't answer, so I continued. "What Egan meant was he was a pawn in the game. Just following orders." I paused once more and then asked again, "Do you now understand what I'm telling you?"

I heard a whispered, "Yes."

She had to have an inkling as to where this was going, so I decided to just hit her with it full on. "The man Egan worked for, Mrs. Garcia, was Derek Cora!"

I heard a sharp intake of breath, then complete silence. The silence told me all I needed to know. I waited a beat, then said, "You know Derek Cora, don't you Mrs. Garcia." It wasn't a question. She remained silent. "And I know, and now you know," I said quietly, "that Derek Cora ordered not only *your* daughter's death, but also *his* daughter's death, as well."

"No," she screamed. "That cannot be." Then nothing but hysteric sobbing. I gazed heavenward and nodded my thanks. It had all become clear.

CHAPTER 54

I stayed on the phone with Mrs. Garcia for the next hour and a half; sympathizing over her loss and talking about what a wonderful young woman Poppy must have been. How she had been so helpful to my nephew, Bobby. It was only after these reminiscences that she finally opened up about how she met Poppy's father, Derek Cora.

"I came to your country as a nineteen-year-old Mexican immigrant with nothing more than the clothes on my back and a pocket full of hopes and dreams. I knew some girls from my town who lived in San Francisco. They offered to take me in. I was lucky to find a part-time job as a maid. My employers were Derek Cora and his live-in girl-friend, a woman named Monica something or other. Three months after I was hired, he purchased a 6-bedroom, 5-bath, 10,000 square foot house on Sea Cliff Avenue They asked me to come live with them as their full-time housekeeper."

"Lucky break."

"Oh, not so lucky. Six months later, I was pregnant with Derek's child." I heard her sigh deeply. "I was very young. Very foolish. I had no experience with men. Especially older men. He filled me with stories about how he was going to get rid of Monica and marry me. I believed him."

"How did he react to your pregnancy?"

"He wanted me to get an abortion. I refused. I was Catholic

and wouldn't even entertain the thought of an abortion. I felt I made the right decision then, and I still feel that way now."

"Cora paid your medical bills?"

"All of them."

"And how about Monica?"

"Around this time, Monica got replaced by a young twenty-something woman named Rachel. That didn't bother me at all because I loved Derek Cora and wanted desperately to marry him. But when I said no to an abortion, his whole attitude towards me changed."

"Did Rachel stay for a while?" I said.

"Until after my baby was born. She insisted from the beginning that Derek take ownership of the baby. And when Poppy was born, it was Rachel who made sure he gave us a place to live. That *place* turned out to be the flats on Kirkham."

"They were the people known as Robert and Judith Gold?" I asked.

"Yes. He bought the flats under those names. He was the Robert and Rachel was the Judith, at least for the year or so they were together. Rachel actually lived in the top flat for the first year of Poppy's life. She told me she'd rather be with me and Poppy than with him. She became like Poppy's aunt. She was there when Poppy first slept through the night, when she first called me *Momma,* and when she took her first step. But then, with absolutely no warning, Rachel was told to move out."

"Why was that, do you think?"

"She never told me. One day she rang our door bell and told me that Derek told her pack her things and move out. That was the last I ever saw of her, though I received a nice card from her when she heard Poppy had been killed."

"Cora let you stay in those flats while Poppy was growing up?"

"Yes. He rented out the bottom flat until Poppy turned eighteen. Then he sent me a note saying he wanted Poppy to live in the bottom flat alone. That he'd take care of both our rents. The last time I saw Derek Cora in person was when he came to Poppy's graduation from high school. Even then he didn't talk to me."

"Can I ask you a question, Mrs. Garcia? It's probably none of my business, but how'd you come up with the name *Poppy*?"

"I came up with it. You have to understand that Derek and I became intimate soon after I moved in with them and became their full-time housekeeper. I fell deeply in love with him. His live-in girlfriend Monica was taking classes at SF State so Derek would often take me to business meetings. As his secretary. On one of those trips, we went to Colusa. Do you know where that is?"

"Of course. Up near Sacramento."

"Correct. There was a place there called Bear Valley." Her voice changed, becoming softer. I was hearing a young woman's voice remembering happier times. "There was a huge meadow filled with poppies. I remember it as if it were yesterday. We made love in that meadow. It's where my daughter was conceived." She went quiet for a minute. I didn't attempt to fill the silence. When she spoke again, it was the voice of vengeance. "And now, he has killed her. That man belongs in hell, Inspector, and I'll do whatever is necessary to put him there."

~~~~~

I thanked her for her honesty, and immediately called Kincaid. "Mrs. Garcia not only confirmed that Cora was Poppy's father, but that Cora used the name Robert Gold as his financial alias."

"Then he's toast," Kincaid said. "You do good work, Inspector. I'm impressed. Her sworn testimony about Cora's finances as they relate to Robert Gold, plus this meeting of his with a Mexican drug lord, is all we'll need to open an investigation. I think the IRS and the FCC would like a piece of this action as well. When can you have her here?"

"I checked flights. Earliest is noon tomorrow. I told her to book it. Can you have someone meet her at SFO?"

"No problem. We'll also book her a room in the city under an alias. An agent will be assigned to her for the duration."

"How long do you think the duration will be?"

"We'll get her testimony done within the week," he replied. "I'll have the formal investigation in place by the time she arrives tomorrow. Now that she gave us the name *Gold*, I'll start looking into all of Cora's financial relationships under that name."

"How quickly can you get an indictment?"

"Not until Monday, at the earliest. I could open the formal investigation today if we had the time. We don't, so I'll do it tomorrow. But we'll go to a judge today with 'probable cause.' He or she will hopefully convene the Grand Jury on Monday. If not, then Tuesday. We should have an indictment by noon."

I hung up and looked at my watch. Five minutes to four. I was dead tired and wanted nothing more than to go home and climb in bed. But I had to check something with CK first. I gave her a call.

"I've got those records you wanted," she told me. "Stay put. I'll bring them to you." No sooner had I taken a sip of water from the half-empty plastic bottle on my desk than she appeared. "You owe me big-time, my friend," she said as she placed a small cardboard box on my desk. "I need this back Monday morning, at the latest."

I carried the box down to the same meeting room I'd used only two weeks before when interviewing Godines' attorney. It seemed like a lifetime ago. I closed the door and emptied the contents of the box on the table.

Ever since the new chief showed up in 2006, SFPD personnel records were kept on an electronic system known as Kronos, named after the Greek god of time. It required every police officer to clock in when they arrived and clock out when they left. If they were out on assignment, they clocked in remotely. If they didn't clock in at all, the system defaulted to either sick or on vacation.

Over time, I came to see the wisdom in the changes. Administratively, it allowed the office to keep track of where officers were on any particular day, at any particular time. Not that anyone cared, but Kronos was a big help to me that day. I needed to find out where a particular officer was on a particular day, at a particular time.

It took me an hour to find and process that information. I put the papers back, deposited the box on CK's desk, and asked her about Bristow's schedule for tomorrow morning. She told me that except for my "coronation," his calendar was empty. I asked her to book me for 8:30 a.m. When she asked how long I thought the meeting would last, I replied, "Tell him right up until he puts the crown on my head."

CHAPTER 55

It was five-twenty by the time I got back to my desk. I had one more piece of the puzzle to insert before this whole drama would come into focus. I pulled out my cell.

"Hey, Sherm. It's your favorite homicide inspector. You're still in the City, aren't you?"

"I am. What's up?"

"Was wondering what you got going on for the next hour or so. Would love to buy you a drink or two or three, or even dinner."

"Must be pretty important for you to be springing," he said with a laugh.

"Important enough I can expense you. You're going to be the guest of the City and County of San Francisco."

"Well, hell, man," he replied, "I got nothin' doing 'til eight. You at the Hall now?" I answered in the affirmative. "Then I'll pick you up out front in twenty minutes. Can't have my favorite 'wounded warrior' overexerting himself. Wanna go to Cora's place?"

"Given what's going on with him, probably not a good idea."

"Whoa, sounds interesting. Can't wait to hear what's been going on since you got shot."

I called Becky and told her I had a dinner meeting with Sherman, and I'd be home no later than eight. Forty minutes later, Sherm and I were being seated at a comfortable restaurant in South San Francisco.

After the waitress took our drink order, Sherm leaned across the table and said in a conspiratorially low voice, "Let's cut to the chase, okay? I'm guessin' you musta had a good reason to invite your old friend Sherm out to dinner. Especially on such short notice and apparently on the City's tab. Something to do with that Garcia case you've been working on? Am I guessing right?"

"You're too smart, old friend," I said with a laugh. "Yeah, we just need a few more pieces to button up the damn thing."

"I figured. What can I do to help?"

"Well, there are two threads still flappin' in the breeze I need to tie up. And they both have to do with you."

"Is this an official interrogation? Do I need to lawyer up?" He laughed.

"I hope not," I said, meaning every damn word of it. "Just a few questions."

"Shoot."

"This is a case that goes back to June of 2007. I know you were already working for Derek Cora by then. Did you by any chance attend San Francisco's Pride Parade that year? I know Cora was there. I need to know if you were with him."

"Geez, Deck, what the hell kind of question is that?" he asked, irritation now evident in his voice. "You think Cora's involved in that Garcia woman's murder?"

"I'm just snipping off all the loose ends, Sherm. Stay with me, okay? You'll understand where I'm going. So, I have to ask you again, this time on the record. Did you attend the San Francisco Pride Parade in June of 2007?"

"You've got to be kidding." He looked at me through squinty eyes. "I hardly remember what I did yesterday, let alone thirteen years ago."

"I've got to ask, Sherm, and you've got to answer."

"I've never been to a 'Pride Parade' anywhere in the world,

let alone in San Francisco. Ever! That good enough for you?"

"Good enough for me, Sherm. Thanks. I believe you. But just so you know, the FBI is going to want to talk to you, too. They're going to ask for dates and times."

"I'd be happy to talk to them. Clear my name, so to speak. Just so you know, however, from the end of May 2007 all the way through the first week or so of September, I was in New York and the Caribbean. If you need them, my accountant still has the receipts and telephone logs that will prove I was there during that time."

"That's a big relief to me, Sherm. I knew you weren't involved, but I just had to have proof. The reason this is important is I'm in possession of the pictures Poppy Garcia took at that year's parade. They show Cora and Egan in an office building along the Parade route having drinks with Ismael Zambada, the second in command of the Sinaloa Drug Cartel. Those pictures got Poppy Garcia murdered."

"Son-of-a-bitch," Sherm muttered.

"Yeah. Son-of-a-bitch is right. And there is a fourth person in that room. Unfortunately, because the image was in complete darkness, even the FBI's ultra-sophisticated equipment couldn't make an identity."

"And you thought maybe that could be me?"

"Hoping to hell it wasn't, but had to make sure."

"And you're paying for dinner just so you could find out?"

"Well, that and one other thing. Remember I told you a few minutes ago that it was the pictures she took that got her murdered? Well, that wasn't quite true. What got her murdered was her reaction to Facebook taking them down. If she had just let well enough alone, you and I wouldn't be here today about to eat on the City's dime."

"Hmmm. What am I missing?"

"The only reason she got herself offed was because she told Facebook she'd put up a fuss on social media if they took them down. Cora couldn't allow a backlash to make Poppy's pictures famous. And you know who called in the complaint to Facebook that the photos were homophobic?" When Sherm didn't react, I said, "Brigitte Le Pendu."

"When did Facebook get that call?" Sherm asked.

"Early the next morning. About 5:30 am. When I talked to Facebook yesterday, I was told the photos came down on the complaint of Advisory Board member, Brigitte Le Pendu."

"And this is the same weekend we're talking about? The Pride Parade weekend?"

"Well, the phone call would have been made the Monday morning following the Parade."

"The person making that call couldn't have been Brigitte, Deck. On the Monday morning you're talking about, at 5:30 west coast time, Brigitte and I were just descending into Lanseria Airport, outside of Johannesburg, South Africa. I remember it so well because it was that trip that solidified our relationship and made possible our leaving Cora."

"Music to my ears, Sherm." I came around the table and gave him a hug. "Thanks be to God. Poppy Garcia can now rest in peace."

I flagged the waitress over. "We're going to order dinner now," I told her. "In the meantime, two more gin and tonics."

CHAPTER 56

I was up bright and early the next morning. Not because I wanted to primp for my big day at City Hall—well, maybe that, too—but mostly because I knew the person I wanted to talk to was at his desk by now. Never wanting to miss an important story is how he built his reputation as the best investigative news reporter on the West Coast, maybe even the country.

"SF Chronicle, Ransom Peak speaking," the voice said.

"Ransom," I said. "This is Reg Decker. Remember me?"

"Well, sheee-it," the voice responded. "Of course, I remember you. The famous SFPD homicide inspector walking around with a bullet up his ass?" A wheezy, garbled laugh followed.

"Not up it, Ransom. In it."

"Whatever! Anyway, I plan on being at the awards ceremony this afternoon. You gonna be there?"

"Well, hell ya, I'll be there," I said. "Wouldn't miss it for the world. Heard they were honoring the greatest SFPD homicide inspector since Harry Callahan."

"Dirty Reggie, that be you," he wheezed. "What can I do for you?"

"Ask not what you can do for me, but what I can do for you." I paused. "I'm going to feed you information no one else in this city, or county, or country for that matter, has but me. You have to promise never to use my name or my affiliation with the Department."

"You know me, Reg. I've made my bones because I speak only to invisible people. Deeper than deep throat."

"The very the reason I'm coming to you."

"Whatcha got?"

I told him about Cora's financial empire being investigated by the FBI and other Federal agencies. About allegations related to illegal off-shore accounts he uses to finance his nefarious business enterprises, including being a major player in the world-wide distribution of drugs coming out of Mexico. I told him to be at the ceremony this afternoon and bring photographers.

~~~~~

Manny picked me up and drove us to the Hall. I poked my head in Bristow's door at exactly eight-thirty. "You got time to see me?"

He jumped from his chair and almost ran to the door. "Well hell, yes. Here, let me help you."

"No need, Matt, but thanks." I held up the donut Sherm gave me. "Have seat, will travel." He laughed, closed his office door and escorted me to a chair around his conference table.

"I know you told me you were shutting down the Garcia case, Matt, but since I was on official leave, I thought I'd try to piece together all the loose ends—of which there are many."

"Hey, good for you. Any luck?"

"Actually, lots of luck." I spent the next hour telling him about the events leading to Poppy Garcia's murder. I finished by laying out copies of the photographs that Poppy took at the Pride parade. "She took these at the Pride parade on June 24, 2007 and posted them on Facebook late in the day on the 26th," I explained. "Early Monday morning the 27th, Facebook was notified that a suit was about to be filed against them by a prestigious city law firm, alleging the photos were homophobic. They asserted if they weren't taken down immediately, the plaintiffs would pursue a suit."

"Where'd you get all this, Reg?"

"I'm not making it up, Matt. The guy I talked to at Facebook confirmed what I'm telling you. Not surprisingly, they wanted no part of a suit accusing them of being homophobic, so they immediately took her photos down. When Poppy saw her pictures had been removed, she called to complain. They told her they would look into the matter. They did, and put them back up the next day. She never got to see them reposted, because early that morning Poppy Garcia was murdered in her own home." I let that bit of information sink in, then said, "As you and I know from experience, Matt, that's too much of a coincidence to let ride."

Bristow shrugged his shoulders as I spread my hands over the photos. "You see anything here that can be construed even remotely as homophobic?" He silently looked at each picture.

"Looks to me like a bunch of people having fun. Don't know what else to say."

"Exactly. Just people having fun. Why would anyone object?" He shrugged his shoulders, while looking at his watch. I knew he was getting bored, and I knew I didn't have a lot of time to convince him. "Look at some buildings in the background Matt. Buildings with windows. What if there was somebody in one of those rooms that didn't want to be identified. In fact, not only didn't want to be identified, couldn't afford to be identified." I took out the two pictures that Kincaid's people had processed and slid them across the table. Pointing to one of the window pictures, I said, "In that room there are four people, three were identified through FBI facial recognition software from Poppy Garcia's pictures." I pushed the FBI file toward him.

Bristow studied each picture carefully and then read the FBI file. "Son-of-a-bitch," he said. "I recognize Barry Egan and Derek Cora, but who the hell is this guy? This Zambada character?"

"The Sinaloa drug cartel's second in command."

"Geez. You sure about this? I mean, Cora? Come on."

"Matt, there's more. First of all, you know Facial Recognition software is allowed in murder trials. If it's good enough for juries, it's good enough for you and me." I paused a minute, then said, "You know much about Cora?"

"As much as anybody, I guess. He's a celebrity, I know that. A friend of our Chief, the Mayor, the Governor, Hollywood movie people, DC politicians and probably half the rich people in the country."

"Wanna know something else about Cora? He's Poppy Garcia's father."

"You're kidding me!"

"Well, Matt, I just spoke to Poppy's mother in person. I won't go through their history together, but she identified Cora as her daughter's father."

He looked at me, his face plastered with skepticism. "You sure about all that? I mean she could be lying."

"I'm as sure as I can be without ordering a paternity test, Matt. But I don't think the mom would lie to me about something so easily traceable." I fidgeted in my seat trying to get more comfortable, then continued, "So, back to Derek Cora. It was his then sweetheart who phoned Facebook threatening a suit unless they took Poppy's photos down." I let that sit for a minute before I continued. "Funny, you know? My hang-up on this murder has always been the motive. I couldn't see any reason why someone would want to murder a twenty-five-year old cab driver. I do now. I'm convinced the SOB called a hit on his own daughter and got Egan to carry it out."

"Boy, this is a boat-load full of '*where do we go from here*?'"

"I'll do whatever you want, Matt. I'm not going to make a stink today in front of an *adoring* crowd." Matt and I both chuckled at that one. "Right now, I'm expected at the FBI office. Kincaid might still be able to do a facial recognition job on the fourth person in that room."

~~~~~~

Becky and I arrived at the Federal Courts Building just after 1:00 pm. We parked in the underground garage as instructed, and called Kincaid. He said to take the elevator to the thirteenth floor and he'd meet us. After the obligatory handshake for me and the peck on the cheek for Becky, he escorted us down a long aisleway to his office.

I knew I'd been invited so I could meet Maria Garcia, but felt slightly awkward, almost bordering on the embarrassed. I could only think it was because of how intimate we'd become with each other over such a short period of time. I'd never set eyes on the woman, but had dug into her life, scolded her for not being forthcoming, accused her of not loving her daughter, chided her for not wanting to find her daughter's killer and ridiculed her for protecting the man who had dumped her with a child of his own making.

I shouldn't have worried. Maria Garcia was an extraordinarily refined and pleasant woman. She had light brown skin, humorous eyes with just a trace of eyeshadow, and tiny, slightly protruding, ears.

I shook her hand and introduced Becky. Kincaid had us sit around his conference table and offered coffee from a carafe sitting on a warmer near his bookshelf.

Because we all knew, and lived through, the connection that brought us together, it didn't take long for our conversation to get personal. Both Becky and I told Mrs. Garcia how sorry we were about her daughter. I told her the story of my nephew Bobby, who still credited Poppy with getting him cheerfully through two or three horrific years filled with operations followed by recovery, followed by more operations, followed by more recovery, not one of which led to him being able to walk. She in turn expressed her gratitude that I reopened Poppy's case, as well as her sympathy that I sustained a bullet wound for my efforts.

I asked if she was coming to the medal ceremony. She looked over at Kincaid for an answer. Kincaid, in turn, looked at me. "What do you think?"

"I think there's a good chance that Cora will show up," I said. "If he does, would you advise Mrs. Garcia not speak to him?"

Kincaid shrugged. "We haven't talked about that yet. Given all that has happened in the past twenty-four hours, we're going to look more carefully at both the pros and cons. I don't want the case against Cora to be jeopardized by some chance meeting, nor would I want Mrs. Garcia to be verbally abused by Cora in public."

"I'm going to Inspector Decker's award ceremony whether you want me to or not, Mr. Kincaid," Maria Garcia said. "And if Derek Cora gets near me, I'll kill him with my own hands."

CHAPTER 57

It's a little more than two blocks from Federal Building to Civic Center Plaza. Becky and I decided I was in good enough shape to hoof it over. Fifteen minutes later we found ourselves in the ornate Rotunda of San Francisco's City Hall among forty or so city employees scurrying about putting the finishing touches on the ceremony's setting. They'd already made sure the TV cameras and lights were working and were now checking to see if the one hundred or more guest chairs were properly aligned. I had no idea this event was going to be such a big deal. I was glad Becky made me bring a tie.

At two-twenty, I was ushered up the stairs to the first landing where I stood beside the Chief of Police who in turn stood beside the Mayor. In front of us were a bank of microphones so every precious word any of us spoke would be saved for posterity, or until the start of the next news cycle, whichever came first. I reflexively patted my coat pocket, making sure for the umpteenth time that my prepared remarks were still there.

People continued to file in. The front row, reserved for the police brass, hadn't yet been populated. *Probably will stay empty*, I thought with a wry smile. I looked down to my right and saw Morales, CK and eight of my *magnificent fourteen* brethren. I saw Kincaid enter through a side door accompanied by Maria Garcia.

Looking along the back wall where the press was stationed, I picked out Ransom Peak having an animated conversation with a television reporter I recognized from Channel 2. I glanced at my watch. Two minutes to showtime. People were still arriving as the Mayor rose and walked to the microphones. One group caught my eye as they walked quickly to the front row and took their seats. I recognized them all—Chester McMann, the Deputy Mayor; Bill Maher, the Chairman of the Port Commission, and . . . Derek Cora.

How the hell could he be here, I thought. *He's supposedly under house arrest.* I smiled inwardly. He must not have gotten the message yet.

The Mayor began by welcoming everyone, and then complimenting the police department for the exemplary job they're doing in bringing to justice people who commit crimes against the innocent. The next five minutes was a political advertisement highlighting what a great mayor he'd been and how his policies were keeping the city safer.

Next up was the Chief of Police, Harry Peterson. He spent twenty minutes giving the audience an overview of the Garcia case, most of which came from my deposition taken in the hospital during recovery. He covered the phone call from my nephew that triggered the probe as well as Bristow's wisdom in allowing me to reopen the cold case of a young Hispanic woman who was murdered in one of the most violent years in City history. He then called me to join him at the microphone. With me by his side, he guided the audience through the twists and turns the investigation took before my "exemplary police work" finally identified the murderer. He went through my being shot and how, even though incurring a nearly fatal wound, I summoned the strength to shoot and kill my attacker. He put his arm around me as the audience gave me a standing ovation. Then, to everyone's delight, he told the crowd that I was really getting this award as a tribute to an ass that would never make it through airport screening again. He waited for the laughter and catcalls to die down before he slipped the Valor in the Line of Duty medallion over my head.

Then, it was my turn. When I was first prepping for this, I decided just to thank everyone for coming and call it a day. I knew most of the people in the audience hoped I'd do exactly that. Give them the opportunity to applaud politely, shake my hand, pat me on the back and then get the hell to the nearest bar. Another case closed. But seeing Cora in the crowd prompted me to travel in a different direction.

As I approached the microphone, I lifted the medallion over my head. Holding it up in my right hand, I said, "On behalf of the San Francisco Police Department in general and my fellow officers in the Homicide Unit in particular, I want to recognize Maria Garcia, Poppy Garcia's mother, who flew in today from Mexico to be with us. Can you please stand Mrs. Garcia?" I pointed to the back of the room. All heads swiveled to where she stood, and then everyone rose and gave her a loud and long round of applause. I glanced down at Cora. He was standing and giving a few perfunctory claps with his hands, but he never turned around to look. *Gotcha, you son-of-a-bitch*, I thought.

When the applause died down, I said, "While we know who pulled the trigger of the gun that killed Poppy Garcia, we are not ready to close the investigation just yet. There are still loose ends we are looking to tie together. If all goes well, we hope to have them tied up by the end of next week. And, at the conclusion of the investigation, I'm told the Department will issue a press release as to its findings." I thanked them all for coming and turned the mic back to Chief Peterson.

After the chief's closing remarks, I limped down to the main floor, deliberately sidestepping the hoard of television cameras and reporters waiting to interview me. I walked slowly to where Manny was standing with Becky and a number of others.

After giving Becky a hug, I told the group my interview with the press would last about thirty minutes, after which we could all go to dinner at the restaurant around the corner. Ten of the twelve present said to look for them at the bar.

I turned back to the reporters who were waiting patiently to interview me just in time to see Cora approaching the Mayor and the Chief as they maneuvered their way through the crowd. Both men walked straight past him without even acknowledging his presence. My heart fluttered in delight. The word was already out. Stay away from Cora; he's toxic.

CHAPTER 58

It took close to an hour to satisfy the press' curiosity about my being shot by a former member of my own unit. Once they filed out, I found myself alone with Becky, Manny and the City Hall clean-up crew as they returned the Rotunda to its normal configuration. However, I was mistaken about only Becky and Morales being there.

Retrieving my coat that I'd hung on the back of a chair, I heard a voice behind me say, "Hey Inspector Decker, got a minute?" I turned and saw Derek Cora walking toward me, big smile on his face. "Been a while, huh?" he said, putting out his hand.

"Yeah, awhile." I said, not accepting his proffered hand. He looked quizzically at me, then shrugged like it was no big deal and withdrew his hand. I turned to find where Becky was, pointed to my watch, flashed ten fingers, and feigned eating. She nodded, gave me a thumbs up and started for the door. I turned and faced Cora.

I hadn't seen him face-to-face in over a year. His light brown hair, worn longer than I remembered, was now speckled with gray. While most people in the Rotunda that day came dressed in business attire, Cora came casual—a light blue Under Armour t-shirt, khakis, loafers with no socks, and a Joseph Abboud sports coat.

"I'm surprised you're still here." I said.

"You shouldn't be," he countered. "Most of the people here

today are good friends of mine."

"You sure about that?"

My question surprised him. He fumbled for a few seconds, frowned and then said in a mildly unfriendly tone, "Where'd that come from, Decker?"

"You saw Mrs. Garcia here today," I replied. "Thought maybe you'd already made the connection."

"Not sure I understand what you're talking about," he said, his tone now edging toward the hostile.

"Well, it's not hard to understand, is it Derek? I saw the pictures you blackmailed Facebook to take down."

Cora's frown deepened. "Not sure where you are going with all this. Blackmailed Facebook? Why would I do that? I'm one of their largest shareholders." His tone now outright unfriendly.

"Well, let me tell you *where I'm going with all this*. We have a photograph of you in a room with your good friend, Ismael Zambada. You may also know him as El Mayito Gordo. In either case, you and I both know he's a big player in the Sinaloa drug cartel. Shame on you, Derek. What do you think your 'good friends' who were here today are going to say when we make that photograph public?" I saw his eyes flicker for just an instant. "And that ain't all."

"You're toast, Decker," he spit defiantly. "You have no idea who you're playing with."

"Let me finish before you start threatening me. First of all, I know exactly who I'm playing with. I'm playing with the slimeball who had his own daughter murdered."

"Who do you think you are accusing me of murder? You have no freaking proof for any of this."

I tilted my head forward, feigning to whisper in his ear. "Before you get too cocky, Derek, don't forget who came up all the way from Mexico just to talk to us about you."

"That whore?" He nodded his head back to where Maria Garcia had been seated. "What's she going to tell you, that I knocked her up?"

"She's already told me that. It's the other things she knows that should worry you."

"My word against hers? Come on, who'd take her word over mine?"

"Well, how 'bout the FBI for starters? I've got to tell you, they've heard her story and tell me it's pretty persuasive. She has the FBI on her side, for sure."

"I'll fight them and win, Inspector. And you know why? Because I have friends in the highest reaches of government. Friends that will tell the FBI to forget all about this travesty."

"Won't get that far, my friend. You're through."

He looked at me with pure hatred. "We'll see." He took a step backward, spun around and walked right into Ransom Peak.

"Got a minute, Mr. Cora?" I overheard Peak say. "I've heard disturbing things about you and want to get your comment.

~~~~~

I walked to the restaurant only to find Becky and Manny at the bar alone. "What, no one came? How'd we get so lucky?"

"People just got tired of seeing you," Manny replied with a chuckle. "And lucky? Hell, yes. So lucky, I'm going right home and climb in bed. I'm dead tired and it's been a long-ass day."

"You're lucky," Becky said. "You'll probably be home before slow-poke here even gets us to our car." She squeezed my arm and gave me a kiss on the cheek.

"She's right, Manny. I'll get us home in time for me to turn right around for that meeting Bristow called for Monday morning at nine. He told me he was inviting you, too."

317

"Any idea what it's about?"

"I'm guessing it has to do with Cora being there today."

"Anything I should know about."

"Not that I know of," I lied. "Have a good weekend."

CHAPTER 59

T ime to wake up, sleepy head."
I felt like I was surfacing from a scuba dive—tired, wet, and out of breath. "What time is it?" I croaked.

"Noon," Becky replied, running her fingers through my sweat soaked hair.

"Noon?" I said. "Like Saturday noon?"

"You were a tired boy. Even made whimpering noises a few times. When it got this late, I thought I'd better wake you. Glad I did. The sheets are soaked. Why don't you get up and take a shower while I change them? Then you can go back to bed if you want."

"Thanks, baby," I said. "I hate to be such a damn burden."

"Stop with that talk," she said. "That's what we women do for the men we love." She kissed me on the cheek. "Except for that damn insurance policy I could have collected, I'm glad the bastard didn't kill you." She laughed, peeled back the covers, took my hand and gently assisted me out of bed. "Okay, now into the shower you go."

The shower made me feel almost human again. After drying off and putting on sweats and a T-shirt, Becky took me by the hand and led me to the living room. Sitting me on my donut, she went into the kitchen to get my pills and a large glass of orange juice. In the old days, I'd be having a beer right now. How quickly our fortunes change.

"Heard anything about our little camp follower recently?" I asked. "He's been up there since I was shot, right? So, it's been what, two weeks?'

"Almost four. You missed a whole week." She snuggled into me as best she could with my donut intruding on her space. "Honestly, I miss him. You're still okay to travel up there tomorrow, right?"

"Absolutely. As I remember the set-up, we're only there to observe. He'll never know we were even there. Are you sure you want to go all that way for that?"

"Oh, Reg, of course," she said excitedly. "But I'm worried about you. Are you sure you're up to it?"

"It's no more than a car ride," I said. "You can drive. We'll go to early church tomorrow and then you can lay me in the back seat on my donut."

She laughed. "Never. You and your donut are sitting up front with me. When we get there, I promise they'll be only a few tears." I could already see the first few forming.

~~~~~~

We went to church at eight, got out at nine-fifteen and were on the road with a bag of donuts and a thermos of coffee by ten. We arrived in the town of Mendocino at twelve-forty and were at the Stornetta Ranch by one fifteen.

The SR, as they were known, was a real working ranch run by the City and County of San Francisco's Juvenile Probation Department. The men and women who worked at Stornetta's were hands at various ranches and dairy farms in the area, and donated their time to take troubled youth under their wing. Since most of these juvenile wards were city kids, the objective of the Ranch was to take them out of their sterile concrete environment and

320

give them the experience of getting their hands dirty working with animals and nature, from milking cows to cleaning up hog pens.

After presenting our credentials to the chief administrator, we were introduced to Charlie Schaeffer, a senior staff person who would be our guide for the next hour. Schaeffer ushered us into a room off the main hall. We were offered a choice of sitting on a sofa or individual arm chairs, all of which faced a large TV screen on the opposite wall. Because of my physical infirmity, we thought it best to take the individual chairs

"You understand the rules, right?" He didn't wait for our answer. "Relatives and friends are not allowed to have personal contact with any of our wards. Our experience has taught us that for these kids to grow, they need to be isolated from their past environment so they can immerse themselves in an entirely different life-style. You're here to see . . ." he looked through his paperwork, "Edwin Jones? Can I ask your relationship with the young man?

"I am—or was—his second-grade teacher," Becky replied as we, having collectively changed our minds, sat on the sofa. "My husband is a San Francisco police officer."

"Nice to meet you both," Schaeffer said. "I can report that Edwin, even in his relatively short time here, is a good boy. Like so many of our young ones, he simply needs direction in his life."

"His home life was a disaster," Becky said. "As his teacher, I could see the potential in him. We asked his mother's permission to let him stay at our house for a week or so. She said yes, but when my husband was injured, I knew it would be impossible for me to give Edwin the attention he needed. Since there was no way I was going to let him slide back into his old life, we got a referral up here."

"You're lucky. Referrals are hard to come by. We can take only so many children." He turned to me and asked, "What Unit

321

are you with, Officer?"

"Homicide," I responded.

"You must be well respected, Inspector, to get a referral here on such short notice."

"They just felt sorry for me. She's the one who did all the work," I said, nodding toward Becky.

He smiled. "In any case, you know the rules. Since we don't allow our charges to have visitors, we've placed cameras around the property so parents—or, in your case, a teacher—can see the child. Let me show you Edwin." He flicked a switch and the screen came to life. The camera showed a grainy picture of the inside of a barn. In the foreground were animal stalls. In the back we could see four boys with pitchforks stabbing into a huge pile of hay. "If I'm not mistaken," Schaeffer said, "that's Edwin there with his back to the stall."

Becky got up and walked to the screen. "There?" she asked, pointing to a particular boy. "So grainy, it's hard to make him out."

"I recognize him because he's wearing the plaid, long-sleeved shirt. Those are the shirts we give the boys who've been here less than six weeks. After that break-in period, they can wear anything they want."

Once his pitchfork was loaded with hay, the boy we now recognized as Edwin carried it forward and pitched it into the second stall. Then he returned to get another load.

"He'll do this for the next hour and then we'll switch him to some other form of work. That way, they don't get psychologically bored. But I wouldn't worry about Edwin. He's adapted well to his new surroundings."

Becky reached out and lightly touched the screen with her index finger. The tears on her face sparkled in the backlight. Pushing myself off the sofa, I went to her and dabbed her cheeks with my handkerchief.

We stayed in the room watching Edwin for the next hour. After finishing the hay work, a staff member had Edwin and the rest of his team hitch four donkeys to a wagon. I'd never seen that done before and was amazed Edwin already knew how to do it.

"Hitching up teams of animals to wagons is one of the first things we teach them," said Schaeffer, noticing my body language and facial expression. "Gets them familiar with animals, in this case donkeys. We've found teaching them to care and love four-legged animals carries over into having caring and loving relationships with two-legged animals."

~~~~~

On the ride home that afternoon, all Becky could talk about was getting Edwin back at the end of September. I knew this was not the time to resist her impulse. Truth be told, I found myself looking forward to having him back, too. Even at that, I knew the time between now and September was a lifetime.

We were on Highway 1, just a little above Jenner, when I got a call from Matt Bristow telling me the department received a call about thirty minutes ago from someone at Derek Cora's house. "One of the gardeners," Bristow told me. "Found Cora dead in his bedroom. I'm here now with the coroner. Looks like he committed suicide, Deck."

CHAPTER 60

I had Becky drop me off at Cora's Pacific Heights address. I told her I didn't know when I'd be home so don't wait dinner. The coroner's wagon was still there, as were a half-dozen police cars and Bristow's SUV. About thirty people from the neighborhood were being held behind yellow police tape.

Bristow met me at the front door and took me upstairs to the master suite. We put on the plastic booties the coroner's assistant gave us and walked slowly into the room. Cora's body, in multicolored silk pajamas, was grotesquely stretched out on the round king-sized bed. His head, or what was left of it, flopped over his left shoulder. The headboard behind him was covered in brain matter and blood. I saw a weapon, which to me looked like a 9 mm Glock, lying by his right butt-cheek, possibly carried there by the gun's blow-back when it discharged.

"Did he leave a note?" I asked Bristow as we stood watching the coroner pack up his tools while instructing his staff to tag and bag the body.

Bristow nodded toward the coroner. "Ed hasn't given us permission yet to mess up what he said may be a murder scene."

"He said it might be a murder scene? Did he tell you why he thought that or was he just being obstreperous?"

Bristow shook his head. "Who knows with that guy."

"Just like Ed. He needs to be asked nicely." I walked over to him. "What you got for us, Ed?" I asked with an exaggerated sigh.

"Well, fancy meeting you here, Inspector," Ed Fastbein replied. I'd known Fastbein for years. He'd been deputy coroner when I went joined Homicide. Odd little fellow, but competent. "They call you out because the dead man is Derek Cora?" he asked.

"Yeah. I've had some dealings with the man lately and the brass wanted me to check if his death was really a suicide. You know how important the Cora's of the world are, Ed." I winked at him.

He nodded, then said, "Only too well. You'd expect people like Cora to be victims of foul play. But here . . .?" He paused, sweeping his hand over Cora's remains. "Here . . . this looks like, well, what can I say? It looks very much like a suicide."

I caught the hesitation in his voice. "Did I hear a 'but' somewhere in there, Ed? Like it looks very much like a suicide, *but* could also be a murder?"

"Nothing concrete one way or the other, Inspector. Maybe it's because I went to church this morning." He laughed. "Anyway, I don't know. Just doesn't feel right. Too pristine. Like it was staged."

"What leads you to say that, Ed?" I asked, my antenna now extended to the max.

"Well, again, it's just a feeling, Inspector. Nothing in particular. Suicides are really messy. Don't get me wrong—this was messy, too, but not quite like what I would've expected. Like the body positioning seemed to me just a wee bit off. And the weapon? Too precisely placed. Stuff like that, but nothing I could take to court."

"Hmm. Well, okay. What's your estimation on time of death?"

"A seven-hour window, Inspector, starting about four this morning. Could have happened at four, could have happened as late as eleven. No earlier, though, and probably no later."

"Thanks, Ed. I appreciate your candor. I'll tell the guys to be really careful as they're sifting through all this stuff. Oh, one more thing. You come across a note or anything like that?"

"No, not in here. But I didn't look over the entire house." He picked up his bag and shook my hand. "Good luck, Inspector."

~~~~~

I told Matt what the coroner said, called a cab and left. The ride home was anything but pleasant. While standing in Cora's bedroom, I had a flash of insight. Throughout my career, I learned to pay close attention to those flashes. They almost always led me in the right direction. In this case, though, I prayed to God I was wrong.

I called Morales from the back of the cab. "You're not going to believe what happened," I said. "Derek Cora committed suicide today."

"Come on, Decker. You're kidding me." When I didn't answer, he said, "Aren't you?"

"No, Manny, unfortunately I'm not. But with his suicide, I think I can put this Garcia case to bed. To do so, though, I'm gonna need your opinion on how best to proceed. It's one more thing we can go over with Bristow. We still good to go at nine tomorrow? Let's meet then in the conference room, okay?"

"Sure, Deck. I'll be there for you. Nine it is. Together we can finally get this puppy buttoned up, and move on to more important cases. It's gone on way too long."

CHAPTER 61

I was at the Hall and in Bristow's office at eight the following morning. I'd called him last night and laid out my entire case.

"You're sure of this, huh?"

"I am, Matt. I wish to god I wasn't, but it's all here in my briefcase."

"When do you want me there?"

"Give me ten minutes with him and then come in."

I left his office and went to wait in the conference room. It was fifteen minutes to nine. Manny Morales had been my friend for the past twelve years and my partner for the past five. I hoped I was wrong, but knew I wasn't. I unholstered my Sig and placed it on my lap under the table. Manny didn't appear until nine-fifteen. The longest thirty minutes of my life.

"Sorry I'm late, Deck," he said as he bolted through the door. "Bad traffic." He sat across from me.

"Doesn't matter, Manny." I leaned forward and put my left elbow on the table. At the same time, I brought the Sig up with my right hand. "I hate to do this, Manny. I really, really do. I'm placing you under arrest for the murder of Poppy Garcia and Barry Egan. The look on his face was indecipherable. "You know the drill. I need you to reach in with your left hand, then use your thumb and index finger to pinch that gun of yours out of its holster and lay it on the table."

He sat there stone-faced, then shook his head and said, "Come on, Decker. This is a joke, right? An elaborate hoax. Okay, where're the rest of the guys?" He swiveled his chair back towards the door.

"Hands where I can see them, Manny. Flat on the table." I placed the Sig in front of me pointing at him to show I was serious.

Just then Bristow entered the room and sat at the head of the table. Morales turned to him and said, "I don't know what the hell is going on here, DC. Can you explain?"

"I asked him for his weapon, Matt. He hasn't complied yet."

"Your weapon, Manny," Bristow said, his hand outstretched.

Holding his hands up like a stop sign, Manny said, "Okay, okay." He slowly brought his left hand around, pulled his weapon out with two fingers, and placed it on the table.

Bristow reached over and pulled it to him. "You're not carrying a back-up are you, Manny?" he asked. Morales shook his head. "Well, just in case you are, from now on keep both your hands, palms flat, on the table."

"You're actually placing me under arrest for the murder of Garcia and Egan? This is ridiculous. You've absolutely no proof." He paused, looked at me, and said, "Do I need an attorney?"

"You'll no doubt need one," I said. "But there's really no hurry. He or she won't be able to do you much good." I paused, then said, "The three of us should put our cards on the table, don't you think?"

Manny had his head down and didn't respond. "Okay," said Bristow, "then I'll start. We do have proof, Manny, you murdered Barry Egan. In fact, we have an eye witness." Hearing that, Morales' head jerked up. "You must have forgotten, Manny. Inspector Decker was actually in the room that day." I saw the muscle under Morales' left eye twitch. I smiled inwardly. The seeds of uncertainty were starting to break down his defenses.

Morales looked at me. "You've told everybody who would listen that you don't remember a thing. That you were unconscious the whole time. I've got at least twelve homicide inspectors who'd swear to that. Hell," he continued, his voice rising in anger, "I'll swear to that, too. After all, I was the one who saved your sorry ass."

"Easily explained," I said. "Repressed memory brought on by the trauma of being shot." I smiled at him. "You've been around long enough to know a jury's gonna believe the heroic police officer who almost died, but who, thank god, recovered from the trauma you and Egan inflicted on him to clearly remember seeing you shoot Egan."

"If your 'repressed' memory is the extent of your 'proof', I think I'll take my chances."

"Well, Manny, I'd think again." I reached in my briefcase, pulled out a large manila envelope, and plopped it on the table "Here's the case against you. Sixty-seven typed pages, single-spaced. You know what a bad typist I am, so you know it took me most of the night to finish this report. One of the reasons I'm in such a foul mood this morning." I paused and, for effect, pulled out my entire report. While yawning, I rifled through the pages.

"Over the weekend," Bristow interjected, "at our behest, the Sacramento PD conducted interviews of all the people living around Egan's old neighborhood. You know, the block where you say you waited for Decker to finish his business with Egan. In your deposition, you told SFPD that you parked on a particular street. In that interview, you told the interrogator that you waited for over two hours before you went looking for Decker."

"That's exactly what happened. You're not going to tell me you've corralled some neighbor saying he remembered me, and actually kept tract of the number of minutes I sat there before driving off? Again, if that's all you got, I'll take my chances."

"We'll see," Bristow challenged. "On Friday, I requested Sacramento PD to conduct interviews. They found a neighbor who was walking his dog that particular day and remembered you. Even described the make and model of the car you were driving. Actually, gave a pretty accurate description of you, too. Says he became suspicious when you just sat there looking straight ahead. Not moving. Not reading anything. Just sitting. He thought maybe you were up to no good. But when he got back from walking his dog, approximately twenty-minutes later, you were already gone."

"This is crazy, DC," Morales said, shaking his head. "You know as well as I do if you took that testimony to a jury, they'd laughed your ass out of the courtroom."

"We'll take our chances," Bristow said with a smile, mimicking Morales' response. "In your deposition, you claimed that you waited over an hour before you decided Egan had left. This guy's testimony contradicts you. Also, in your deposition you say you got to the farmhouse by following the signal from Decker's cell phone app—which you presumed was in the farmhouse." I could see the slight slump Manny made when Bristow mentioned the cell phone. It was his Achilles' heel, and he knew it. "You want to take over, Deck?"

"Gladly, Matt." I looked at Morales and said, "What you couldn't have known, Manny, was Egan turned off my cell phone at his house. Didn't want to be distracted, as he put it, from 'doing his duty.' Which as we all know now was to kill me."

Manny was silent. I was sure by this time he was calculating that the best way out of this dilemma would be for him to control the narrative. He started to speak, but I stopped him.

"My turn," I said. He went silent, and slumped back into his chair. "Here's how I see the case against you. Manny. Let me finish before you interrupt. If you wanna play hardnose, then we'll lock your ass up right now, and let the chips fall where they may. Capiche?" He stared at me for a few seconds, then nodded. "Good. The way I figure it, you needed Egan dead to eliminate the one person who could finger you as Poppy's killer."

Morales snorted, shaking his head vigorously back and forth. "You don't know what the hell you're talking about, Decker."

"I'm afraid I do, Manny. Over the weekend, I went back into the files. You remember when whoever the chief was back-in-the-day put all our personnel records on Kronos?" Manny didn't respond. "I don't know about you, but I hadn't thought about that system in years. You'll probably remember it was designed to keep an electronic record of every officer; when he arrived in the morning and when he left at night. I'm sure it was put in to curb overtime abuses."

"Yeah, I remember," he said quietly, still looking at his hands on the table.

"It wasn't long before they purchased a plug-in to the system that allowed the office to keep track of where officers were on any particular day, at any particular time." I paused, judging from his body language that he knew it was all over. "You know where I'm going with this, don't you, Manny?"

Morales' shoulders slumped visibly, and he sat back in his chair. "I want an attorney," he said.

"You sure you want to go that way, Manny?" I asked. "A good attorney could probably get you some of the minor charges dismissed, but the big ones are gonna stick. You and I both know that."

He looked at me. "Can we be alone?" he asked in a barely audible whisper. I looked at Bristow and shrugged my shoulders in a way of conveying "it's your call." Bristow thought for a moment, then said, "Sure." He put out his hand. "And give me your weapon." I did. When he got to the door, he turned and said, "I'm going to station someone outside the door. You need anything, Reg, just yell out."

CHAPTER 62

W e sat there in silence staring at one another for what seemed like an eternity. Finally I said, "How could you do this, Manny?" I looked him in the eye and shook my head slowly back and forth. "You betrayed me. You were my partner. My brother, for god's sake. And you betrayed me."

His face started to crumble, one sector at a time. He looked down at his hands and said,

"How'd you figure I was the shooter in the Garcia case?"

"Went back and had the system check out both Egan's time-card and your timecard for the day Poppy was murdered. Egan's card showed him on a homicide assignment that day in the outer Mission District from 7 a.m. to 4 p.m. Your card, on the other hand, showed you didn't report to duty that day until three in af-ternoon. It was a no-brainer on my part."

"And stupid on mine. I should have remembered and gone back and changed it."

"Yeah. It's always the little things that get you, isn't it?"

There was a silence before Manny spoke again. "You know I'm a changed man, Decker. Ever since Egan left in twenty-ten, I've been clean. In all the years you and I have been together, I've been clean. Always trying to outlive my past." He paused and then said, "I've suffered the pangs of hell every second of every day for what I did back in those years."

"It never stops, does it, Manny? The sins of the past! Finally, they all come back to bite us."

We both sat there in silence. I was mad at him. I didn't know why exactly, except I'm a cop and he's a criminal. Goes with the territory. There was no reason why I shouldn't be mad. So why was my heart splintering inside my chest? Why did I feel such a deep sadness for him? Before these feelings could go any further, Matt rescued me. Sticking his head in the door, he asked, "Everything okay in here?"

"Just fine, Matt. Thanks," I answered. "Don't know about Manny, but I could sure use some coffee."

Bristow reappeared a few minutes later with two cups of coffee and put them on the table. "You sure you're okay?" he asked me. I reassured him that I was, that we were just reminiscing about old times. I asked him for another ten minutes. He understood the dynamic and left.

I took a sip, looked across the table at Manny and said, "Cora! Did you do him?"

He put his cup down, wiping his lips with one of the paper napkins Bristow had brought. He nodded. "A bad man," he said. "I'm sorry I ever got involved with him."

"Bad choices have a way of compounding themselves."

"Yeah, tell me about it! I'm sure you learned a lot about Cora this past week, huh?" I nodded. "So, you knew his being rich allowed him to do most anything he wanted. Even getting a slap on the wrist for pimping out twelve and thirteen-year old girls. I had to stop him, and I did."

I nodded through another sip of coffee. "I'm gonna guess Egan was in his hip pocket."

"Oh, big time. I always felt sorry for Egan."

"Don't. He wasn't worth it."

"Yeah, I know." He took another sip, looked down at the table, and said, "You were right, Decker. I did the Poppy girl." He went silent, then: "I didn't know at the time it was Cora's own daughter. He had her killed because, innocently enough, she caught him on film with the cartel guy from Mexico."

"Speaking of the 'cartel guy,' was that you in the photo the FBI can't decipher?"

"I was in the room that day, yeah."

"Did you kill McGinnis?"

"No. That was Egan. Ran the guy down late at night."

"The fire?"

"The fire, yeah. The fire was on me."

I shook my head. "I have to tell you, Manny, hearing this really hurts. You were my partner, man. Like my freaking brother. I know this all happened because of things done thirteen years ago, but there is no statute of limitations on disappointment—or hurt. Just like there are no statutes of limitations on murder."

"I know, Deck. All I can say is I saved you at the farmhouse. Egan knew he only wounded you and was going to shoot you again when I walked in. I told him just to let it go, that you'd bleed out. But he wasn't having any of it, so I picked your weapon up off the table and shot him. In fact, shot him twice so you'd look even more like a hero."

"The two-fer," I said.

"Exactly. Then I stopped your bleeding as best I could, knowing intuitively that I had to make it look like you did it. It was only then that I arranged the scene to make it look like you and he had a shoot-out."

I didn't know what to say. Thinking to myself that "thank you" was not the appropriate response, I stayed silent.

The room remained silent for a few more moments, and then Morales leaned closer to me and whispered, "I know you carry a hideout on your ankle." He saw my surprise. "Come on, Decker. No secrets between partners, remember?"

Stupid, stupid me! I'd forgotten he knew I carried that damn Sig P365 in an ankle holster. I had mindlessly strapped it on today like I do every day. Just second nature. Bristow was not going to be a happy camper when he finds I'm still carrying. What the hell was I thinking?

"I want to ask you a favor, partner. You know as well as I do that if I'm put in Quentin, being a cop or even an ex-cop, I'd be stone cold dead before the sun went down. I don't deserve that, Decker, being beaten to death, or a shiv stuck up under my ribcage. You can empty that Sig except for one bullet and then look away. I'll hit you hard enough to stun you, grab the gun and shoot myself. Let me end it right here, right now. You're my partner. I saved your life, for god's sake. That's gotta mean something. Now you can save mine." He paused, then said with a dim smile, "So to speak."

It did mean something, but unfortunately for Morales, not enough. I wasn't thinking about the law. That I should let the legal system work. No, I was thinking that suicide would too easy of a way out for this person I used to call my partner. My mind flashed on the YouTube video my nephew sent of Poppy Garcia as she helped him walk to school in a driving rainstorm, covering him with her umbrella while she herself got drenched. I thought of all the good works Poppy Garcia could have done in her life had it not been cut short by Manny Morales. I became so caught up in anger that for a quick second I considered drawing my Sig and ending Morales' life then and there.

But instead, I opened the door and called Bristow.

Edwin returned to the City in mid-September and was placed in a foster home in the outer Mission. He no longer attended Becky's school, but she knew where he'd been placed and kept in weekly contact with his new teacher. From her reports, Edwin was doing well. His case worker told us he was absolutely amazed at what the Stornetta experience had done for the child.

At Christmas, we invited Edwin over to our house. He was, indeed, a changed young man. A win for the good people, I mused. A *win* that was made possible only because Becky recognized early on the good in him and acted on it.

~~~~~

In early March, we received an invitation from Sherm inviting Becky and me to Brigitte Le Pendu's opening of her new flower exhibit at San Francisco's Botanical Garden. Both Becky and I were curious as to why we'd been invited, and it was that curiosity that prompted us to RSVP in the affirmative.

We arrived at the Garden at 9 a.m. for the 9:30 a.m. tour. At least one hundred people were already gathered, and we knew more than half of them, including Matt Bristow who waved and walked over.

"Fancy meeting you here," I said with a smile.

"Come on, Decker. The Mayor's here. The Chief's here.

Damn if half the City's pols are also here. Even you and your wife are here." He clapped me on the back. "You didn't think I'd miss this, did you?"

"With all this brass here, Matt, I'm surprised you were even invited."

He laughed. "Cute. Hey, did you know Maria Garcia is here? Right over there." He pointed over my left shoulder. I turned. She saw me and waved.

"No, I didn't know she'd be here," I said, waving back. "But now I understand why Becky and I were invited."

"Yeah. Gonna be a dedication," he said.

I'd read in the brochure that the Botanical Garden comprised some fifty-five acres of landscaped gardens and open space. Staying on the path, the group walked through a meadow filled with every variety of flower imaginable. To add to the ambiance, little pink butterflies flitted lazily about in the soft morning air.

After walking for ten minutes, we turned a corner and were met by an enormous field of beautiful red and gold poppies. It reminded me of a scene right out of the Wizard of Oz. I quickly looked into the distance expecting to see the Emerald City. It wasn't there. In its place, though, was a large engraved plaque: REMEMBERING POPPY!

I put my arm around Becky, pulled her close and whispered, "Perfect."

~~~~~

In April, Manny's trial for the murder of Poppy Garcia begins. I'm numero uno on the Prosecution's list of witnesses. It's not something I'm looking forward to.

###

Acknowledgments

To my friends and family who have been with me through the writing of this novel.

Thank you for purchasing this
Pen Books paperback.

Please remember to leave a review at
your favorite retailer.

DENNIS KOLLER is author of
the popular Tom McGuire suspense series including *The Oath*,
Kissed By The Snow, and *The Custer Conspiracy*. Mr. Koller and his
wife live in the Dallas area.

Learn more about his work at www.DennisKoller.com

Made in the USA
Middletown, DE
08 October 2020

21358190R00199